A Secret Visitor

I heard the footsteps crunching on some old snow outside. They came closer and closer. I stood in the middle of the warming kitchen, arms folded across my middle, trying to steady myself.

Then came the soft knock on the door. Three raps, silence, then two, as Elizabeth had described it. I hesitated for one awful moment, then walked clumsily across the brick floor and lifted the latch.

In the moon-washed night, I could see him as clearly as if it were day. He was tall and dressed in a shabby British officer's coat. The sleeves were too short on him. From under the tricorn hat, his face stared down at me, gaunt and unshaven, haggard, with sunken eyes.

There was no doubt about who he was. The man had the look of sickness about him. But I must be sure. "Yes?" I asked.

"I'm here to see Becca."

"I'm Becca."

FINISHING
BECCA

FINISHING
BECCA

A Story about Peggy Shippen
and Benedict Arnold

Ann Rinaldi

GULLIVER BOOKS
HARCOURT, INC.

Orlando   Austin   New York   San Diego   Toronto   London www.HarcourtBooks.com

First Gulliver Books paperback edition 1994
Gulliver Books is a trademark of Harcourt, Inc., registered in the
United States of America and/or other jurisdictions.

Library of Congress Cataloging-in-Publication Data
Rinaldi, Ann.
Finishing Becca: a story about Peggy Shippen and Benedict
Arnold/Ann Rinaldi.
p. cm.
"Gulliver Books."
Summary: In 1778 fourteen-year-old Becca takes a position as
personal maid to Peggy Shippen, the daughter of wealthy
Philadelphia Quakers, and witnesses the events that lead to General
Benedict Arnold's betrayal of the revolutionary American forces.
Includes bibliographical references.
1. Philadelphia—History—Revolution, 1775–1783—Juvenile
fiction. [1. Philadelphia (Pa.)—History—Revolution, 1775–1783—
Fiction. 2. Arnold, Benedict, 1741–1801—Fiction. 3. Quakers—
Fiction. 4. Spies—Fiction. 5. Pennsylvania—History—
Revolution, 1775–1783—Fiction. 6. United States—History—
Revolution, 1775–1783—Fiction.] I. Title.
PZ7.R459Fj 2004
[Fic]—dc22   2003056708
ISBN 0-15-205079-5

Designed by Trina Stahl
Text set in Stempel Garamond

Printed in the United States of America

A C E G H F D B

For Aunt Julia, my biggest fan,

who remembers when all

my books were just dreams

Acknowledgments

One of the definitions for the word "acknowl-edgment" in *Webster's New World Dictionary* is "to admit as true."

I admit as true, therefore, that I never would have thought of doing an historical novel had it not been for my son, Ron. I admit as true, that some of the best years of my life were spent "at-tending" the War for Independence, when I and my husband and our daughter, Marcella, followed Ron around the thirteen original colonies to restage its battles and the encampments with the Brigade of the American Revolution.

I admit as true, that on Christmas Day, 1993, as I watched Ron standing in the cold in tricorn hat, regimental coat, breeches, heavy cloak, boots, and sword, playing the role of General Nathanael Greene in the annual reenactment of Washington's

Crossing of the Delaware, I thought, *This crossing is the end and the beginning of the year for us, has been since Ron started reenacting it seventeen years ago now.* And, in spite of the hectic rush it causes on Christmas morning, with my husband and son both in the boats, it has become part of the holiday for us. And it has reached further across the years and into our lives than I ever thought was possible.

I admit as true, that I am indebted to all the good people I have met in our reenactments over the years for what I have learned, to the field of journalism for teaching me how to be a writer, to my husband, Ron, for being the wind beneath my wings.

I admit as true, that without the many scholarly books on research I could never attempt to write an historical novel, and I am indebted to their authors.

I admit as true, that I was at Valley Forge many times when my son, Ron, worked there with the National Park Service while in college. But that I still feel I fell short in doing Washington's army's tenure there justice in this book.

I admit as true, that for this particular book I am indebted to Anna Coxe Toogood, historian at Independence National Historical Park in Philadelphia, not only for her help but for her permission to allow me to use her nickname, "Coxie," for one of the servants in the Shippen household.

The name came across as so strong and compelling to me that I simply had to use it.

I admit as true, that David Dutcher, chief historian at Independence National Historical Park in Philadelphia, was tireless in advising me about reading material.

I admit as true, that Ann Curran of the Oakland, New Jersey, Historical Society not only advised me as to what kind of wedding gown Elizabeth Shippen should be wearing, but is a longtime friend and believer in my work.

I admit as true, that my editor, Karen Grove, and her assistant, Erin DeWitt, have been tireless in their patience, understanding, and emotional support.

All this I admit as true and am not only glad, but consider myself blessed to be able to do so.

—*Ann Rinaldi*

FINISHING BECCA

Merlin heard them first. All I heard was the low, threatening growl from his throat as I was pouring the milk into the container in the springhouse.

Then came the voices, ever so soft but carried in the mist that settled over everything. I looked out the window.

It was hard to see. The weather had turned warm, and steam was rising from the snow that had covered the ground all winter. Then I saw them, figures half there in the white air. Three men sitting their horses right outside the pasture gate.

Two had muskets. My heart slammed in my breast. *They are going to take Opal. How dare they?*

I started out of the springhouse and stopped. Were they American or king's men? Worse yet, were they marauders? In these times every sort of scum pretended to be with either army when for a fact they were reaping the benefits of the chaos all around us and just plain stealing.

The men had gotten off their horses and were pointing at Opal and conferring. I went to the door and peeked out, shushing Merlin behind me. But I could not understand their words.

Hessians. I felt the terror course through me. Hessians. A plundering party. Hessians had been swarming over the area outside the city for the last two months, stealing, burning, looting.

Why had I put Opal in the pasture where she could be seen? Because the day promised to be sunny once the mist burned off. Because she needed the air. Because I was stupid.

I drew in my breath. Even if they were Hessians, they weren't going to take *our* cow. I knew that much. Why, Opal was all the cow we had. And she was more than a cow. Anybody could see that. She was part of the family.

I didn't know what I could do. Here I was, a girl. And only fourteen, but I would do something. I had the element of surprise on my side. My brother, Blair, who was with Washington, had said that it was the element of surprise that had helped the Americans rout the Hessians at Trenton. Hessians were stupid anyway, Blair had said. All that fierceness was one thing when they were together, marching with their French horns, trumpets, and drums, but separate they were cowards.

I had no musket, no protection. No help from the house. My stepfather would be sleeping, Mama making breakfast. I didn't want to bring Mama into this.

I stepped out of the springhouse. A pitchfork lay against the wall. I picked it up. They were in the pasture now, creeping up on Opal. She saw them from the corners of her eyes and was moving away. Her bell tinkled softly.

They were cajoling her. In German. Beside me Merlin gave another deep-throated growl. I hushed him. Now Opal was running, her bell clanking in the misty morning air. She was terrified, mooing.

"Stop, stop! Don't hurt her, please!" I made my presence known.

They stopped, taken with my sudden appearance. If I'd had a musket I could have sent them running. They turned and stared. I must have looked like some demented witch girl, coming out of the mists at them like that, brandishing a pitchfork. My mob cap had come off, my shawl was hanging, my hair flapping. "Don't you put a hand on her!"

One of them already had grabbed Opal's halter and was holding her firm. The other one had his musket aimed at me.

The man in front had drawn his pistol. "Not to move. Call back the dog," he said.

Merlin had dashed forward and was running and barking around them, nipping at their heels. I called him. He came, reluctantly, complaining. I grabbed his collar. They were Hessians, all right, I could see that, though their green uniforms were dirty. They all sported those black, curving mustaches.

I minded the day last September when I'd stood on a hillock with twelve-year-old Jacob Morton on his father's farm and watched the Hessians marching down the Germantown Road on their way to Philadelphia. The British had led the march. But it was the fearful Hessians who had frightened us so.

"You're Hessians," I said. It was stupid, and they laughed.

"*Ja*," the one in front allowed. He wore a sword. An officer. His uniform distinguished him only because it was a little less ragged. They all had that look of wariness in their eyes that I'd seen on the faces of people in the city who were not American or British.

"She's our only cow," I said. "Please don't take her. We need the milk."

They laughed at that and spoke German to each other. It was a large joke.

"This is American household?" the officer asked. "Or Tory?"

"Loyalist," I lied quickly. "We're a good Loyalist family. We're loyal to King George III."

"Then you give cow to feed his men, yes?"

"No!" I stepped forward. The barrel of the musket was raised higher.

For an awful moment we were at a standstill. There in the early mists of the February morning in our own cow pasture, where I'd been a hundred times, I faced the enemy. This was war then, I minded. Not all those battles we only heard about after they were over. But standing in your own front yard, defending your cow. This is what Trenton had been about, and White Plains, Brooklyn Heights, Lexington, Brandywine, Saratoga. All so we could keep what was ours, what we'd earned, no matter how paltry.

A crow called in the distance. I felt the weak sun climbing in the heavens, moving across time. One warm day, I thought, one warm day in this whole frozen, benighted winter, and this has to happen.

"She be stout *und* young," the man holding Opal's halter said. He was not speaking of Opal. He gestured his head toward me. I felt fear-quickened. I was not stout, but he meant me.

The officer looked at the house. "Who's to home?"

"My stepfather. And he has a gun."

They laughed again, said something more in German about me. I felt their eyes go over me. I heard the word *Fraülein* and blushed. Then the officer reached inside his coat and drew out something. "I give notation," he said.

"No. No paper. I want nothing from you. Your quartermaster doesn't pay. Our neighbors have told us. Just go." I raised the pitchfork.

"Ve have no food," he said, holding forth the paper.

"You have food in Philadelphia. General Howe got control of the rivers from the Americans in late November. And brought in provisions before the waters froze."

The officer raised his eyebrows and shrugged. "Ve, how you say, borrow," he said.

"No, you take. And I won't give."

They laughed again, enjoying my challenge. It gave savor to their day. Then they grew serious. "You vant ve go and take from house?" The man who offered the paper put it back in his pocket and shrugged. "You vant ve should burn?"

"It would be the last thing you ever burned." A wellspring of anger gave me foolish courage.

He scowled. Then he turned, strode across the frozen ground, withdrew his sword from his scabbard, and lifted Opal's tail.

"Stop!" I screamed and shut my eyes tight.

There was a bellow from Opal. I opened my eyes. He held the end part of her tail in his hand. She'd broken away and was running like some demented thing, her bloody tail flapping, her bell ringing crazily. I threw the pitchfork at him. It fell wide of the mark. I covered my face with my hands, heard Opal's terrified moans, Merlin's barks, and then the Hessian commander shouting orders at his men to bring her in hand.

Then another sound. "Halt there. Or I'll shoot!"

A door slammed at the house. And through the morning mists I saw my stepfather, Henry Job, holding his fowling piece.

"Get away from that cow." He strode across the road between the house and the pasture and came to the gate. He held the fowling piece steady. "I'm fair to middling with this thing. Can hit the frozen apples off that tree yonder and make sauce of them. Or I can make sauce of you. Now get. You damned jägers."

They stood staring at him. "Ve are under orders from Knyphausen."

"I don't care a pig's tooth whose orders you're under. You damned king's hirelings have raided enough farms. I go into Philadelphia. I see your women sitting in the market house selling the plunder you stole the night before. Now get off my farm!"

"*Nein*," the sergeant said.

"No *nein*. Three. I'll give you to the count of three." He was half-dressed, roused from sleep, and mean. But Henry Job was mean enough under the best of circumstances. It was his way. *You don't know who you're dallying with*, I said to myself, *so you'd best light.*

Henry Job started to count. "One."

The officer stared in disbelief. Opal had come to a standstill in the back of the pasture and was lowing piteously. Deep growls were coming from Merlin's throat. I was hard put to hold him, lest he charge and be shot, too.

"Two," my stepfather said.

They did not move. "You vould shoot the soldiers of your king?" the officer yelled.

"Three."

"You vill be put under arrest. You vill be hanged! Ve vill burn the house!"

The fowling piece exploded. The report carried on the mist like a cannon shot. I smelled the black powder.

The Hessians ran by me in a blur, boots clomping, spurs jingling.

They didn't stay to find out how fast Henry Job could reload. Their horses' hooves beat on the cold ground as they rode away. Then silence, except for Opal's lowing. And the tramping of my stepfather's feet as he walked by me.

"I've told you, girl, and I've told you, not to let that cow out." He paused beside me. "Didn't I tell you?"

"Yes, sir." I was trembling. I let go of Merlin.

"Then why did you do it?" he screamed at me.

"I thought she needed some sun."

"Sun!" He raised his eyes and his arms to the heavens with the fowling piece still in one hand. "We all need sun! We all need food. We all need this godforsaken war to be over with! Go into the house and get me some rags. Now!"

So this was the war then. Not prettified British officers walking on Philadelphia's streets. But Opal with a sheared-off tail. Blood all over the snow. I shivered and ran to the house.

Chapter 1

MARCH 1778

*M*ove over, Opal, move over."

She was being stubborn again. I could swear that cow knew, all of a piece, that since her tail had been lopped off, she could make us feel sorry for her and get her own way. Mama had stitched the tail back together that morning while Henry Job and I held her and I talked to her. I suppose Henry Job could just have bound it up. But he said she needed it long to switch the flies in summer. She would always have to wear the rags on it, he said. So now it caused considerable damage when she swished it in your face.

She swished it often. I discovered that talking to her becalmed her, so I'd taken to conversation while I milked.

"We all miss Blair," I said. "Be happy you're not with him now. His men would butcher you and make a good stew."

Blair wouldn't allow any such thing, of course. Because she was Blair's cow. He'd raised her from a calf. But I didn't tell her that. I just went on talking and blowing on my hands, because it was cold. The brief warm spell we'd had last month when the Hessians had come had lasted only two days. Then the bitter cold set in again.

She was fixing to come at me with that tail again.

"You hit me with that tail, Opal, and I'll deliver you myself to the American army this day. Sick to the teeth they are of fire cake and turnips. Although we hear that Washington did manage to get them some spirits. I know how to get to Camp Valley Forge, you know. I went with Mama on Christmas, remember?"

Not that I wanted to remember, but I told her about it just the same. "An ungodly place it is, Opal, where the Americans have been holed up since mid-December. Never did I see a place so frozen and sad. Why, the sound of the wind whipping across the hills is enough to make a person mad as a March hare! And the snow!"

The milk made a pinging sound as it hit the sides of the pail. "Mama drove the wagon right down the main street. If you can call that frozen mud hole a street. And there was Blair, waiting for us. Oh, Opal, be glad you didn't have to see him. He's grown taller and his wrists stick out of the regimental coat Mama made. And it's ragged. But he was so happy. And do you know why?"

She turned to gaze at me, listening. I stopped milking. Tears were coming out of her great brown eyes. She *understood!*

"Because they were soon to have huts. The soldiers were already building them when we were there. You know how Mama knitted him the hose and muffler for Christmas? Well, all he wanted was the tools we brought. They made him so happy. He cried when he saw them!"

I finished milking in silence. I was pure talked out. It wasn't until I was standing outside the barn in the cold and dark, with the first faint light streaking in the east, that the thought came full-blown to me, like a flower in the snow.

How had Mama known to bring those tools to Blair? I'd seen every note my brother had sent via Robert Morton, our Quaker neighbor.

DECEMBER 11TH: *We cannot stay at Whitemarsh much longer. We are too exposed to the elements and the British.*

DECEMBER 15TH: *The precise position of winter quarters is not yet fixed upon and will likely be determined this day.*

DECEMBER 20TH: *We are in a place of wooded slopes, heavy with slushy snow, past the*

17th milestone from Philadelphia. It seems deso-
late, but we have plenty of wood and water.

Something nuzzled my hand. Merlin. Ever
since the day the Hessians had come by, he waited
outside the barn door for me when I milked. It
seemed Merlin would never forget those Hessians.

I sighed and shook off my thoughts. There were
too many things to confuse a body these days. I
tramped through the snow to the house.

· · · · ·

Mama was in the kitchen already, bending over
the hearth, stirring a pan of eggs and ham. I saw
indigo stains on her fingers. So, she'd been up
early, working in her dyeing shed.

"Was the springhouse broken into last night?"

"There were no footprints in the snow, Mama.
And I didn't hear Merlin bark." We hadn't been
raided since the Hessians. Not even irregular militia or deserting Continentals. Blair had spoken
up for us, of course, so that foragers from Washington's army stayed away. But since the Hessians,
Mama worried.

"Why didn't you sleep late? I'd have made
breakfast," I said.

"I wanted to dye the linen for Rebecca Franks's
spring cloak. Don't tell Papa Henry."

Mama's dyeing was a bone of contention between them. It was her latest business experiment.

"It smells like the hounds of hell are breathing on us!" Papa Henry would yell coming into the kitchen of a morning when Mama had been mixing her colors. Papa Henry could be very descriptive.

To be fair, the smells did seep in from the lean-to shed off the kitchen. But Mama persisted. All the good dyers had fled Philadelphia when the British came last fall. And she saw a chance to make more money. She now not only sewed for the fine Loyalist ladies, she supplied them with colored fabric. Mama had a first commandment: "Nothing we learn is lost to us."

"It will serve me well, this knowledge of dyeing," she'd told Papa Henry when he ranted and raved over the smells. But Henry Job Claghorn hated the poisonous mordants, papery onion skins, crumbling leaves, and pieces of bark that sat in the shed. To say nothing of the stinking indigo pot and stores of stale urine. I think that secretly he hated her dyeing because she made good money from it. And he didn't, running goods to the British.

"Did you finish sewing the blue dress?" I sat down to eat.

"Yes. It's the most elegant I've ever done."

Mama was taken with elegance. She'd come from a well-placed family and my father, Phillip Syng the silversmith, had been a wealthy man before he lost his money. Mama carried the signs of her breeding and past life with her. Like one who has had the smallpox carries the scars. Given her life here on the farm and her marriage to Henry Job after my father died, her elegance was a weight around her neck. Her need to reach for things she felt she had a right to, things always out of her grasp, caused all the trouble between them.

She satisfied the need by rubbing shoulders with the rich people she sewed for.

"Who's the blue dress for?" I asked. "Mrs. Loring?" Mrs. Loring was General Sir William Howe's American mistress.

"Hush. Not to speak her name in this house. It makes Papa Henry angry."

"Everything makes him angry. You don't have to whiten silk stockings anymore since she gave you her business and told her friends about you. Why is it wrong for you to sew for her and not wrong for him to supply the British with food?"

"He needs the money. A man has his pride. How do you think he feels when I bring in money and he doesn't?"

"He could sell to the American army. They're in need."

"He should sell for worthless Continental currency? This year all the Pennsylvania farmers had their best crop ever and they won't sell to the American army."

"He should sell so your son can have food, Mama."

"Bah! The food would never get to him. Like those fifty wagons of clothing from Lancaster never got to them."

"One of these nights Washington's dragoons are going to kill Papa Henry when he's on a run to the city," I said.

"Blair has spoken for him. Washington's men will not touch him," she said.

"Why? When he's selling to the British? Blair can do only so much, Mama. Sooner or later they'll catch him and kill him." Her blind faith in Henry Job made me angry. She was so concerned with his pride that she dismissed out of hand that he was selling to the army her son was fighting against.

"Washington's men will leave him be." The subject was closed. She spoke with such fierceness that I fell silent. What did she know that she was not telling me? That Henry Job's twice-weekly runs into the city were covering his activities as one of Washington's spies? That would be funny if it were not so sad. Because Henry Job Claghorn was a dolt. He put in a day's work on the farm, yes, but barely. Since Mama had married him, he had allowed her to put food on the board by selling off all her possessions from her life with my father. Only after most everything was sold off did he rouse himself with this scheme of selling to the

British. He was always scheming, convinced there was a magical way out there to make a fortune, if he could only stumble upon it.

And he criticized Mama in trivial matters constantly, yet gave her no succor with important problems. Mama soon learned to make her own decisions. And she was becoming good at it.

Blair and I were her world. Blair more than I. All the dreams she had lost were bound up in him. She had used the last of my father's money to send him to the College and Academy of Philadelphia. She intended him to become a merchant.

Then those New England Puritans started their war, as Mama put it. That enraged Henry Job. He was from Boston. And they had a running argument going between them, each defending the virtues of his own city.

Blair was made a lieutenant in Captain Sharpe Dulaney's Third Battalion. Mama was shameless about reminding those who gave out commissions that her first husband had served in the Provincial army with the young George Washington. Blair acquitted himself well at Long Island, White Plains, Harlem Heights, Trenton, Princeton, Germantown, Brandywine. He was now a captain. Mama was so proud of him, betimes it made me jealous.

"Eat," she said now. "I need your help in the city today."

I was full taken back. What was amiss? I loved

the city. But I did not trust Mama. She kept too many secrets.

I watched her eating. She had the manners of a great lady. My father had owned the Sign of the Silver Cup on Front Street. She'd had plenty of years to be a great lady. But in the lean time, after the end of the French War when the British army was no longer here to spend money, my father found himself overstocked like other merchants. And England still shipped goods to us. Everyone lost money. Mother started sewing for friends.

Then my father invested in a ship exporting grainstuffs to the West Indies. By then the West Indies trade had peaked. That year rains favored the Caribbean and the islands produced enough provisions so they didn't need our grainstuffs.

We were economically ruined. I was three. Mother started advertising herself as "a clear starcher who would also whiten ladies' silk stockings." And she started sewing more.

We removed to our country place near Germantown. Father turned his hand to farming and failed. Henry J. Claghorn was their caretaker. Blair said he just sat back and let Father fail, though he knew farming. Mama says Father wouldn't take Henry Job's advice. I believe Blair.

Father died. Blair said that Henry Job moved right into the house before they were married. So far out, who would know?

Mama held on to her gentleness and elegance.

But they soon became honed with anger and determination.

Sometimes at breakfast Mama would talk about her old house in the city—the wide curved staircase, damask draperies, paneling, and portraits by Charles Willson Peale, the furniture from the shop of James Randolph. She would speak of the table she kept, the entertaining she did, the gowns she wore.

"Prominent people came to that house," she would say. "Charles Thomson and Thomas Mifflin, the merchants. The printer William Bradford. The lawyer John Dickinson. Dr. William Shippen and his wife, Anna. *She* is from the Lee family of Virginia."

My heart hammers inside me whenever she gives voice to her memories. I can see the house, the table with the delicate desserts, the library full of books, the pleasure garden out back.

Of course, I belong there. Not on this farm. I know I could play the harpsichord she speaks of. I know I could do the dances. There is something in me that is drawn to that life. Something that sickens my soul for the lack of it.

Once, we were on our way home from the city at twilight. It was in the beginning of December. Because of "shameful irregularities" by his own soldiers, General Howe had men on the street with orders to take up all stragglers or disorderly persons.

Though we did not wish to be caught as such, Mama pulled up on the reins of Duke, our old horse. "There"—and she pointed—"there it is."

I just stared. "What?"

"Where we once lived. There is the house," she said.

It was three-and-a-half stories high. In the twilight there was a rosy cast to the brick. It had white marble steps and trimmings, iron railings at the front steps and at the garden gate. The front windows had shutters. English ivy graced it in places. I felt a dryness in my throat, looking at it. A pulling at my heart. Candles shone within. I saw a maidservant in white cap and apron walk by one of the windows.

We sat for a while in silence, then Mama clucked to Duke and we went on our way. I was struck dumb. It was still there! Our house! Why had I never thought it would be?

·　·　·　·　·

"Go and get dressed," Mama ordered now. "There isn't much time. I'll be late!"

I left the table. We were going to the city! Joy throbbed in my veins. I ran through the hall to my room, which was in the converted back parlor. We lived downstairs, for this had once been a grand country house. We closed the upstairs off in winter. We could not afford to heat it.

I dressed in my good blue linen, my second-

·　21　·

best woolen underskirt, my good chemise. I put on my best shoes with the silver buckles and grabbed my go-to-meeting cloak from the peg. I was out in the hall in less than ten minutes. My hand was on the handle of the front door.

"You there!"

His voice always brought my world to a stop. Henry Job stood just outside the door of his and Mama's room, roused out of sleep and mean-spirited over it, like the bear of a man he was. "Where're you off to?"

"I'm going with Mama. To help her make her delivery."

"Look at me."

I turned. There was a darkness in this man that I could never put a name to. But I was old enough to know you didn't have to name things to fear them.

"Cow milked?"

"Yes, sir."

"Stall cleaned? Chickens fed? Hogs slopped?"

"I did all of it. There's a pot of soup bubbling on the hearth. I brought cheese in from the springhouse."

He pointed a finger at me. "You're not to see that girl in the city, you hear me? You're to have naught to do with her."

"What girl?"

"You know. The Darragh girl."

"Ann? But she's my friend!" The Darraghs were Quakers. Ann's father taught school. They lived on Second Street in the city. An upstairs room in their house had been taken over by British staff officers as a council chamber. General Howe's headquarters was across the street, and I'd met Ann there one day when Mama delivered a finished gown at the headquarters for Mrs. Loring.

Ann had been sent across the street to secure a pass for her mother to go out of the city and get flour at the mill at Frankford. That day, while she waited for the pass and I for my mother, we became acquainted.

Ann knew a lot about the city. And I was hungry for news of it. "Come visit someday," she'd invited.

I'd spent a whole day with her just before Christmas when Mama was visiting her customers. I'd even taken supper with the family. We were planning another day together soon.

"Why can't I see Ann?" I demanded of my stepfather.

"Her mother's a spy."

I stared at him. He scratched his bewhiskered face and the rasping sound seemed loud in the hallway.

"Ann's mother is a good Quaker woman."

"There are no good Quaker women. Pious hypocrites, the lot of them. Rich as thieves."

He hated Quakers. He hated Philadelphia. In Boston, he said, people dressed and spoke like Englishmen, and they had proper frame houses and not those narrow piles of red brick.

"Quakers keep the town decent," Mama would tell him. "They keep it from being debauched like Boston."

"Quakers are as dull as crows," he would say. "And they favor whatever army comes through, for all their piety!" Oh, he and Mama had their differences, all right.

"I don't like you bandying about town when your mother is working," he told me then.

"I don't bandy."

"Not a decent place for a young girl. Why, you can't walk down the street without hearing an Amish farmer arguing with a German grocer. Or running into a Jew bargaining with someone who has the brogue of a Scotch-Irishman. You're to stay with your mama, hear? Be a help to her."

No profit in arguing. He could forbid me to go, if the humour seized him. "Yes, sir."

"Rumor has it that the Darragh woman has fed to Washington some information she overheard in her house."

Ann's mother? She was so proper and demure. I felt a thrill of excitement. "When?"

He waved a hand in disgust at me. "Last December. When the Americans were at Whitemarsh."

"What has that to do with Ann?"

"It has to do with us!" he shouted. "With the fact that I don't wish any suspicion placed upon us. You think I could make my runs if the British connect us with spies? You think your mother would be allowed in and out of the city? You dare to have a saucy tongue in your head? You think I can't make you mind?"

I thought nothing. Except that the man had need to lord it over someone. And I was the only one convenient. "No, sir." I managed to be sufficiently contrite. And hoped the "no" would properly answer all his questions.

He scowled for a moment, confused himself. Then he nodded, satisfied that he had put me in my proper place, whatever he perceived it to be. He went back to his room. "Tell your mother I want her home before darkness sets in."

"Yes, sir." Mama would come back when it pleased her. You could say that about her, at least. She defended her husband to everyone but stood up to him herself. She paid no heed to him, yet allowed him his rantings and ravings anyway.

"Remember, you've a cow to milk!" he called after me as I went out the door.

I did not answer. Mama was waiting in the wagon.

Chapter 2

The sky was the same blue as Mama's Delft plates that she had hidden away someplace unbeknownst to Papa Henry or me. She had sold off all her good Chippendale furniture, my father's library, her gowns and jewelry, her china and rugs, all Father's silver. The Delft plates were her last hedge against the uncertain future that plagued us all.

A fresh dusting of snow covered that already frozen on the ground. Only those two days in February when the Hessians came around had the temperature risen above freezing. It snowed at least once a week. The Delaware and the Schuylkill rivers were just starting to unfreeze now.

Late in November the British had finally wrested control of the rivers from the Americans. Then they'd had to scramble to bring provisions in before ice clogged those rivers. Many times their ships were damaged and cargoes lost when they tried to get by the *chevaux-de-frise*, the large frames with dangerous pointed spears, that the Americans had sunk into the Delaware. The Americans tied a knot about the city so provisions couldn't get in. Occasionally a farmer bringing food in was murdered by American pickets. So far Papa Henry had been lucky.

Though Mama provoked me with love of elegance, when we went to the city together, we were on common ground. I felt a kinship with her. Was I a hypocrite then? Or just befuddled about who I was? Why did I so often feel like there were pieces of me missing? Where would I find them? Where to look?

I think I always trusted Mama to work things out for me. She had worked them out for Blair, hadn't she?

As the farm smells receded behind us, Mama rested easy in the wagon and I asked her about my friend Ann. "Why did he say I can't see her?"

"He told you, didn't he? There is suspicion that her mother spied for Washington. We can't have that shadow cast upon us. It's hard enough, these days, scraping a living out of this landscape they have given us with this war."

"But, Mama, Ann is my *friend*. How can I explain to her?"

"Hush now. Will you hush? Never have I seen such a provoking child as you. You complain about chores, about our life, then when I set about to make things better, you won't even listen to my plan."

"What plan?"

"Will you keep a still tongue in your head and listen? And forget Ann for now. They are Quakers. Quakers will always manage. They choose no sides but cosy up to both. They know how. Would that we had a little of their common sense. Now, I'll turn and go back if I hear another word about Ann."

I fell silent.

After a moment she spoke. "The gown I made is not for Mrs. Loring. It is for Peggy Shippen."

Shippen, Shippen. I cast about in my mind. "Is she the daughter of Alice, who is of the Lee family of Virginia?"

"No, Alice is Doctor William's wife. Peggy is the daughter of Edward. He is cousin of Doctor William. He is the judge. He has four daughters and a son. You must keep this straight."

I nodded. She frequently spoke of the people she sewed for, the houses she went into, the matters discussed therein. How would I ever keep it all straight?

"Soon all the Shippen girls will be needing new gowns," she said. "But it is Peggy we will see this day. Not only for the gown. But for other business."

"What business?"

"She would meet with you."

"Me?"

"Yes. She is very pretty, and she lives in a fine house. She is in need of a maidservant. The British have lured away the best servants from all the households. At her last fitting, she asked me about you."

I felt a tremor of excitement. This very pretty young girl, this daughter of a judge, who lived in a fine house, had asked about me! "What did you tell her?"

"That you are lazy and slovenly and disorderly."

"Mama!"

"All winter she has been partying. Sleigh-riding parties, theater parties, assemblies, and balls. While our men have been suffering in that valley without a forge. And prisoners on both sides languish in hunger and cold."

"And you would have me work for her? A Loyalist?"

"She's no Loyalist but a Quaker. All the Shippens are. Judge Shippen is doing his best to remain neutral. But he has kept open house for General Sir William Howe and his staff since they came here."

"I'm confused."

"So are they. Don't worry the matter. He's a judge, and he doesn't know what to do about things. His cousin the doctor is ashamed of him. His cousin is running the medical department for Washington."

I listened in rapt attention as these bits of gossip rolled off Mama's tongue.

"Peggy's father is a harried, frightened man. He once invited Washington to his house when the Continental Congress was in session. But he lost all his positions on the king's bench and the Provincial Council when the Rebels took over. He lost a lot of money, too."

"Rebels! Mama, don't call them Rebels. They're Patriots. We're Patriots!"

"We're nothing of the kind."

"What *are* we, then? Blair's in Washington's army!"

"We're waiting, like everyone else, to see what will happen."

"Mama, you *know* you're a Patriot. So am I!"

She gripped my forearm until it hurt. "You're *never* to say you are a Patriot in any of these houses I take you to! Do you understand?"

She was so fierce it frightened me. "Yes, Mama."

She let go of my arm and went on with her recitation. "Peggy's father was at one time placed on parole by the new Rebel authorities. Peggy's older sister Elizabeth has a beau with the American army. Peggy's only brother, Edward, rode right into the British lines in Trenton last year to renew his allegiance with the king. He was captured and sent to Washington's headquarters at Morristown."

"What happened to him?"

"Washington had him sent home to his father."

She was intimate with all of it, I minded, all the goings-on with Philadelphia's best families.

"Make no mistake about it," she said. "Peggy Shippen, who has asked for you as a maidservant, is one of the prettiest girls in Philadelphia. And no matter what is happening to her father, she is enjoying this war. She has come into her own. This is her time. She was the guest of honor at a dinner and a dance given by Captain Hammond on the British frigate *Roebuck*. And she's ofttimes been seen sleigh riding with Captain John Andre of the Royal Fusiliers."

I thrilled to his name. And the name of his regiment. And the easy way Mama spoke them. "You know so much, Mama," I said.

She sighed. "I have had to learn. But what I had to learn most of all, and what you will have to learn if you take this position, is to keep your ears open and your mouth shut. Do you think you can do that?"

I shivered in excitement. "Yes."

"She only wants to speak with you today. To see if you are suitable for her needs. She has need of a friend more than a maidservant. Someone to accompany her and hand her things, to lay out her clothing, to fix her hair and listen to her. It's a genteel position. You'll be like a lady-in-waiting. So remember your manners. Curtsy when you meet her. The way I taught you to. Be amiable. And *don't make mention of your brother in Washington's army.*"

"Yes," I said again.

She pulled up on the reins and looked at me. "I do this for you, Becca. I have not been able to do anything for you. Being in such grand company, you will learn their ways. It will be as good as the best finishing school."

Tears came to my eyes when she said that. "Finishing school?"

"Yes. Like I had. Like Peggy Shippen and all the well-placed girls in Philadelphia have. You need this, Becca. You need to be finished."

Finished. Yes, I minded, Mama was right. But how had she known there were pieces of me missing?

"It isn't for the king's shilling that I send you there. It is so you will learn to speak softly and well. To mind your diction. To see how they do their needlework, how they dance, perhaps even pick up some French."

Was that all I needed then? Were such things my missing pieces? I pondered for a moment.

"What is it?" she asked.

I searched her face, looking for answers. But I did not even know the right questions. "What about Papa Henry?" It was all I could think of to say.

"Leave him to me."

"Who will milk the cow?"

Mama then did something she scarcely ever did. She hugged me close for a long moment. "Loving our children gives us such pain," she said.

Never had she told me she loved me. I was struck dumb, afraid to break the spell.

Then she released me and smiled and pointed. "Just look at that house. Couldn't you learn to be finished in a house like that?"

We sat in the wagon, staring at it. Rosy red brick with shutters the color of fresh cream. Tall arched windows that shone in the glint of the morning sun. They had beautiful moldings. The bare limbs of great trees hovered over it protectively. Its chimneys rose majestically. A thin crust of snow iced its grounds. There was a garden in back, now only frozen sticks of grapevines, jessamine, roses, and weeping willows. But what a garden it would be come spring! I could see Peggy Shippen taking tea there with this Captain Andre.

A great sense of peace washed over me as I sat looking at the house. It was as if someone had clapped his hands and all my fears had turned into birds and taken flight. I could almost hear the rushing of their wings as they flew away.

I had dreamed of such a place. Stately, orderly, commodious. Here I would find my missing pieces, yes. "I'll do my best to make her like me," I said.

"Good." She clucked to Duke and we drove to a wrought-iron gate on the side. A servant opened it. Mama drove in.

Chapter 3

$\mathcal{T}$he wrought-iron gate clanged shut behind us, and I minded that one could hear the sounds from the cobblestone street outside, but here it was secluded and sealed off. Here was its own world. One had the feeling of being in a more gracious place and of a gentler time.

Servants came running to meet us. One helped Mama from the wagon, another took Duke's reins, still another Mama's package. Two of the servants were nigra. Mama knew and conversed with them all.

There was a stately brick carriagehouse out back behind carefully groomed garden paths. Mama pointed to a small brick building to the side. "The servants' quarters," she said. "You may be living there."

What can I say of the house? It welcomed me.

We were brought in through a small back room and invited to sit on benches by a nigra woman. "How you this day, Miz Jane?" she asked.

"My bones hurt, Coxie."

"Do they now?" She laughed. "My bones is dead an' doan know 'nuf to lie down. You like some chocolate?"

"Hmm, yes, that would be nice." Mama took off her cloak and bade me do the same.

I looked around. This was a kitchen, yet it was not a kitchen. Large windows let in sunlight that glowed on copper pots and pans. A scrubbed oaken table sat in the center of the room. A fire burned in the hearth. Soup bubbled there. The woman called Coxie put more wood in the beehive oven, but I smelled no cooking bread.

"What is this room?" I whispered to Mama.

"It's a waiting place," she said. "For the food. After it is brought from the kitchen out back. They keep it warm here. Coxie keeps it warm in the brick oven."

"This be a waitin' place for food an' people," the woman called Coxie said. She handed us mugs of steaming hot chocolate. "This your little one, Miz Jane?"

"Yes, this is my Becca."

Coxie folded her hands across her ample belly and appraised me like I was a side of bacon. Sprigs of graying hair peeked out from under her mob cap, but her face did not seem old. "So, you be wantin' to work in this house, then?"

"If they'll have me," I said.

"Oh, they'll have you, chile. They'll have you in many ways. Servants scarce as talcum powder in town these days." And she laughed. "You hear 'bout the duel, Miz Jane?"

"No, what duel?"

"One of those dandies of Miz Peggy's, one of those king's men, wanted to fight a duel. Said if'n he was to die, he wanted to die made up proper like. But couldn't find no talcum powder fer his wig in all of Philadelphia. So he fought this mornin'. Miz Sarah, she went an' watched wif Miz Peggy. They say he weren't hurt, but there be so much cookin' flour flyin' 'round from his wig you could scarcely see him fightin'." Her laugh was deep and real.

"Peggy and Sarah went to *watch?*" Mama was horrified.

"Yessum. They be in the liberry now wif their daddy. He's havin' high words wif them 'bout it. From what I hears, this dandy king's man kissed Miz Sally. Right in the open, in the Lord's good sunlight!"

"Oh dear," Mama said.

"Yessum. Doan you worry none, Miz Becca. They'll be havin' you in this here house. They'll be havin' you. Sweet little thing like you, why wouldn't they be havin' you?" She kept a running one-sided discussion going, asking and answering her own questions while she went about her duties.

I sat there sipping my hot chocolate in the waiting place for food and people. After a few moments the door to the hallway opened and another servant stood there. This one was white.

"You may come into the hall, madam," she said.

We left our cups and went into the wide center hall. As we did so, the house's welcome turned into an embrace. With each step I took on the lush carpets, I felt it. The faces that gazed down at me from gilt-framed portraits seemed benevolent. I felt truly as if I had come out of my own waiting place and come home.

From up the sweeping stairway came the sounds of a harpsichord. Its echo set something to stirring in my blood. Did I dare call it memory? I dared not.

We sat on straight-backed chairs in the center hall. From behind a carved door came muffled voices raised in argument. A man's, then a girl's. The maid knocked, opened the door, and stood waiting to be acknowledged.

"On the street! In broad daylight! Like a common doxie!" the man was saying.

"He meant no harm, Father," came a female voice.

"No harm? By God, he'll know what harm he's done before I'm through with him! Whatever made you go to watch is what I want to know. I can understand *you*, Peggy, with your capricious ways, but you, Sarah? You know better!"

"I wanted to bring him some talcum powder for his wig," came the tearful reply, apparently from Sarah.

"Talcum powder?" The man was incredulous.

The one called Peggy had a voice that was lustier and firmer. "He was determined to die like an Adonis, Father. But he could find no talcum powder. It was the *least* we could do."

"Romantic nonsense! Yes, Dorothea, what is it? I told you we did not wish to be disturbed."

"Sir, the mantua-maker is here for a fitting with Miss Peggy. And she's brought her daughter for an interview."

"Good Lord, is it time already? All right." He cleared his throat. "We'll discuss this later, girls. I *will* have an apology from that young scamp, or know the reason why. Peggy, go upstairs for your fitting. Sarah, to your lessons."

We were led forward by the maid. I stood there dumb and bedazzled. My eyes could not take it all in. My senses were assaulted. Rich wainscoting. A silver tea tray on a polished table held the remains of some delicate sweetbuns. A massive fireplace gave toasty warmth, and elegant chairs beckoned.

Richly bound books lined the walls; damask draperies, imported carpeting, polished floors.

I had not known that people lived in such a manner. All we heard of was deprivation, sacrifice, and hardships because of the war. Here, in this house, there was no war. The distinguished-looking gentleman in the well-cut frock coat was keeping it at bay outside the wrought-iron gate.

Early last fall, Blair had stopped by our house with a young fellow officer, a colonel. His name was Alexander Hamilton, I recollect. They were on a mission for Washington, to get everything they could out of the city that would be of use to them before it fell to the British.

I had been sent out to the well for fresh water. Before I came in I heard Blair telling Mama of rapes by the British soldiers in the countryside in the Jerseys.

Here, the man of the house was outraged because a king's man had kissed his daughter on the street.

I felt a small knot of anger in me. And then I looked at the girls themselves. And the small knot grew.

The girls moved amongst these rich trappings as if they were commonplace. Shining curls tumbled around their heads. Velvet cloaks were strewn carelessly over chairs. Delicate hands sported rings. Soft, rich folds of fabric fell back from their young arms as they reached up to hug their father.

The blond girl turned from him to look at me. Then she looked back at him. "But I'm to interview the girl," she pouted. "Why do you send me from the room?"

"Go for your fitting, Peggy," he ordered. "Don't you think Mrs. Claghorn has other duties this day?"

"But, Daddy!"

"I will speak with the girl first," he said. His tone brooked no argument.

Peggy puckered a delicate mouth, picked up the skirts of her beautiful dress, and stomped from the room. Mama followed. The maid closed the door. And I was alone with the man who was filled with righteous Quaker anger because his daughter had been kissed right out in the open, on the street, by one of the king's men, like a common doxie.

"Sit, child, do." His manner was most gentle.

I settled myself into the soft chair he offered. The fire crackled. Through the long windows, the sun shone on the silver candelabra. He picked up the shining silver teapot, then a delicate china cup. He poured a cup of tea for me. Something was inscribed on the pot. It was Latin. *Vigilans*, it said.

He stood before the hearth. His breeches and frock coat were of velvet. His hands were strong but well kept. His hair was almost all silver. His face was etched out of years of genteel living. He conducted himself as one who was accustomed to being obeyed. Yet he had no pretensions. He had a broad brow, intelligent eyes, and a very patrician nose.

He went with the house, I decided. I would not have been surprised to find something in Latin inscribed on his forehead.

"You are younger than I expected," he said.

I sipped my tea. "I can act older."

"I have no doubt, being your mother's child, that you are responsible. I am looking for a young woman of prudence, forbearance, and firmness. If the girl I hire is anything less, Peggy will make mincemeat of her."

I smiled.

He did not. "The girl I employ must be from good people, yet willing to work. She must be honest, sober, earnest. She must not have a loose tongue concerning what goes on in this house."

I understood. "I can do that, sir."

"She must have a sunny disposition yet be able to exert a mild influence of common sense over my Peggy. I understand you were raised to have such common sense."

I allowed, dismally, that I was.

"It goes without saying then that you must be both circumspect and outspoken. This morning, for instance, if you had known my girls were setting out to witness a duel, what would you have done?"

I gaped. "Done, sir?"

"Yes, would you have advised them against going? Said nothing? Or come and told me?"

His blue eyes bore into me. For all his gentle demeanor, I felt an icy reserve. So then, he was asking me to declare where my loyalties would lie. With him or his daughters? I thought quickly. But all that came to mind was that if he wanted forthrightness from me, I would give him forthrightness. I would enter into no games. He would know me for what I was.

"Likely, sir, I would have advised her against going, then once she decided on her course of action, I'd have kept a still tongue in my head."

He scowled. "Do you think that a proper answer?"

"Sir, I'm not always a proper person. I only know what I would likely have done. It's the way of me. I can't dress my character up in plumes and feathers."

He smiled. "I don't want plumes and feathers. But truth. You have the position."

I could not believe it! "But wouldn't you rather I said that I'd tell you of her plans?"

"Yes. But I'd rather, more, that you be circumspect. When can you start?"

My head was spinning. "Whenever my mama says so."

"Good. Then I shall write her a note." And he strode across the room to a desk, where he wrote something on expensive vellum. Replacing the quill pen in the silver inkstand, he turned to me. "Your father made this inkstand. And I paid him fourteen pounds sterling for this silver tankard. See how much I use it? The hinge of the lid is near worn through."

I beamed.

"He was an excellent silversmith."

Tears came to my eyes. He was a decent man to mention my father's accomplishments to me.

"Here, take this note upstairs to your mother."

I took the paper. It was of handmade linen. I had seen the kind once before in a note the young American officer Alexander Hamilton had sent around, thanking Mama for her hospitality. The paper had the watermark of a Continental soldier, musket in hand, pointing to the legend *Pro Patria*. I was surprised to see such paper used in a Quaker house where British officers were frequent visitors. A small thing, but it said something about the man. What, I did not know. Perhaps that his loyalties were torn by this war.

He smiled. "Yes, it's a note telling your mother that I will provide your clothing for the position."

I hadn't even looked at the written message.

He walked me to the library door. "Peggy is my baby. I have indulged her. She is headstrong and impulsive. I would ask one thing of you."

"Yes, sir."

"I am doing my best to keep chaos at bay now that the social order is disrupted. I am of limited financial means because of the war. When my girl starts talking of new gowns, more frippery, discourage her. Remind her of how beautiful she is in her present finery."

I was touched that he should ask such. "Yes, sir."

"My Peggy is most impatient with me these days because I have had to put restraints on her spending."

I went up the stairway to find Mama, thinking how if this very caring and loving man were my father, I would not be impatient with him. I would read to him, serve him tea. I felt the absence of my own father like a hole in my heart.

Chapter 4

*W*hy does the girl need to be finished?" Papa Henry asked. "She's fine as she is."

It was the only compliment he had ever paid me. And he said it to Mama, not me. As if I were not there at the table.

"There are things she needs to learn, Henry." Mama had wisely allowed him to finish his soup before she brought up the matter of my working at the Shippens'. The soup, which had been bubbling on the hearth all day, soothed him.

"What does she need to know, more than she knows now?"

"Some French, a little music, perhaps, how to give her arm to a fine gentleman so he can escort her in to dinner."

"And what does she need to know these things for?" he asked. "What fine man will be escorting her to dinner? It'll only give her ideas. And you don't have to come from Boston to know how dangerous ideas are in the wrong heads."

Mama was firm. "Ideas are wonderful things, Henry. And who says her head is wrong for them?"

"She's a girl," he said simply.

"Well, I'm not one to think my girl knows enough if she can make a shirt and a pudding."

"Such fancy schooling is all right for fancy folk. But we're not fancy folk. Where will we get the money to dower her if she meets a fine man to escort her to dinner? I suppose you'll be selling off the Delft and the silver coffee service? You think I don't know that you've got them hidden away someplace?"

Mama got up to serve the ham and squash. I did not know of the silver coffee service. I watched her slice the ham. What else did she have hidden away?

Papa Henry held out his plate. She served the ham slices and buttered squash. "It would be like an Adventure School," she said, "of the kind they run in private homes, where the girls learn music, dancing, drawing, and needlework."

"Isn't life enough of an adventure, Jane? You need to send her to school for it?"

"You know of what I speak, Henry. They have them in Boston as well as Philadelphia."

"You've made the arrangements without asking me, then?"

"I'm asking," Mama said.

"And if I say no?"

"You won't say no, Henry," Mama said wearily. "No more than you did when I sent Blair to college. Or moved all the powers of darkness to get him his commission." She looked at him hard. "Boys can get commissions, go on to college. Girls can't. I want a chance for my Becca, too, Henry."

Mama's words stirred me so that I could not swallow. Papa Henry savagely tore off another piece of warm bread. "A chance?" he asked. "Blair's freezing his toes off in that godforsaken valley without a forge. If he ever gets out of there alive, he'll end up having his brains blown out by a musket ball."

"He'd have enlisted without a commission," Mama said. "At least now he is an officer. He has dignity and respect."

"When they're lying dead on the ground they all look the same," he told her.

Mama's face went grim. A pall settled over the table.

Papa Henry saw his advantage and pushed it. "You've heard of the extravagances and immorality of Philadelphia's leading families. You want your daughter exposed to such?"

"I saw no immorality in that house. They are

good people, Henry, trying to weather this war like the rest of us."

"Cosying up to the British, you mean. That's how Edward Shippen is weathering it. The man was put on parole by the independence men. He dasn't go six miles from his house."

I wondered why Mama did not remind him that in delivering his goods to the British he was cosying up, too. "The man has signed a paper not to do anything injurious to the United States of America. Henry, I ask you. Let the girl go. With this war and our limited circumstances, would you deny her?"

He looked at Mama. "And if I do?"

If he said no, Mama would send me anyway. He knew it. And he knew it would make a hole in the household that could never be repaired. He was not prepared for that, much as he might want to go against her. He knew he could not live in a household with a hole so big he would fall into it every morning when he got out of bed. There were too many other holes a man could fall into these times just trying to make it through the day.

So he came back with another argument. And it was the same as I'd asked Mama earlier. "Who will milk the cow?" he said.

• • • • •

"Mama, why did you marry him?"
"Hush. That is not a seemly question."

Henry Job had gone to bed. I was in my long flannel nightdress and had gone into the kitchen to say good night to my mother. She was wrapping the bread dough that I would put into the oven before I went to milk Opal in the morning.

"Widowhood is not a good state for a woman," she said. "We need the protection of a man. Besides, he cares for us."

"You care for us, Mama. Your earnings put food on the board."

She shook her head and sighed. "He's a good man. There is more to him than meets the eye."

"What more?"

"If you would look, you would see. And there are other kinds of caring. He loves me."

"Do you love him?"

"Betimes I do. Betimes I don't."

"Which times happen more? When you do or when you don't?"

"You're a saucy child." But she was not angry. She looked at me with a measure of sadness. "You aren't sensible of it yet. But in all marriages there are times when the two parties don't love each other."

"I'm always going to love the man I marry. And he'll always love me," I told her.

She smiled. "Silly child."

"I'm not a silly child. Why can't it be so?"

" 'Twas not meant to be. There must be pullings apart if there are to be comings together. In the pulling-apart time, if we are wise, we will go our own way and learn. And bring what we have learned back to the other."

I sat down at the table bench. "Did you have those pulling-apart times with my father?"

She wrapped the last of the bread dough and wiped her hands on her apron. "That question I do not have to answer."

But she had answered it without words. I watched her move about in the kitchen. She missed my father. She had truly loved him, I decided. And there had been no pulling-apart times with him.

"When do I start at the Shippens', Mama?"

"Not soon enough for my liking."

I laughed. "Will you miss me?"

"I'll miss the confusion you cause around here. I'll miss trying to keep you and my Henry from each other's throats."

"Mr. Shippen has an inkstand my father made. And some candelabra."

She turned. Her eyes went soft. "Does he, now?"

"Yes. He said my father was an excellent silversmith."

"He speaks the truth." She turned away from me. Her voice was raspy of a sudden.

"Oh, Mama, I wish he hadn't died. I wish things hadn't gone bad for him and that he could still care for us like Peggy Shippen's father cares for his family. Mama, Peggy and her sisters want for nothing. He gives them everything!"

"Yes, I've seen." She took off her apron. "Your father did not leave you barefoot. He gave you something of great value, Becca."

"What?" I looked at her. Would she tell me what else she had hidden besides the Delft plates and the silver coffee service? Would she divulge the hiding place of these treasures to me now? "What has he left me?" I asked.

She smiled. "Your good name," she said. "Now off to bed. You start in two days. We've much to do."

Chapter 5

I stood in my plain little winter room, looking around. Always I had hated its worn floor-boards, narrow lines. I yearned for my commodious upstairs summer chamber, private and away from everyone. But it was closed off in winter. This room was warm, being close to the kitchen. And suddenly it was very dear to me.

I was leaving home! I could not believe it. I smoothed the comforter, feeling a sense of dread. I wanted to crawl back into my bed and snuggle under the covers and forget the whole business.

I was all packed. I had dressed by the light of one candle, for it was still dark out and bitter cold. I wore my best, from the yellow quilted underskirt Mama had dyed and made for me to my best linen apron and short gown. My go-to-meeting cloak lay on the chair.

There was a tapping on the door. "Come in, Mama, see how I look."

It was not Mama. It was Henry Job. "You look right fine," he said.

I was embarrassed. "Thank you."

He just stood there, shifting his weight from one foot to the other. He had something on his mind. Why didn't he say it? I looked at him and minded more than ever what a great plodding, dull bear of a man he was. I had always seen that. But it came to me for the first time then that he was trapped by his own dullness, by his own plodding movements, his meager ability to put things into words.

Of course, I thought. *He is like a prisoner in that body of his, embarrassed by his clumsiness, his lack of grace.* Why had I never seen that before? And what good did the revelation do me now?

"I milked the cow," I said. "I fed the chickens and slopped the hogs. I've left everything in the barn neat and clean."

He nodded, disinterested. "I've not come for that."

"For what then?" I faced him square. Wasn't that all he saw me as? Someone to care for the livestock?

He ducked his head, jingled whatever it was inside his fist even more. "You mind who you are," he said.

I just stared at him. "I don't understand."

"Who you are!" he said gruffly. "You always mind who you are."

I could not keep from the saying, "Who am I?"

"Your mother's daughter! And your father's. You're nobody's servant. You're as good as the lot of them. 'Tis circumstances that bring you to their house in such a manner. Such circumstances can befall the best."

I stood there disbelieving.

"You don't dishonor yourself. In any way. You hear?"

"I know how to behave."

" 'Tis not behaving I speak of. There are other ways of dishonoring yourself. By selling bits of yourself off"—he tapped his temple—"here. And here." He tapped his heart. "What you believe to be true, what you know to be true, you don't question. Or let anyone's fancy notions or high style of living make you ashamed."

I took full measure of the man. I could see the cost of the effort of those words to him. His face broke out in a sweat. He mopped his brow and stood silent.

I nodded, struck dumb by his words. Never had I heard such sentiments from him.

"Promise me you'll not allow them to corrupt you," he said.

Before that moment I would have laughed at him. Now my heart constricted and I could not speak. So I nodded, yes.

Then he took a few steps across the floorboards. They creaked under his weight. He held out his hand. "Take these and keep them somewhere safe. So you never have to ask for a thing from them if you're hungry. Or at any time you can get a ride home in one of those fancy Philadelphia chaises, if what you need to fill you is more than food."

I held out my own hand. Into it he dropped some coins. They gleamed in my hand. Guineas. Newly minted with the profile of George III on them. I stared at them. The profile of the king blurred for the tears in my eyes.

He closed my fingers over them gently. "Don't ever allow the begging words in your mouth," he said.

"But," I protested, "you and Mama need these!"

"Hush, girl. Do ye never know when to hush? It'll be the death of you, that loose tongue of yours." And with that he turned and left the room.

I stood staring after him. I felt his presence even after he was gone. And then I thought of something. There had been none of the usual cloud over him just then, none of his darkness of manner. It was as if for once he had pushed aside the darkness to say what he truly felt.

"Becca? Come have breakfast."

I picked up my cloak and small trunk. Think of it! Henry Job had given me money!

I slipped the coins into my crewel-worked pocket that I wore around my waist. I was caught off guard and a bit put out. Now that I was leaving, Henry Job decided to treat me kindly. Why couldn't he have acted so all along? And something else plagued me, too. Always, I had thought I had known what he was about. Now I was not so sure. And I did not like that at all.

But I forgot him as I ate breakfast, for he'd gone back to bed. By the time we got into the wagon, I gave him scarce a thought. A streak of orange was announcing the sun in the eastern sky, and thanks to Mama's breakfast, my spirits were high. I was taken with the excitement of the moment. A new life was starting for me. I hugged Merlin, who had jumped into the wagon at the last moment, sensing, as dogs do, that something was going on and wanting to be part of it.

·　·　·　·　·

When Mama reined Duke to a stop in front of the Shippen house an hour or so later, the sun was above the horizon. The eastern sky was a weak blue. And strangely, in the west a large pale full moon still hovered. There was something eerie about the morning. For one thing, it was not as cold as I had expected.

The cobblestone street was snow-crusted and

deserted. Behind shuttered and draped windows, an occasional candle shone from the lower floors as servants brought the houses to life.

A dog barked in the distance. A cart's wheels ground toward us. "Fish!" the fishmonger called. "I've got shad. Fresh shad!"

Side doors of the fine houses opened. House servants came out bearing buckets and baskets and crowded around the man driving the cart. Mama nodded. "The spring migration," she said. "It has started early this year. Thank God. The weather has warmed. The shad are running. Our men at Valley Forge will eat."

We sat in silence for a moment and watched the house servants buying up the shad. "Good with onions," Mama said. "And a bit of butter and herbs." Then she reached into her things and handed me a small leather-bound Bible. "Read it every night as we do at home." She kissed me.

I felt panic. "You aren't coming in with me?"

"It isn't as if I'm sending you across the ocean."

I climbed down from the wagon. She handed me my small trunk. "Remember," she said. "Out of everything that befalls us in life, we can learn. Even if what befalls us seems like the most dolorous situation. Nothing we learn is lost to us."

I hugged her. Something strangled my innards. Then I hugged Merlin. The thumping of his tail and low whine meant he was beset by my leaving.

He would miss me. How could I explain to him? I had to make myself put him aside.

They drove off. I stood in the empty street, watching. Mama did not look back. I watched her straight back recede in the pale light. Soon I couldn't see Duke's ears anymore, and all I could hear was Merlin's confused bark.

"Becca Syng? Be that you? You look lost, chile."

I looked up into Coxie's round, dark face. She was holding a bucket of fresh shad. The other maidservants were going back into their houses, clasping their buckets and baskets of bounty.

"Is it shad?" I asked. "Is it running already?"

"Shore is, chile. Early this year. Now you gonna stand here freezin' to death? Or you gonna come on in so I kin fry you some with butter an' onions?"

· · · · ·

I sat at the large wooden table in the warming kitchen, eating fresh shad and warm, buttered biscuits, and drinking hot cider as if I'd never eaten before in my life. Sun poured in the large windows. A fire burned brightly in the hearth. Everyone but the servants was asleep still, Coxie explained. In a corner, a tall maid who was near to white stood ironing.

"That be Brilliana," Coxie said. "Let me 'splain to you 'bout all the help."

She, Lettice, and Brilliana were slaves, she told me. "But I gots the keys to the cellar, where they keeps the preserves, dried fruit, maple sugar an' syrup"—she ticked the items off on her fingers— "relish an' ketchup, potatoes, vegetables, bags of flour an' beans an' rice. An' "—she leaned forward to whisper—"in the outer cellar, between stone walls that are filled with ice, they gots butter, sides o' beef an' mutton, milk an' cream, smoked hams an' turkeys."

She stopped, finally, her breath spent. She was over all the servants, she told me proudly. "Nigra an' white. They all take orders from me. 'Cause I had years wif the Shippens. I was wif Miz Margaret Frances afore she married the mister."

She was in charge of procuring the food. "An' that be no small task, 'cause Mr. Shippen, he keep a good table."

I listened, learning. Another nigra servant came in to set down some freshly cooked bread and went out. She did not speak.

"That be Lettice. She do all the real hard work wif the cookin' an' the scourin' up. She make candles, too."

Brilliana left the room for a moment. "Brilliana was sent up from Virginnie," Coxie told me. "Sent by the Lees, else she be killed down there. Sent to

Doctor William, the master's cousin. He ship her over here."

"Why would she be killed down there?" I asked.

" 'Cause she be high yellow, chile. Her master make free wif her mama. She be a Lee. Her mistress like to carve her up wif a knife."

Brilliana came back from the inner regions of the house with a beribboned petticoat and began to iron it. Her movements were languid and her manner filled with contempt.

Ellyn and Dorothea were white. "They is indentured," Coxie said. "They serve the meals an' clean an' fetch fer the womenfolk. They doan talk to us, lessen they have to. Or to badger Brilliana and Lettice. You stay clear of that Dorothea. She be nerved up all the time, given to the miseries."

"Why?"

"Doan know. She here only a short while. Last two white servants we had went over the fence to work fer the king's men. You mind, chile, that servants come dear now. Doan take no sass."

Pepy and Cecil were slaves, too. Pepy spent all his time polishing Mr. Shippen's coach and sweeping out the new red brick carriagehouse. Cecil was the "inside man" who wore red-and-white livery. "An' when the king's men gets too tipsy, he sees 'em out the door," Coxie said.

I learned that her real name was Cox-Anna.

Her first master had been named Cox. "Young master Edward, Mr. Shippen's only boy, named me that when he was a baby. It just sorta stuck."

She was of a political turn of mind, too. And very intelligent. "I'm fer the independence men," she whispered. She nodded in quiet certainty. "The day they read that declaration offa the steps of Carpenter Hall, I was there. Took myself right outa this kitchen and went. And I'se waitin' fer this liberty it promised."

Brilliana spit on her hot iron. "There ain't no liberty for folks like us'n." She had a Southern drawl. "Never will be, either. You will have bones of rust and you never be free, old woman. Best you just forget it and stop waitin'."

"Will be fer me," Coxie told her. "I believe the words of that declaration. If'n you heared 'em, you'd believe 'em, too." She was sure of it. And herself.

She counted off on her fingers the things I must learn if I expected to "keep drawin' breath" in that house. "You doan never say no to Miz Peggy," she said solemnly. "You always duck when she throws things at you. You never say nothin' 'bout her mama in her presence. She hates her mama."

"Why?"

"Her mama be a woman. She hates all women. But you be nice to Mrs. Shippen. You curtsy to her, an' if'n she send you on an errand, you do it.

An' if'n you ever need a friend besides me, she be it to you. She be a great lady."

"Yes," I said.

She counted on her middle finger. "You always stay clear of Captain Andre. He be livin' in Benjamin Franklin's house, so he be here alla time. More than young Edward. He never comes. He practicin' law in Readin'. Anyways, Andre fancies the women, no matter they be servants. Never find yourself alone in a room wif him. If'n you do, you go to the hearth an' pick up a poker."

My mouth fell open. "A poker?"

"Tha's what I say. You say, 'Captain, you like me to fire up the dog fer you?' An' you pick up that poker an' put it in the fire."

"The dog?" I had seen no dog in the Shippen household.

"Yessum. It mean make the poker hot so you kin put it inta his flip. That be his favorite drink, though it be American. He see you standin' there wif that poker in your hand, an' he'll back off. He won't be able to figure if you be fixin' to swipe him wif that poker or if'n you only fixin' to fire up the dog. Come to think of it, you'd best learn how to make flip, if'n you wanna stay on the good side of Captain Andre."

"Why do I have to stay on his good side?"

" 'Cause Miz Peggy be smitten wif him. Now *he* be smitten wif Peggy Chew, her best friend.

Only he wear his coat on both sides where women be concerned, an' your mistress doan wanna hear 'bout him an' other women. You make her think he be languishin' only over her."

I nodded. "How do you make this flip?"

"We keep a mess of it here in the kitchen. The part made out o' sugar, eggs, an' cream." She got up and bent to open a small door to a box outside in the cold and showed me a pitcher full of the mixture. "It gotta stand fer two days. If'n he send you here fer some, you pours four spoonfuls of it in this." And she took a pewter tankard off a shelf. "Then you pours in some strong beer." She opened another cupboard and showed me a wooden barrel with a spout. "Then you pours in a dram of this here rum." And she picked up a flask.

"Then you whip up a fresh egg." She bent to open still another small door. In another box set outside was a ready supply of eggs. "We keep 'em here fer that purpose," she said. Then she walked heavily back to the table and sat down.

"You brings this tankard to him, an' you hold it in one hand, an' then you take up that hot poker you left sittin' in the fire an' you plunge it in. An' that Captain Andre, he'll hold you in high esteem, yes, yes."

She laughed again, at some private joke.

"Is there anything else I should know?" I inquired weakly.

"Oh, yes." She grew solemn. "The master? He be shakin' in his boots every day that he be 'rested."

"Who would arrest him?"

"Who else? The independence men."

"But the British occupy the city."

"Fer now, fer now. But he be under parole by the independence men. And they still be watchin'. They got mens watchin'. He can't leave here. If'n he stay, he gotta cosy up to the king's mens. After they go, what?"

I didn't know what. For Mr. Shippen or for any of us.

"The independence mens, they ain't gonna dis-remember that he was against the declaration. He got no money comin' in right now. An' he be spendin' a whole lot entertainin' the British. An' what he ain't spendin' on that, his daughters be spendin' on frippery. So he gonna be in a whole peck o' trouble if'n the war goes on much longer. So you be kind to him. He be a good man."

I blinked. "That's it?" I asked.

"Uh huh. 'Cept fer one more thing."

"What?"

"You best be learnin' to run when your mistress calls. I hears her callin' now."

Chapter 6

$\mathcal{I}$ ran up the stairs. On the landing I near collided with Dorothea. She had a covered silver tray in hand.

"Mind your manners." Her face was flat, her eyes and nose had a pinched look. "We don't run in this house."

I ran past her to the room at the end of the hall.

"I will *not* wear that ugly cap-hat!"

The cap-hat in question went sailing across a room that was awash in flounces. Great flounces of thin flowered fabric hung around the high tester bed and dripped from the windows like tears. The bed was full of lace-edged pillows.

I stood there staring. It was the kind of room I had only been able to dream about. Without ever having seen such a room, in my heart I had always known it existed.

The girl who had thrown the offending cap-hat stood at the wash basin in a ruffled nightdress beribboned with blue. She was polishing her teeth with a cypress twig.

"I know it's an ugly cap." A dark-haired woman in a blue morning gown stood on the Persian carpet, surrounded by an array of discarded clothing. "But if you put it on of a morning, you'll save your taffeta one."

"For what? Save it for what?"

"The future."

"The future is now, Mama."

The dark-haired woman bent to take up the cap at her feet. I rushed to retrieve it and handed it to her. Up close, I could see a few gray hairs in the lustrous dark ones under her own crisp white cap-hat. She had pleasant crinkles around her eyes. When she smiled, I felt drawn to her. So this was the master's wife then.

"Who are you?" she asked.

I curtsied. "Rebecca Syng, ma'am."

"Who?"

The girl at the wash basin was examining her perfect teeth, smiling at herself in the mirror. "My new maid, Mama." She flung me a disdainful glance. "Come at last, have you? Where were you, on detached duty with Washington? I like my chocolate *before* I get out of bed in the morning. Well, where *is* my chocolate?"

"Here, Miss Peggy." Dorothea came into the room, turning up her nose as she passed me.

"Thank you, Dorothea. Give it to that lazy wench, and I'll get back into bed and have her serve me." And she climbed back into the high bed and snuggled under the feather quilt.

Dorothea thrust the silver tray into my hands. "Well, you were in such a rush. Now serve your mistress, if you know how." And she glided from the room.

I stood there, benumbed.

"New maid?" Mrs. Shippen asked from the foot of the bed. "Since when?"

"Since today, Mama. And she's mine. To be shared with no one. Daddy said so."

"But you don't need a personal maid."

"Of course I do. Just look at this place." She waved a graceful hand in disdain. "Someone has to keep things tidy."

"You could pick up after yourself, Peggy. The rest of us are making all kinds of sacrifices now that your father's circumstances have been reduced."

"Oh, Mama, you're just provoked because you had no say in hiring her. Will you serve my chocolate, girl, and stop standing there like a jackass in the rain!"

I set the tray down by her bedside and poured the chocolate into a dainty cup. Her mother was watching. My face went red and my hands trembled. Just being so close to Peggy Shippen did that to me. Never had I seen such a beautiful face, such exquisite hands. But it was her disdain for all the fine things around her that I was most taken with.

I minded my own hands, reddened from barnyard chores, the nails cracked and chipped. I felt like Opal in comparison.

Apparently Peggy thought I looked disgraceful, too. She took my measure coldly. "Your clothing beggars all description," she said. "I can't have my personal maid looking like such. Come closer." When I did so, she picked up my petticoat. Under it I was wearing my good yellow quilted underskirt. It was very warm. "Haven't you better clothing? With a mother such as you have?"

"Peggy!" her mother scolded. "We don't talk so to the servants. They come dear in these times."

"Well, this one doesn't. She's scarcely costing us anything, Mama. So don't worry your head about it."

"And why is that?" Margaret Shippen asked.

Her daughter shrugged. "Oh, I don't know the bothersome details. Daddy does. He's made some arrangement with her mama. We're supposed to allow her to learn French and drawing in her idle hours. God knows why. Such pursuits will only give the lower classes notions."

Margaret Shippen turned to level her full blue

gaze at me. "Syng. Of course, how stupid of me. Your mama is our mantua-maker. Her name was Syng before she remarried."

"Yes, ma'am."

"And your father was the silversmith Phillip Syng."

I nodded yes.

"Dear child! He made a silver rattle for Peggy when she was born! And my tea service! I was to your house several times. When your parents were"—she hesitated—"in better circumstances."

"In heaven's name, Mama, must you?" Peggy scolded.

But there was no stopping her now. "Jane's girl. You have a brother with Washington's army, do you not?" she persisted.

I blushed in misery.

"Don't be shy about it, child. My brother Tench is a captain in the Philadelphia militia. My nephew, Tench Tilghman, is aide-de-camp to Washington himself."

I did not know what to say to this passionate outburst of patriotism.

Peggy did. "Mama, for heaven's sake, Daddy is killing himself to remain neutral, and you are bandying about such information. Besides, all American militiamen are worthless drunkards."

Smiling, Margaret Shippen stepped forward and

took my hand in her own. "Welcome to this house, child. I would be glad to help you with your French and drawing. And anything else."

I was taken with her dignity. In comparison, her daughter was like a shrew. In spite of her years, Margaret Shippen could still be wide-eyed in surprise, still had a lilt to her laugh. Where her daughter was hard, she was girlish. "Thank you, ma'am," I said.

"How about some decent clothing?" Peggy put in. "Captain Andre is coming this morning. I can't have her looking like a camp woman. The only decent thing she's wearing is that yellow quilted underskirt." She had taken a pendant from inside her nightgown and was twirling it on its silken cord.

"Your father has provided, miss," I said. "I haven't had time to change yet."

"What is that pendant you wear around your neck?" her mother asked.

Peggy fingered it lovingly and smiled coyly. "A gift from Captain Andre."

"Do you think that wise, Peggy? To accept such gifts?"

"No, but it is great sport, Mama."

"He exceeds the boundaries of proper behavior, Peggy."

"Oh, Mama, don't be tiresome. It's such a glorious morning. Go down and have breakfast with

Daddy. I'm sure he wants to discuss the household accounts with you."

The woman turned to leave. At the doorway she paused. "I am no one's fool, Peggy. Don't ever suppose such. Neither is your father. He may coddle you, but the day will come when you will step over the line. Then you will be sorry."

"Yes, Mama," she said with feigned contriteness.

Margaret Shippen swept her skirts up into her hands and left the room with a dignity worthy of Queen Charlotte.

The moment the door closed, Peggy Shippen set down her cup and glared at me. "You listen to me, you little guttersnipe," she whispered savagely. "I don't care who your father was. You are in this house as a maidservant. Mind that."

The vehemence in her brought me up short.

"And mind this. You are my maid alone. And no one else's. If my sisters, Sarah or Elizabeth or Mary, ask you to so much as fetch a lace handkerchief, you are to say no. Do you hear me?"

"Yes," I said.

"As for my mother, she is nothing in this house. She is a convenience for my father and most times not even that. I am his true confidante, the one he turns to in times of trouble. Listen to *nothing* my mother says. Have naught to do with her. And don't curtsy to her again. It will only give her airs."

Her words made me tremble. But what troubled me more was the sharpness her face took on as she said them. It was as if up to this moment she had been wearing a silk mask of the kind some ladies wear to protect their faces when they travel about the city. And now she had taken it off. And the real Peggy Shippen was revealed.

At first I had been shocked by her ready display of languid voluptuousness that mocked everything the Quakers stood for. But I saw now that it was a thin veneer for a hardness and viciousness in her that hid right beneath the surface. But more important, I recognized a darkness in her. I recognized it because I had seen it in my stepfather.

The difference was that his darkness was a plague to him, something he labored under, which betimes got the best of him. In Peggy Shippen I sensed that the darkness was something she reveled in. And it spring-fed her cruelty and hunger.

Hunger for what, I asked myself. *What does she need or want that she does not now have in profusion?*

"Another thing," she snapped. "When you are in the room with me and Captain Andre, you will stand in the farthest corner and make yourself scarce. And you will *never* tell a soul, not my mother or father or my sisters, what transpires between us. Disobey me and you will soon be cleaning the necessary."

I could not respond. I could scarcely breathe.

I felt suspended between this world and a nether world that I could not name, but that I could feel pulling me in. A strange sensation came over me. *Knowledge.* I felt the knowing in my bones.

This girl, I told myself, *is in league with the devil.* And the knowing was a terrible thing. I wanted naught to do with it.

Fortunately for me there was a commotion then. Shrieks and giggles from out in the hall. Two girls came in.

"Peggy, Peggy!" A round-faced girl with honey-colored hair bore something on a tray that was covered with a white linen napkin. "You can't imagine what we have here."

Peggy sat up straight in the bed. "No, I can't, Mary, but it had best be good, for you to barge into my room like this."

"Guess!" It was Sarah. She was dark-haired and looked something like her mother. I remembered seeing her that first day I'd come. When the king's man had kissed her.

"How can I guess, Sarah? Don't be a goose. Tell me."

"Guess first who brought it just now."

Peggy's blue eyes went dark with excitement. "I've not time for games. Is it a gift for me?"

"Yes!" they said in unison.

"Then it's from Captain Andre." Panic seemed to overtake her. "Is he here? *Now?*"

"He's downstairs at the breakfast table!" Sarah squealed.

"Give it to me this instant!"

Her sisters handed over the tray. Peggy whipped off the napkin and screamed. "A London baby!"

Her sisters jumped on the bed and exclaimed over it. I could not see. I stood on tiptoe. On the silver tray was a doll of a type I had seen before. It was no plaything. It was about twelve inches in height and dressed in the latest fashion from London. It was in this manner that high-placed ladies kept up with London fashions. The dolls came in on British ships, and I had heard Mama say that since Howe had occupied Philadelphia, his officers had gained entrance into many a Loyalist household by bringing such a gift.

"Look at the sleeves!" Peggy was saying. "I love the sleeves. I must have a gown like it."

"Captain Andre said we should tell you that he hopes to see you in such a gown soon. That you should pay special mind to the color."

"Yellow," Peggy wailed. "There isn't any yellow dye to be had in all of Philadelphia. What will I do!" Then a thought struck her. She climbed out from under the feather quilt, pushed her sisters aside, and crawled over the bedclothes to look at me.

"You are wearing a yellow quilted petticoat."

It was an accusation. Nothing less. I backed away.

She gestured to me with her index finger. "Come here."

I went forward.

"Lift up your outer garment."

I did so.

Her two sisters gasped.

"Yellow!" Sarah said. "Is this your new maid-servant, Peggy?"

"Yes. Leave her be. She's mine alone."

I felt like a *thing*, a piece of chattel. And for the first time in my life I minded what it must feel like to be a slave.

"What's your name?" Sarah smiled at me.

"Becca."

"Where did you get the yellow dye?" Peggy scrambled off the bed and stood before me.

Sarah got off the bed, too, standing a bit behind her sister. "Oh, don't frighten her so, Peggy. I like her. She looks like a decent sort." Then to me. "Don't let my sister make you cower so. Her bark is worse than her bite. Stand up to her. I tell you for your own good."

"Hush your mouth, Sarah," Peggy ordered. "Tell me, Becca, where did you get the yellow dye?"

"My mother had some laid by," I said.

"Your mother does dyeing? She made no mention of it to me."

There was nothing for it but to tell her. "Before the war, Mama had no need to. She imported fabric. But then she honored the nonimportation agreement and refused to buy English fabric. So my stepfather has been growing flax, and Mama's been weaving her own quality cloth. Sometimes I help her. Before the British came, she took it to a clothier's shop to be dyed. But he fled the city when the British came."

"Where does she do her dyeing?"

"In a shed at home. It's a messy business. It requires the storage of poisonous mordants as well as stale urine and other unpleasant things."

"Does she have the makings of yellow?"

I knew Mama had the peach leaves, goldenrod, butternut bark, smartweed, and hemlock to make yellow. But I hesitated.

"Mayhap you don't understand," Peggy said distinctly. "There isn't any yellow dye to be had in all of Philadelphia. I know women who would kill for it. My grandmama in Lancaster near drove my cousin Neddy Burd daft, sending him about town to find some yellow for her quilt silk petticoat. But even Mr. McDermott, who's the best dyer in town and from Scotland, had none. Grandmama had to have it dyed *blue*."

I stood there feeling guilty because of her grandmama's blue quilted petticoat.

"What makings does your mama have for yellow?" Peggy asked.

All three of them were staring at me, waiting. "Those are my mama's own secrets," I said.

"You refuse to tell me?" Peggy was aghast.

I ran my tongue along my lips. Sarah gestured to me from behind her sister, smiling and nodding in encouragement.

"Yes," I said.

Peggy stepped forward. She raised her hand. For a moment I thought she would slap me. Then of a sudden her manner changed. And I was to learn something about this young woman. When she could not at first get her own way, she resorted to every device to do so.

"I don't want to know your mother's precious dyeing secrets," she cajoled. "She can keep her poisonous mordants and stale urine. I only want you to ask her to dye some fabric yellow for me. And make me this gown as quickly as she can. Now tell me what you want from me in return."

I hesitated, struck dumb. But Sarah came to my rescue. "You ought to allow her to sleep in your chamber with you, Peggy. You know the servants will rob her blind. Especially Dorothea. For some reason she has taken a dislike of her. I heard her talking. And you know they smuggle men into the servants' quarters at night. Old Coxie sleeps like the dead, good intentioned as she is."

To my surprise, Peggy listened to Sarah. "Would you like that?" she asked me.

Sarah was nodding yes vigorously.

"Yes," I said.

"What more?"

I looked at Sarah. She stood very straight and held her head proud and raised her upturned nose in a most haughty manner.

"I am not a chattel slave," I said. "My father was a leading silversmith, my mama once a fine lady whose circumstances were reduced when he died. It could happen to anyone. I was hired as more than a maidservant, but I will serve you well. However, you must stop degrading me, and treat me with a fair amount of dignity. That is what I wish."

Peggy's blue eyes widened and grew darker at the same time. She was taken aback. She drew in her breath. Then she took my measure with those eyes, and I saw a gleam of appreciation in them. "You have spirit," she said. "I like that. You're not a noodle-head. Very well."

"There is one more thing," I said.

Peggy narrowed her eyes. "Don't press me."

But I felt brave. "I would like, when my chores are finished, to be able to seek out your mother and take her up on her offer to teach me French and drawing."

She considered it. "Very well, as long as your loyalties remain with me."

"They shall." I meant it.

She saw that I did. She gave a disgruntled sound. "I may be a fool, but I believe you. Very well, we have an agreement. Now, if my sisters will leave the room, you can help me dress so I can go down and meet with Captain Andre."

Before her sisters left the room, Sarah clasped her hands together and raised them triumphantly over her head and smiled at me.

I had made a friend.

And so it was that my yellow quilted underskirt purchased my dignity from Peggy Shippen. As well as my freedom to learn. I wore the underskirt whenever I could that winter. And I minded Mama's fight with Henry Job to keep her dyeing shed. And how she'd said, "It will serve me well, this knowledge of dyeing."

And her first commandment: "Nothing we learn is lost to us."

Chapter 7

I helped Peggy dress. However, she would wash first. She sent me to the warming kitchen for more warm water.

I took the servants' stairway. In the kitchen I near dropped my pitcher. Brilliana had just come in the back door with a steaming platter of fish. She raised the platter up high and stood there shrieking.

"What is it? Get it outa heah!" Fear made her accent thicker. For a moment I thought she would drop the platter.

Dorothea stood before her, laughing. Between them, on the red brick floor, was a large green turtle. It raised its head and hissed at Brilliana.

"What's the matter with you, Brill?" Dorothea asked. "You never seen a terrapin before?"

"Terra-what? I'll terrapin you, Dorothea. You been bedevilin' me since I been heah!"

"He's from the Bahamas," Dorothea announced. "Captain Andre brought him around this morning."

Brilliana set down the platter of fish. "Then he's no terrapin. I knows a terrapin when I sees one. They be only freshwater or tidewater turtles."

An argument ensued about what a terrapin really was. They were yelling at each other's faces. The argument, I perceived, was about more than that turtle. Animosity boiled out of them both.

"Hush!" Coxie scolded. "No fightin' in my kitchen. Mistress doan tolerate fightin'. Dorothea, you git outa here now. Brill, go an' fetch Pepy. He's gotta kill this thing so's I kin make soup."

"He be polishin' the coach," Brilliana said.

"Well, tell him to stop polishin' fer once an' do somethin' helpful, afore I make soup of *him*. Go now." Coxie all but pushed the girl out the door. "What are you doin'?" She whirled on me.

"Filling this pitcher," I said. "Miss Peggy wants water to wash."

"She's not dressed yet? Everybody's at the breakfast table. How long am I expected to keep this food warm? Hurry up, go. An' make her hurry. That lazy girl. That's what comes from stayin' out late an' goin' to balls wif them fancy king's mens. No good will come of it, I'll tell you now."

I went. She was raving about debauchery as I

climbed the back stairs. Breathless, I opened the door to Peggy's room and stopped dead in my shoes.

She was standing there in God's good sunlight with only a long piece of flannel half covering her naked body.

"Well, it's about time. I'm near freezing, waiting. Pour the water into my basin and go put another log on the fire. Then fetch my green velvet out of the clothespress."

I did her bidding, trying not to look shocked at her nakedness. I sensed, somehow, that she did not have to linger in such a state, but that she was so proud of her lush figure that she wanted to display it to me. She had no shame. I was the one with the shame, because I could not countenance her behavior.

Thank heaven, she kept me busy while she washed. She had me tripping about the room, fetching one garment after another for her inspection.

"Oh, God, it's as I thought, the green is dirty around the hem. I wore it to the horse races on the Commons with Captain Andre the other day, and it needs brushing. Get the scarlet silk."

That had a spot on the front. She'd been helping Captain Andre paint scenery in the Southwark Theater on Cedar Street the other day. "He paints scenery as well as writing and producing the plays," she confided. "The scene he painted was beautiful, with cascades of water and groves of majestic trees. But the dress needs cleaning. You'll see to it, won't you, Becca? And don't tell Mama how it got stained. She isn't fond of the theater. No Quakers are. Get my white flannel petticoat and the purple-and-white striped silk short gown."

I did so. And finally she dressed. The ruffles of the chemise were not the only thing spilling out of the low neckline of the short gown.

"How do I look?" She stood and preened in front of the mirror.

"Very fetching," I said.

"My mother will say I am showing too much bosom."

She was. But she did not ask my opinion, so I did not venture it.

"Take the London baby and come down," she ordered. "Just stand in the dining room with the other servants. After breakfast you may tidy my room and clean my gowns."

As we entered the dining room, her father and the young officer at the table got to their feet. The officer came to take her hand, bow, and kiss it. "My dear Peggy, you seem surprised to see me."

She pouted. "After the ball last evening I thought you would not be able to abide the morning sun."

"You are my morning sun, dear lady. I couldn't

abide not seeing you." He pulled the chair out for her. She sat down. Dorothea poured her tea. Ellyn and Cecil were serving fresh fish, slices of honey-dipped ham, eggs, and hot muffins with fruit preserves. There was no war or deprivation in *this* house.

"Are you here to invite me to another ball this evening?" Peggy teased.

"This evening I have planned a lavish board for my colonel. It is long overdue."

"Oh posh. And what am I supposed to do?"

"Rest for the Thursday night ball tomorrow at Smith's Tavern." He stood behind his chair for a moment. He was very tall, and he wore his soft red coat, with its gold trimmings and white lace at his throat and wrists, with casual indifference. He had a beauty of form and movement that I had never before seen.

His boots gleamed with polish. He had every permissible grace and an air of practiced gentility that came from knowing he was superior to all beings.

I felt like an insect in his path. I was sensible, suddenly, of the fact that I had not changed from the clothing that Peggy had said "beggared all description." I moved to a far corner of the room.

Yet at the same time I could not believe I was allowing myself to be so bedazzled by a king's man. What had come over me? I kept sneaking glances at him. Oh! Surely he belonged to a world that did not exist anymore, a world of knights and ladies fair.

"I suppose there will be gambling tonight?" Peggy chided.

"There usually is."

"I heard at the ball last night that Lieutenant Evans was so deep in debt from losses at the Pharao bank run by Captain Wreeden of the Hessian jägers that Evans had to sell his commission."

"I play to win, Peggy, never fear," he said. "I shall not be selling my commission."

"There's too much of that going on in your army, I hear," Mr. Shippen put in.

"You are correct, sir. The harmful effects of gambling have been the ruin of many fine officers who might have rendered years of honorable service to Great Britain."

Peggy played with her food. "And yet, Captain Andre, gossip has it that you are going to the cock fights this afternoon."

He smiled. "Gossip has it wrong."

Peggy made a face.

"I went yesterday afternoon. How else would I have won that fine green turtle I brought to your house for soup?"

"Turtle?" Peggy asked.

Sarah squealed. "You should *see* him, Peggy. He's in the kitchen. He's a giant!"

"He's just off a merchant ship in from the Bahamas," Captain Andre said, smiling. "So is the French wine I brought." Then he sighed. "The first ship to get through since the ice broke up."

"You ought to be able to dress up your provisions now," Mr. Shippen said.

"We ought." Andre sighed. "Howe is sending a joint army and navy expedition to the lower counties of New Jersey for forage. The ice is no longer a problem, but we still have those pesky armed Rebel boats infesting the creeks around Wilmington."

Mrs. Shippen had been silent through the whole meal. Now she spoke. "Captain Andre, have you heard any news of the *Mary and Charlotte*?"

"The only word, madam, is that she sailed on February tenth from London. Loaded with a cargo of beef, pork, butter, biscuits, meal, peas, cheese, and coal."

I saw something different in Andre's eyes as he addressed Mrs. Shippen. A respect that was not in them when he spoke with Peggy.

"The London and Irish Quakers have responded generously to our committee's appeal for help for the poor," Mrs. Shippen said.

Andre nodded. "I shall keep an ear out for any intelligence, madam. And pray the ship reaches our port soon."

She awarded him a genuine smile. "Thank you, Captain."

He lowered his eyelids and inclined his head and shoulders in a bow.

"And what word have you had about the apology I demanded from Captain Watson for kissing my daughter in the street?" Mr. Shippen asked.

"Oh, Father!" Sarah reddened.

"He has been soundly reprimanded, sir. Some wanted to court-martial him, but I spoke on his behalf. You will soon be receiving a formal written apology."

"That isn't necessary," Sarah said.

"Hush, Sarah, it is." Her father's voice was stern. "You are not some abandoned little wretch but an upstanding young woman from a good family."

"Your father is right," Andre told her. "Lieutenant Howse of the 389th received five hundred lashes for dragging a nigra woman from the middle of the street and robbing her. You have a name to uphold."

Sarah hushed.

"Now tell us what intelligence you have of the French alliance with the Rebels," Mr. Shippen prodded Andre.

"All rumors and intelligence indicate such an alliance is in the making," he said. "However, the king has empowered a peace commission to make certain concessions to the, ah, Americans."

I came out of my stupor to perk up my ears. An alliance with France? It was what Blair had hoped for in his last letter to Mama—that Benjamin Franklin, over in France, would be able to get the French to come to our aid. But a peace commission from King George III? I had not heard of that.

"What concessions?" Mr. Shippen asked.

"Most everything, short of independence," said Andre.

I heard a gasp. Silence descended on the gay group at the table. Dorothea came in to serve a second round of tea from the silver pot. As she passed me with the tray, I could smell the brew and it bedeviled me. I loved my tea, and at home it was in short supply.

"God's bones, I could abide that," Mr. Shippen said. "After near three years of war and ruination, I could abide that. It is most generous of the Crown," he gushed to Andre. "But do you think the Rebels will be smart enough to accept? I, for one, would never want to be beholden to the French. And I have many good friends here who feel the same."

"The French alliance will never be." Andre sounded bored. "But I will give you some intelligence you have not heard yet, which *will* be. And very soon!"

"What?" The girls spoke in turn. "Tell us?" And "Oh, we're tired of this talk of politics!"

So Captain Andre told them. And the three

Shippen girls, as well as their mother, sat be-numbed as they listened to him. Their eyes glistened. Their bosoms rose and fell beneath lace and silk.

"Well, you know that General Sir William Howe has requested the king to relieve him of his command and allow him to return to England?"

"Yes, yes." Peggy was near beside herself. "Is he going?"

"Has he been recalled?" Her father's concern was more serious.

"Rumor is he will be by spring," Andre said. "And my fellow officers and I have decided it would not be right to let him go without a proper farewell."

"What kind of farewell?" Sarah asked.

"What are you planning, Captain?" Mary pushed.

Only Peggy did not question him. She smiled at him across the table.

"A party." She breathed the words. Her eyes glistened.

He leaned toward her, and for a moment it was as if they were the only two people in the world, let alone the dining room. "The most lavish affair you have ever seen, or will see, in your life," he said to Peggy. "And you shall help me plan it."

"Yes," she said. And she was already planning. But it was more than that. They were planning together without saying the words. It was as if they were reading one another's mind. As if they had no need for words to know what the other was thinking.

They understand each other, I thought. *They are of a kind, cast from the same mold.* It frightened me.

I saw Mr. Shippen's eyes meet with his wife's. His brow furrowed. She bit her lower lip. But they said nothing.

Chapter 8

*Y*ou are all mad," Elizabeth Shippen said. "The frivolity and expense of this party are ridiculous when you think of all the men, American and British, starving in prisons."

She came into the sun-filled upstairs room, bearing a tray of food and tea. At twenty-four, she was the oldest daughter in the family. She had been away when I had arrived a week ago, visiting her grandmama in Lancaster.

"Why so?" Peggy asked. "Howe wants his officers to take their pleasure. It helps their spirits."

Elizabeth sat down and poured herself a cup of tea. "If Howe's officers took a walk to the jail at Sixth and Walnut, their spirits would be improved. Simply by seeing they aren't as miserable as those wretches inside."

"Those wretches are Rebels," Peggy reminded

her. "They deserve what they get." She and Sarah and Mary were on the Persian carpet, poring over sketches of dresses for General Howe's party. The sketches were drawn by Captain Andre.

"Like my Neddy? Don't you remember what I went through when I thought he was killed at Long Island? And then afterward when he was on that British prison ship? Did he deserve what he got?"

"No," Peggy allowed, "but he's *our* Neddy, too, you know. He's our cousin. So he's different."

The two girls glared at each other for a moment. Then Peggy faltered in her resolve, dropped her gaze, and went back to studying the sketches. Whatever design she picked I was to bring home to Mama on my day off tomorrow.

I'd been sitting in the background doing some crewel work, as Mrs. Shippen had taught me in my spare hours this past week. But since Elizabeth had come into the room, I could not take my eyes off her.

She was wearing men's breeches and shirt, a black silk stock, frock coat, and tricorn hat. Never had I seen a woman so dressed. The clothing not only flattered her slender, tall figure, it gave an aura of mystery. Earlier this day, I'd discovered that aura was not without substance.

I'd been in the warming kitchen, fetching Peggy's hot chocolate, when Elizabeth alighted from the carriage in back. "Who is *that?*" I'd asked Coxie.

"Why it's Miz Elizabeth! She's home!" Coxie had rushed out to meet her.

Elizabeth had brought baskets of provisions. "Neck beef and greens," she'd told Coxie. "Make some of your broth. You know the kind."

"Bless you!" Coxie had said.

Elizabeth had gone directly upstairs to see her mother. It was then that Coxie told me that she "always wears those clothes when she goes out an' about on one of her missions." What those "missions" were, Coxie didn't say. She was busy exclaiming over her bounty of neck beef and greens. "I'll make a proper broth for those poor souls in the Walnut Street Jail."

"You might at least ask after Grandmama and Grandfather," Elizabeth said to her sisters now. "They haven't been well, you know."

Sarah and Mary made inquiries. "They're over the quincy throat, but their rheumatism is still bad," Elizabeth said.

"Did Grandfather get the job with the Rebel government?" Peggy asked.

"He's being considered for it," Elizabeth said. "And he should. He's been paying them taxes to acknowledge their authority. Grandfather did not get to be the leading political figure in this commonwealth by being a fool."

"Don't mention such to Captain Andre—please?" Peggy asked.

Elizabeth laughed and sipped her tea. "That fop? I don't bother to speak to him, in case you haven't noticed."

"Don't call him a fop," Peggy begged. "He's a darling."

"All right, he's a darling fop," Elizabeth said.

"Lizzy!" Peggy looked near to tears.

"Well, would you rather I called him a sadistic butcher?"

"He isn't!" Peggy's mouth trembled.

"He is. Even some of his own men said that the way he had over two hundred Americans killed and wounded with bayonets at Paoli last September was the most grievous horror they'd ever seen."

"This is war," Peggy said gamely.

Elizabeth looked at her hard. "Be careful with him, Peggy. His friend DeLancey has already fathered two children here. They are saying that for every American they kill in battle, they will father a child."

"I don't believe it," Peggy said.

"Believe what you wish. You always did and you always will." Elizabeth's eyes fell on me then. "Who is this?" she asked.

"My new maid, Becca."

"Can we talk in front of her?"

"She's my maid, Lizzy, why ever not?"

"You little fool," Elizabeth chided. "You hire a new maid without asking her politics?"

"Maids don't *have* politics, Lizzy," Peggy said haughtily. "They are of the inferior sort."

"You're not only rude, you're wrong, little sister. It's the common people who stand to gain from this revolution. They are going to be running things, if the Rebels win. That's what it's all about. Very well, I shall ask." She looked at me. "Forgive my sister's rudeness. She's a noodle-head. In no way do I consider you inferior. Tell me, are you one of the warm people? Otherwise known as the freedom-loving Patriots?"

There it was, what no one had asked me since I'd come here. They were all staring at me. I hesitated.

"Don't be afraid," Elizabeth said kindly. "My intended, Neddy Burd, was in the Pennsylvania Rifle Battalion. And you've already heard what my politics are. Tell me your full name."

"Becca Syng."

"Her mother is our mantua-maker," Peggy put in. "Her father was a silversmith."

Elizabeth's face brightened. "I recollect him. He would come here when I was a child and bring me maple sugar candy. You have a brother in the Rebel army then, do you not?"

Something quickened my senses. How did she know? I met her eyes. They were friendly. Don't be afraid, they said. And they said other things, too. What, I did not know yet. But I did know that I would not lie to this young woman. "Yes."

"Well, why didn't you say so? Welcome to this house." She poured herself another cup of tea. I went back to my crewel work. But I noticed, looking up once, that her eyes were still on me.

"I like this one." Peggy held up a sketch.

"Let me see." Elizabeth put out her hand and Peggy handed it over. A frown came across Elizabeth's delicate brow. "You *are* mad. You can't wear this!"

"Why?" Peggy asked.

"It's the costume of a Turkish slave girl!"

"They all are." Peggy picked up the other papers to show her.

"Mother said you were to wear the gown of a medieval knight's lady."

Peggy colored and bit her lip. "Captain Andre wanted such a gown at first. But it's been decided that we can't wear them."

"Why?"

Peggy exchanged glances with her sisters. No one answered.

"Sarah?" Elizabeth asked. "You're the only one in this group with a shred of common sense. Tell me."

"Well," Sarah said, "if you don't tell Daddy, Lizzy."

"What you say stays right in this room. You know we've never tattled on each other. I count on you not to tell him of my mercy missions to the jail."

"Well, it was decided," Sarah explained softly, "that American girls are not ladies in the English sense of the term. They must be associated with the lower orders. That's why we will wear the costumes of the Turkish slave girl."

The silence in the room seemed to take on a life of its own, to feed on itself, it lasted so long.

"*What?*" Elizabeth whispered in disbelief. "Is this true, Peggy?"

"Yes," her sister answered meekly. "But after all, Lizzy, we *are* American girls. Would you have us deny it?"

Elizabeth set down her teacup and got up. She strode across the room to look out the window.

"It's going to be a wonderful party, Lizzy," Peggy said. "General Burgoyne dressed people up as shepherds and shepherdesses a few years ago when his brother, the Earl of Derby, got married."

"May I remind you that Burgoyne is a fool?" Elizabeth turned from the window. "He lost the battle of Saratoga last October. It was all the French needed to offer an alliance with the Americans."

"Andre says there will never be a French alliance," Peggy recited knowingly.

"Does he? Then ask your precious Andre how many of the cannon that the Americans left behind at Brandywine way back last September were made in France."

"It's to be called *Meschianza*," Peggy went on without flinching. "It means medley." Her eyes were wide with excitement. "There will be fourteen jousters: the Knights of the Blended Rose and the Knights of the Burning Mountain. Every knight will have a girl to joust for. Only fourteen girls in all of Philadelphia are chosen to take part, Lizzy. And we have three girls in one household. It's a great honor!"

Elizabeth looked benumbed. "You're *all* going to be wearing those gowns? Sarah? Mary?"

Her other two sisters admitted, softly, that they were.

Elizabeth picked up some of the other sketches. "Gauze turbans," she said in amazement, "pearls, and tassels of gold. Feathers. The waist is low."

"Yes, and with a large bow on the left side. And the sleeves are long. The whole dress is of the polonaise kind and of white silk," Peggy put in.

"Where will you get the fabric?" Elizabeth asked.

"Coffin and Anderson's, the great English shop on Second Street," Mary said. "We're all going this afternoon."

"And Becca's mother will sew them, as she sews

all our dresses," Sarah explained. "Becca is to take the designs and the fabric home tomorrow on her day off."

"And the money?" Elizabeth stood over them, sketches in her hand. "All this frippery will cost a fortune. Daddy is giving you money for this?"

"Well," Peggy hedged, "we have yet to ask. We hoped to do that this morning. We hoped you'd take up for us and help, Elizabeth."

"Not I." And she flung the sketches down on the floor. "He's downstairs right now, ranting and raving about selling off two carriage horses to get some hard specie. I'd as soon go up against Andre's bayonets."

"Lizzy, we were *depending* on you," Peggy wailed.

"Why me? You're his favorite, Peggy."

"But you're the strong one," Peggy said.

But Elizabeth was adamant. Gingerly, she stepped over the strewn-about sketches to take another sip of tea. Then she had another thought. "Have Daddy or Mama seen the sketches?"

"No." Peggy avoided her sister's eyes.

"You mean you intend to get money out of him for these unseemly dresses without showing him what they will look like?"

"You aren't thinking of telling him, are you, Lizzy?" Peggy gathered the sketches and stood up. "After all, isn't it just as unseemly for Neddy to come over from Reading to Grandmama's for extended visits with you? In light of the fact that Daddy has refused to let him marry you until the war is over?"

Elizabeth studied Peggy coolly. There was a light of indignation in her gray eyes. She had a quiet dignity much like her mother, I minded.

"And how do you know Neddy visited me there?"

"Oh, come, Lizzy." Peggy yawned lazily. "Why else do you take these visits to Grandmama? Only *she* would countenance such visits, with *her* past."

Now I saw anger in Elizabeth's eyes. "Don't speak ill of Grandmama! Don't you dare!"

"I speak the truth," Peggy said. "They had to flee to Lancaster years ago to escape the scandal of her first husband being alive in Barbados when she married Grandfather, didn't they?"

"Don't speak ill of her. He was reported dead! Didn't they suffer enough with her being threatened with whipping for bigamy? And they both made up for the scandal by devoting their lives to their family. Speak ill of her and I'll go to Daddy and tell him about these ridiculous dresses. I will, Peggy!"

The strength of Elizabeth's anger made Peggy retreat. But she did it with pouting. "Well, you've spoken ill of Captain Andre. And he's been nothing but charming and attentive to me. He treats me like a grand lady."

"You're a fool, Peggy," her sister said coldly.

"And I say you are just jealous. Because *we'll* be in the pageant. And you won't. I'll be by Andre's side."

"Will you, now?" Elizabeth gave a little laugh. "I wouldn't count on that. I hear he's chosen another."

"Another?" Disbelief suffused Peggy's lovely face. It went white. Then anger came and her face went ugly. "Who? Who would he dare choose instead of me?"

"Peggy Chew, your friend," Elizabeth told her.

"You lie!"

"Mayhap." Elizabeth shrugged, picked up the silver tray, and made ready to take her leave.

"Why?" Peggy wailed.

"Why?" Elizabeth turned. "Because of our dear father's neutrality. He's been just as neutral with the British as he has with the Americans. And because of it, we've become poorer and less powerful. Peggy Chew's family is in better standing."

And because he loves her, I minded, or so Coxie had told me.

Peggy burst into tears.

Elizabeth paused, set down the tray, and went to her. "This, too, is war, I suppose," she said. "Oh, Peggy, don't be a silly little fool." She put her arms around the younger girl.

"How could he *do* this to me?" Peggy wailed out her misery on Elizabeth's shoulder.

"Does it matter so much?" Elizabeth asked soothingly.

"Yes. I wanted to be at his side! I belong there. He's given *me* a lock of his hair!"

"You'll be there. You're going, aren't you?" Elizabeth looked at them. "This is the only house in Philadelphia with three sisters invited. And if you insist on going, then I insist that you hold your heads high and not let Peggy Chew know it bothers you. You can do that, can't you all? You're all prettier than her, by far."

I watched in amazement as Elizabeth mollified them all, changing from the angry older sister to the comforting one. Demanding, even, that they uphold the family honor.

Finally, Peggy stopped crying. Then Elizabeth surprised me even more.

"Would you loan me your maidservant for an hour, Peggy? I need to unpack my things."

Peggy hesitated. She was about to say no, but she did not have the mettle to go against Elizabeth. Her older sister was stronger, more sure of herself.

I saw then that Peggy had a weakness in her. She not only looked up to Elizabeth, she needed her approval. Besides, Elizabeth had said she was prettier than Peggy Chew.

Chapter 9

I followed Elizabeth down one flight of stairs. On the landing she stopped. "God's bones, what are you doing in this Loyalist house?"

Her outburst took me by surprise. "My mama says I need to be finished."

"Finished?"

"Yes, you see there are pieces of me missing."

"Missing?" She was puzzled.

"Yes. So my mama has come to an agreement with your father that I should learn French, diction, and dancing in return for my services. I don't know if such things will help me find my missing pieces, but I trust Mama. It was she who got my brother his commission."

A look of amusement came into her eyes. Why, I could not ponder. "Well, they'll try to finish you in this house. But I sense you can take care of yourself. Am I right?"

"Yes."

"Look here, as you are Captain Syng's sister, I assume I can trust you. He and Neddy were in the Battle of Long Island together. He bound Neddy's wounds and would have stayed with him, but he was ordered away. Neddy was captured."

I waited for what was coming next. Something was.

"Come into my room," she said.

She closed the door and flung herself down in a chair. "I love my sister Peggy," she said. "Do you have sisters?"

"No."

"Then it may be difficult for you to understand how I can love her and quarrel so. But hear me out. We're on different sides of the fence with this war. This whole family is divided about it. Truth to tell, I don't think Peggy *has* a side. I think she'll flirt with any officer who pays court to her, be he British or American. And right now, he happens to be British. Be careful. She uses people. You don't have to say anything. I know you must have loyalty to her."

I nodded.

She smiled and went on. "She has a burning ambition to be the most popular woman in Philadelphia. She already is. Andre has helped her. But I despise him. He and his fellow officers, with their plays, gambling, and parties, are making a mockery of this war. And they look down on American women even while they entertain themselves with them. I almost spit wooden pegs when I saw those Turkish slave girl costumes."

"I know you did."

"They think the Americans are fools. They see all this as a game of cricket. The Americans see it as dying for their liberty. When people come to such a turn, they'll do anything to endure. The Americans are biding their time at Camp Valley Forge. They are not beaten. When the French join forces with them, the British will get their comeuppance."

She stopped and gestured that I should sit. I did.

"I believe in the revolutionary government." She leaned forward. "Like Neddy and my grandfather, I'm willing to take risks for it. I'm taking one this night. I would ask your help."

There it was. I hesitated.

"Nothing that would harm your position. Can I confide in you? Or would you have me stop now?"

"Go on," I said. Never had I heard a young woman speak with such force and certainty. If I could learn from her, I decided, instead of doing French and needlework, I would certainly find my missing pieces.

"Neddy has a friend who was a prisoner in the Walnut Street Jail. His name is Lieutenant Persifor

Frazor. Since the third week in January, he's been on sick parole at the Golden Swan on Third Street. He's allowed out for exercise. He has a lung illness."

She got up and pulled a bundle of clothing from under her bed. "He wants to rejoin the army at Valley Forge. But he needs clothing." She held up the bundle. "I won't be here tonight. I'm telling my parents that I'm visiting with friends. I'll be getting a wagon and a horse. Frazor will come to the door of the warming kitchen about eleven tonight. He'll be dressed as a British officer. I'll be down the street with the wagon, in my most proper Quaker clothing."

"And I?"

"You can hear the tall case clock in the hall strike every quarter hour. I understand Peggy will be out at a ball, which means she won't be home until the small hours of the morning. If you could slip downstairs a bit before eleven on the pretext of not being able to sleep and wanting some warm milk, you could give this bundle to Frazor. It will be in the cupboard. All you need do is hand him the clothing, go back upstairs, and let him change in the dark. Then he'll meet me. Will you do it?"

"Why can't he meet you in the street?"

"Because it wouldn't be seemly for a proper Quaker girl who's on a mission of mercy so late at night to be seen with a British officer. But it would be seemly for her to meet with another Quaker girl."

My eyes went wide. "Those are *women's* clothes in the bundle?"

"Quaker women's clothes. He won't be the first American officer to escape captivity from this city as a Quaker woman. My friends have gotten us passes so we can get through the lines. We are on a mission of mercy, remember? Are you afraid?"

"No. I'll do it for Blair," I said.

"I would have thought it was because you were Henry Job Claghorn's stepdaughter," she said casually.

"What's *he* to do with it?"

"If you don't know, mayhap I shouldn't say."

"Tell me," I insisted.

"Very well. Since there must be trust between us. Washington has had to step up his intelligence. He has all kinds of spies. Many are in the city masquerading as loyal subjects of the king. And others bring food into the city, mix with officers and Loyalists, gain information, and pass it on."

I felt the blood pounding in head. I could not believe it! Henry Job? My dolt of a stepfather? I could not think.

"Are *you* a spy?" I asked.

She scowled. "Never ask anyone that. The fact is, no, I'm not. I wish I were. I've been asked, but

I can't endanger my family. Look, all kinds of people you would never fancy are spies for Washington. It's not sport. They are just ordinary people who can't abide what the British are doing to us and have decided to make things right in their own little way. They may do just one act of spying, as the opportunity arises, and do no other."

I thought of my friend Ann Darragh's mother.

"With this business tonight," she said, "I'm just doing a good turn for an old friend of Neddy's."

We talked a bit more, and I left her then. At the door, she smiled. "Do you know the British are so vain, they won't even call Washington 'General'? They call him Mr. Washington."

"My brother told me that."

"And General Howe is a failure. He doesn't deserve this party. He failed to support Burgoyne in Canada. He prefers illicit pleasures in the arms of his paramour, Mrs. Loring, to serving his country. Look here, mayhap you shouldn't tell your stepfather you know of his activities."

I said I wouldn't. And we parted. But I did not know if I believed her about not being a spy. I put the thought from my mind, however. I was too busy pondering the doings of Henry Job, my very ordinary dolt of a stepfather.

Chapter 10

I trembled, thinking of the night and what I had promised to do. Surely it was a simple task. But how would I get through the day anticipating it?

Fortunately Peggy had plans enough to push the thought from my mind. When I went back to her room, she had sent her sisters from her and was waiting for me. "Help me dress. And I wish you to come with me when I ask my father for money for the new gowns."

"Me?"

"Yes. He likes you. All I'm hearing these days from both Mama and Daddy is how industrious and efficient you are. If I get the money, you can come with us this afternoon to Coffin and Anderson's for the fabric. Now hurry! I'll wear my green silk. It needs mending, and I want Daddy to see he's got to spend money on new clothing if he expects me to keep up my standing."

. . . . .

I had never in all my life asked my mother or stepfather for anything. So when Peggy led the way into Mr. Shippen's library, and when that somber-faced man turned from his ledgers to scowl at us, I wanted to run.

"Daddy, how are you this day?" Peggy went to him and gave him a kiss. I stayed in the background. He was dressed in somber Quaker gray. It was not a good sign.

He stood up. "I'm beset, Peggy. My store of hard specie is growing smaller by the day. Everything is triple in price. We're keeping too rich a table these days. And it seems there is no remedy for any of it. We must abridge every article of expense that does not actually supply us with some real comfort of life."

She pirouetted before him. "I'm abridging. Look at this gown. It's threadbare."

"Our clothes can be mended," he said. "And you will always look beautiful to me, no matter how plain the garment."

"Thank you, Daddy." Now she stood on tiptoe to kiss him again. "And you know I'd wear home-spun to please you."

"Daughter, we have not come to such a pass

yet. You are still from one of the leading families in the province."

This was all Peggy needed. "Then would you have me go in rags to the *Meschianza?*"

He scowled. "You're going, then?"

"Daddy, all *three* of us are going; Sarah and Mary, too. You have the only household in Philadelphia with three daughters invited. Aren't you honored?"

He was considerably less than honored. "How much will the gowns cost me?"

"Daddy, is that all you can speak of? The cost?"

"It's all I can *think* of these days, Peggy! I don't sleep nights for worrying about money. Where will it come from? I've had no income since a year past, when I refused to renounce the king."

"If you'd do business with the British, you could have an income."

"I will *not* do business with the British. I remain as neutral with them as I did with the Americans. Unfortunately, that seems to mean keeping as rich a table as I did before the war, to feed the officers who keep flocking to this house."

"You have four beautiful daughters, Daddy."

"I mind that. I mind it every week when you ask for some new frippery. Last week you said you'd perish if you didn't get that yellow fabric dyed to be made into a gown. Well, you got it. Why can't you wear that?"

Peggy looked devastated. "That will be good enough for a ball. But this is *Meschianza*."

"I don't care what it is. Put any name on it you wish, Peggy. I simply cannot give you another shilling. I stand firm on my decision." He planted his feet apart, clasped his hands behind his back, and presented his daughter with as formidable a countenance as Henry Job had ever shown me.

Had his anger been directed at me, I would have shaken in my shoes. Peggy did not. She had long since discovered what I had yet to learn. That when you are wrong you should go on the offensive.

Her offensive took the form of hysterics. Never had I seen the art so perfected.

"You stand firm on your decision, Daddy?" she asked in a high-pitched voice. "Well, how do you stand on your honor?"

"What is that you say?"

"Your honor!" She flung the words at him. She stamped her foot. She picked up the folds of her skirt and paced up and down. "How do you feel knowing that Peggy Chew is to be Captain Andre's fair damsel at the party instead of me? He will joust for *her!*"

The corners of his mouth turned down. "You jest."

"I speak the truth."

"The bounder! After I opened my house to him

and his officers. Why, I accorded him every courtesy. How can you go, now? I cannot permit it!"

Peggy gasped. "No! We *must* go, don't you see? We must hold our heads high. Don't blame Andre. The fault is yours!"

"Mine? How so?"

"Likely Andre heard that you are selling off two of our carriage horses. Word like that gets about. So we are now considered one of the poorer and less powerful families in Philadelphia. That is what your scrimping and saving has done for us!"

Then as if on cue, she burst into tears.

Her father immediately was beside himself. The poor man looked under siege. "Peggy, darling child. You are my heart and soul. Please don't cry. I can't abide it."

The more the poor man begged, the louder she wailed. Her father hushed her to no avail. Mrs. Shippen and Coxie came running. "What is it?" her mother asked. "What's happened?"

"He won't give me any money for fabric and trimmings for our gowns for General Howe's farewell party." Peggy ran to her mother, sobbing out the story, embroidering it so that by the time she was done, the family name was in a sorrier state than it had been in when Peggy's grandmama was threatened with whipping for being a bigamist.

Mrs. Shippen was so taken by the fact of Peggy's arms about her that she likely would have given the girl permission to elope with Andre if the request was put to her. She became agitated at first, then she held her daughter tenderly for a moment.

"Mr. Shippen," she said, addressing him as all wives of quality addressed their husbands, "surely we can spare some hard specie so that our daughters can be properly attired and our family can maintain its position."

He knew he was beaten. As thoroughly as General Wayne had been at Paoli. The blood that ran from his wounds was not visible, but in my tongue-tied stupor I was sensible of the whiteness of his face. The life blood was draining out of him.

"Certainly, Mrs. Shippen," he said. "Come, Peggy, I shall give you the money. Becca, you shall accompany my daughters this afternoon and help them with their purchases."

It was the first he had acknowledged my presence. Was he disappointed in me because I hadn't talked Peggy out of this folly? I did not know.

"Yes, sir," I said.

The ledgers were gone over with a fine-tooth comb. We waited. He unlocked a drawer in a massive cherry desk and we discreetly looked away. I heard the sound of coins. Peggy smiled. The money was given. Peggy kissed him and allowed herself to be mollified and to be instructed on caution and discretion as far as spending the money.

"Mind Becca," he told her. "She knows fair prices for fabric, do you not, child?"

I said I did. It was not an untruth. I had learned enough from Mama to feel confident in my answer. That afternoon we went to Coffin and Anderson's.

．　．　．　．　．

Fair prices for fabric seemed to be the furthest thing from the minds of the young women who crowded the fancy English shop that bright March afternoon. What they wanted, every mother's daughter of them, was attention. And from behind the large oak counter where the bolts of colorful fabrics lay, two portly gentlemen, who I assumed to be Mr. Coffin and Mr. Anderson, were trying to keep order and becalm them.

"One at a time. Each will get her turn. Ladies, ladies, we have the best of everything. We have all your silks and gauzes, feathers and tassels. We have all the king's favors in this shop, such as you have not had in your city in months. The brig *Opportunity* arrived just yesterday. You shall want for nothing."

The man was sweating. He mopped his brow. "Take the chairs, ladies, please. We will bring out the samples and Lacy will serve tea."

A male nigra servant was bringing out extra velvet-cushioned chairs. Another took their wraps.

Most of the young ladies were accompanied by elderly women.

"Look," Peggy whispered, "there's Peggy Chew. And Frances Auchmunty, and Jennie Craig." She knew them all: Nan Redmond, Pamela Bond, Becky Franks, Amelia Smith, Grace Bond, Anne Smith.

Peggy and her sisters exchanged polite hellos. Peggy Chew seemed to be the prettiest. She was dark-haired and no more than seventeen. *Sleek* was the word for her. Well cared for. Full of her own sureness. Most of the girls in the room had some measure of that quality. *How do they get so sure of themselves at so young an age,* I wondered.

And then I knew. And was ashamed of the knowing.

Money. They got that way from never knowing need, never having to mend a dress or milk a cow in a freezing barn, never having to see their mothers work in a damp shed mixing mordants and urine to make dye.

I felt filled with anger as the knowledge flooded me. But I was hard put to know where to aim my anger. At my father for dying? At Henry Job for being a dolt? At Mama for marrying him? With no direction, my anger turned on itself, fed on itself, curled up into a ball and went to sleep inside me. But what would I do when it came awake again?

I diverted myself, watching the two Peggys,

rivals now, exchange polite smiles in the manner of the highborn.

"Do you know how much fabric goes into a gown?" my Peggy asked me.

"Yes," I answered. But I wished Mama was here to advise me.

"We'll buy more than we need, just to be on the safe side. Don't hesitate when our turn comes," she directed.

Lacy, a nigra serving girl, came out with tea. With her was a nigra boy, about five, holding a tray of iced cakes. He was dressed in red-and-white silk. Everyone fawned over him, saying he was precious. Then word went round that he was Lacy's son.

"I want to take him *home* with me!" Peggy Chew cried. "I want him for a pet!" And everyone laughed. The little boy just stared ahead. His mother's face remained solemn.

I hesitated as she paused before me with tea, then saw the other mantua-makers and elderly female relatives taking it. So I did, too. Sipping it, I felt restored. I looked around. Never had I been in such a fancy shop. There was a thick Persian carpet on the floor. Colorful bolts of fabric, bunches of feathers, and rows of delicate laces were draped on tables in front of the multipaned shop windows.

Marble-topped tables all around us were strewn

with London baby dolls, sketches of gowns. An elderly woman wearing a white wig and a low-cut green velvet gown busied herself behind another table, setting out pots and jars of powder and creams, even lip rouge! From a small leather-covered trunk studded with copper nails and lined with satin, she took a collection of hair combs.

Still another woman, who looked to be her daughter, was arranging a selection of women's feathers, tassels, and pearls on a table covered with blue satin. Above, a chandelier with what seemed like hundreds of candles glowed, rivaling the light of day.

I became caught up in the moment. There was no war in here. No talk of deprivation. The girls had settled down now to sip tea and nibble on little iced cakes and talk about the *Meschianza*. I felt a delicious feeling creep over me—that of belonging with a group of females my own age. I didn't *belong*, of course, but the pretending that I did was as good, and it was a new sensation. I liked it.

I heard one young girl say that the late Joseph Wharton's mansion, near the old battery, was to be the site of the pageant. Everyone oohed and aahed at this information.

Not to be outdone, another girl spoke up. "My parents are providing the bunting for the boats," she offered.

Everyone knew something. No one knew

anything for certain. But every freshet of news was shared and devoured. "Did you know," said a dark-haired girl who seemed no older than sixteen, "that a cadre of twenty-two officers was formed to run the pageant? And they have raised 3,312 guineas?"

"My dear papa says such a sum would feed the entire American army for a week," said a small, round girl with large gray eyes.

Silence for a moment. Everyone looked uncomfortable. "Oh, don't be mean-spirited," someone put in. "We deserve a little sport. Tell them, Peggy. Tell them where you were on your sixteenth birthday, near two years ago. And how you missed all the festivities because of the war." She addressed Peggy Shippen.

"We were in Amwell, New Jersey," Peggy said drearily. "With all our elegant furnishings packed away. On a farm! We fled there when British warships were reported in the Delaware. Amwell is a country town. Card-playing old maids and people who know nothing of the genteel life. I thought I would perish until we came back here. Yes, I'd say we deserve a little sport. And I, for one, refuse to feel guilty!"

They all applauded her and the gaiety continued.

While all this was going on, Mr. Anderson was displaying fabric. Mr. Coffin was taking orders.

And money. Elderly female relatives and mantua-makers were arguing softly with their charges.

Finally, Mr. Anderson stood in front of us with his wares. As he had with every other girl, the first thing he did was ask: "Is your knight of the Blended Rose or of the Burning Mountain?"

Knights of the Blended Rose would wear red-and-white silk. The others would be in black and orange. Their ladies' white silken robes, to be worn over the Turkish gauze, would be trimmed in the colors of their knights.

Peggy's face was eager in anticipation. Mr. Anderson leaned over her. Mr. Coffin's pen was poised for her answer.

"The Blended Rose," Peggy whispered. "All three of us." She spoke with the fervor of one taking vows.

"And how much of the silk and gauze will you require, then?" asked Mr. Anderson.

"Becca?"

Everyone looked at me. I calculated, as best I could, as I had seen Mama do so often. So many yards for a ballgown. One half that amount for a silk robe. To be tripled.

I gave my answer in a sure, clear voice. It was not a judicious one. It allowed for extra fabric. Mr. Shippen would think I had failed him. Too much of his small reserve of silver would be spent this day. But I had to think of Mama. If she was to make these absurd dresses, she would want to do them up proper. No shoddiness. She took pride in her work.

After our order was taken and the money was carefully doled out by Peggy from a small silk drawstring bag, we got up and walked to the table where the daughter of the elderly white-wigged woman sat, to purchase tassels, feathers, pearls, gloves, fans, and all the other furbelows that were necessary so that General Howe would be properly seen off from America.

"Did you know," a girl in line behind us whispered, "that word is going about town that Anderson and Coffin will take in twelve thousand pounds sterling before they are finished servicing everyone for this event?"

"That could feed the Rebel army for a year," came the soft whisper of the small, round girl with the large gray eyes.

"Hush, Anne," the older woman with her scolded. "It's an honor for you to be a knight's lady. I know girls who would kill to be in your place."

"They can have it," said the brave little Anne.

"Hush!"

Anne hushed. And thereby went the only voice of reason in the room.

Chapter 11

When we were finished with our purchases and were out again in the bright wind-whipped March day, Peggy was too agitated to go home. "Let's go to Southwark Theater," she said to her sisters. "Captain Andre is there painting scenery this afternoon. He's invited me to drop by."

"Do you think that wise?" asked Sarah. "You know how Mama and Daddy feel about the theater. They say it promotes wickedness."

"Oh posh!" Peggy said.

"Posh?" Sarah looked beset. "Mama is on the committee to present a grievance to General Howe about the vain and wanton exhibitions of his Strolling Players."

"Mama's on every do-good committee there is," Peggy said in exasperation. "She's on so many, she can't keep them all straight. Anyway, I never heard her say a word to Captain Andre against the theater. And she *knows* he's one of Howe's Strolling Players. And that they're putting on thirteen plays this season."

"It isn't her place to care about what Captain Andre does," Sarah argued. "It is her place to care about you."

"Nonsense." Peggy picked up her skirts and climbed into the carriage. "The theater is a glorious tradition in England. It could be here, too, if these stupid Quakers could see past their indignant blue noses."

"Are you calling Mama and Daddy stupid?" Sarah asked.

"No. But the members of that committee are. And they're leading Mama around by the nose. Give those bundles to Pepy, Becca, and let's not stand here arguing. It's a glorious day. I feel spring in the air. Pepy? Take us to the theater on Cedar Street. As for you and Mary," she said to her sister, "you two can wait in the carriage, if you wish, and not taint yourself with wantonness. But I intend to go inside."

The Southwark Theater was a red brick and wooden building with a pitched roof and a belfry on top. It had been used briefly as a hospital after the battles of Brandywine and Germantown. The arched windows in front made it resemble a church.

But we did not go in the front. And the touch

of illicit excitement inside as well as the air of trembling expectancy made it the furthest thing from a church I had ever seen.

Peggy had been there before. She knew her way around. She had Pepy park the carriage in an alleyway across the street, so her father's coach shouldn't be seen near the place. And she knew just the right knock to give at the discreet side door.

Her summons was answered by a tall, fair-haired young man. "Peggy! Delighted to see you. He's on stage."

"Captain Charles Phipps of the frigate *Camilla*," she introduced him to us. "He plays the Mock Doctor. And he gave a wonderful performance as Percy in the first part of *King Henry IV*."

"You're too kind." Phipps bowed to us and led the way.

Sarah and Mary had apparently, on the ride over, put aside their scruples, for they were now as eager as Peggy.

Once the door closed behind us, the darkness was like the inside of the devil's ear, and we stumbled after Phipps. Just ahead we could hear some hammering. And a lady was singing.

Phipps led us around some pillars that supported the roof and the gallery. Once around them we could see the stage.

I heard Sarah and Mary gasp in unison. And my own eyes were bedazzled. Dozens of oil lamps, without glass around them, lighted the rim of the stage.

"Ohhh," Mary said. "Look at that scenery!"

"Andre painted it," Peggy whispered. "I helped him."

We stood there entranced by the spectacle, which appeared like an oasis in the dark. Several workmen were raising a large piece of board on which was painted a rural scene. A small stream was in the foreground with a beautiful cascade of water. Surrounding it was a grove of beautiful, graceful trees. The colors were bright, yet the effect was one of serenity and beauty. It was the painting Peggy had described to me.

In front of the gigantic mural, a group of people were conferring over some papers in their hands. At the other end of the stage was the young woman who was singing. After a moment I realized it was a bawdy street ballad.

"Oh, if Mama could hear that!" Sarah said.

"Hush," Peggy ordered. "These plays are full of bawdy sentiments. But then, so is Shakespeare. Andre says that though such sentiments are indelicate to a modest ear, most women can bear a little, either very publicly or very privately."

"Who is the lady?" Mary asked, obviously in awe.

"That's Miss Hyde," Peggy told us. "She sings 'Tally Ho' between the play and the farce. They're doing *Constant Couple* and *Duke and No Duke* tonight."

"How do you know so much about the theater?" Sarah asked.

"John Andre has told me. Oh, there he is. Let's go into the pit."

And she led us down to the front, where we had to look up at the stage. "John!" she called. "John!"

He was in breeches and shirt, his stock off, directing the placement of the scenery. He turned, grinned on seeing Peggy, and came to the edge of the stage to give a sweeping bow. Then he got down on one knee. "How do you like the way it turned out?" he asked her, gesturing to the scenery.

"It's beautiful. How is the play going?"

"Tickets are near sold out, even at one dollar for boxes and the pit, and a half dollar for the gallery. We've printed a thousand handbills and 660 tickets for each performance. The gentlemen are doing their parts very well, but I'm afraid the ladies are rather deficient. Many of them are common soldiers' wives, and they're of no character to begin with. I'm so glad you could come! And you've brought your pretty sisters with you."

Sarah and Mary blushed. Andre's eyes fell on me. "I say, who is this lovely little Philadelphia flower? Not fair, Peggy, to keep her from me."

"You hopeless flirt, she's my maid, Becca. You've seen her about the house."

"Maid, is it? Well, I always said American girls were beautiful. But now I find their maidservants are, too. But how like you, Peggy, to surround yourself with nothing but beauty. Like a flower in the midst of others, waiting to be plucked."

"I'm not for plucking, so watch your tongue. But how is it that when it came time for plucking you didn't pick me? You picked Peggy Chew for your partner in the pageant."

A scowl darkened his handsome face. "Listen, darling, I had to do that."

"Did you, now? And pray, why?"

He leaned forward, as if to confide in her. "Judge Chew has cooperated beautifully with the British army since we've been here. You know your father has gone out of his way to remain neutral. It was politically expedient, my picking her. It had nothing to do with what was in my heart."

Peggy tossed her head. "If I could believe that."

"Do."

"Why should I?"

He looked past her at us, then back to her again. "May I speak plain?"

"Do."

"It stays here? Amongst us?"

Peggy was instantly flattered. "Yes. And I will vouch for my sisters and my maid."

· 128 ·

"Well then"—and he reached out a slender, graceful hand and touched her head lightly—"I was ordered to pick Peggy Chew. By General Howe himself."

Peggy could not believe it. "*Ordered?*"

"Yes. We are duty bound to return favors done for us by the leading Loyalist families. Howe considers it of the utmost importance to keep up these relations."

Peggy had what she wanted. She was mollified. Her pride was still of one piece. The slight was not of Andre's making, but the result of a military command.

He could be lying, but it could not be proven. A military order was out of everyone's hands. I saw her breathe a sigh of relief and gaze up at him adoringly. "Very well, I shall forgive you," she said.

"You will go with me then to the ball tonight at Howe's headquarters as we planned?"

"Yes."

"Darling!" He jumped off the stage and stood beside her. He smelled of paint. There was a smudge of it on the side of his face, which rendered him most endearing somehow. His shirt was open at the neck, low enough to show some dark hair on his chest. No gentleman ever appeared before a lady without his stock, but he had been caught in a charming state of disarray and that, too, somehow heightened his appeal.

He stood between me and Peggy, and I felt overcome with dizziness being so close to him. He smiled at her. His smile was dazzling. His teeth were even and white. A lock of dark hair fell over his forehead.

I recollected then what Elizabeth had told Peggy about him that morning. *Even some of his own men said the way he had over two hundred Americans killed and wounded with bayonets at Paoli last September was the most grievous horror they'd ever seen.*

I could not reconcile that description with Andre. Was Elizabeth mad?

"How did you come here?" he was asking Peggy. "You didn't walk, did you? May I see you home?"

"Pepy drove us. My father's carriage is across the street. We went to Coffin and Anderson's for fabric," Peggy explained.

To my complete bedazzlement, he put one arm around Peggy's shoulder and one around mine and began to walk us out of the pit and up the side aisle. The pressure of his hand burned through the fabric of my cloak. I told myself his touch meant nothing, that I just happened to be on one side of him as we walked. I told myself I should pull away, step back and walk with Sarah and Mary, who were trailing behind.

But I did not. His touch afflicted me. The

warmth of his charm was as a live thing. I could feel it take hold of me. My throat went dry as I felt myself quicken in his presence. I was blushing by the time we reached the door.

He opened it for us, and we stepped out into the bright March sunlight. I gasped, for it was like a rude assault on my senses after the comforting dark of the theater, where, I suddenly minded, every gesture was magnified, every word carried a greater weight, every glance had significance. And every lie was believed.

He bowed to Peggy, picked up her hand, and kissed it. "Until tonight then, at seven. I can scarce wait."

She laughed scornfully. I thought it most unkind of her. If a man like Andre bowed and kissed my hand and paid me court, I would likely be jelly in his hands. But he seemed amused by her scornful laugh. It challenged him. His eyes sparkled as he watched us go.

In the carriage on the way home, I slumped in a corner, plunged into depths I did not know my soul had. Being inside a theater for the first time, coupled with seeing Peggy's ease in such surroundings and witnessing her exchange with Andre, had only put me on notice.

There was a whole world of glittering women and charming men right under my nose, indulging in clever banter, practicing sophisticated morals and manners, ignoring all the rules of proper behavior and only being rewarded for it.

They appreciated and understood each other. They spoke some rare and refined language of romance that I was doomed never to understand. And was certain never to partake in.

I felt a mortification of the spirit all the way home, as my anger at my own deficiencies roused itself from where I had stuffed it away. Once again my deficiencies paraded before my eyes to the background music of Peggy's chatter. She went on without mercy about what she would wear that night, about the cultural refinements of the theater, about Andre and how he really wanted her for his partner at the pageant and how she had known it all along.

My meeting that morning with Elizabeth was as from another time and place. As was my promise to her. I could not believe I had made it.

* * * * *

But I kept my promise. Because I had been brought up by Mama to do so.

The rest of the afternoon was spent readying Peggy's clothing for the evening and fixing her hair while her sisters, who were also going to the ball, each with her own dashing escort, ran in and out of her room, asking advice about hair, borrowing ribbons, and existing on an edge of excitement that had the whole house in an uproar.

Brilliana made dozens of trips below stairs to press out one more wrinkle in a gown or petticoat. Ellyn and Dorothea were conscripted from below to assist Mary and Sarah. Since she would likely not be home "before first light," Peggy gave me detailed instructions for the gowns my mother was to sew.

"I'll be sleeping all day tomorrow," she said, "so it's just as well it's your day off."

Finally the hour of seven arrived. In the parlor downstairs three dashing British officers waited. Mary and Sarah had gone below already. Peggy would make her entrance, sweeping down while everyone stared, open-mouthed, with worshiping looks on their faces. "Peggy, you're so beautiful!" Even her mother and father said it. Mr. Shippen had tears in his eyes.

Andre came to meet her at the bottom step, took her hand, kissed it, and led her into the parlor, where the light from dozens of candles in wall sconces reflected off polished furniture surfaces and gleaming silver.

Mr. Shippen served his best Madeira for the officers. Mrs. Shippen said all the right motherly things. "Remember, you must only dance with the gentleman who brings you," she cautioned.

Wraps were brought out. Peggy's was trimmed with white ermine.

"Oh, Mama, those are the American rules," Peggy said.

"All that is antiquated now, madam," Andre said. " 'Tis a fixed rule that ladies never dance but two dances with the same person. But I assure you, all rules are made to be broken."

Mrs. Shippen looked as if she did not know how to take his meaning. But the other two officers agreed. The three couples went out the front door. Pine-knot torches gave illumination in the front roundabout. Liveried servants opened the doors of three different coaches. The horses had bells on their harnesses, colorful plumes on their heads.

I watched them drive away. A sense of loss stabbed at me, worse for the knowledge that I had lost something I had never possessed. I would never drive off in a coach like that on my way to a ball. Never, if I lived to be a hundred.

The knowledge made me so desolate I wanted to die.

"Come in now, it's cold. Becca? If you're not too tired, I could work with you on some French tonight. After my husband and I finish supper," Mrs. Shippen said.

"Yes, ma'am, thank you," I said. And I went into the warming kitchen to have leftover stew with Coxie.

* * * * *

That night I lay in the trundle bed beside Peggy Shippen's own large one, bundled against the cold.

The March night had turned blustery. I had gone to bed at ten, after spending an hour learning French verbs with Mrs. Shippen. I lay on my side, gazing into the flames licking at the logs in the hearth. The quiet sputtering of the fire had a timeless quality that soothed me.

I must not sleep. I lay listening for the next chiming of the tall case clock below stairs. The room was flooded with brightness from the near-full moon reflecting on the snow.

I was not concerned with getting into trouble, not even if Mr. Shippen was downstairs in his library reading, as he so often was when Peggy or her sisters were out. Even if he heard the signal, well, some poor, starving soul was always begging at the back door. The poor posed a great problem in the city. Churches constantly asked for subscriptions to help them, and rumor had it that even General Howe was going to hold a lottery to give them aid.

I decided to get out of bed and light my candle. It cast my shadow, larger than life, on the walls. I put on a warm wrap and my moccasins, and opened the door. Just as I did, the clock chimed. Fifteen minutes before the hour. I made my way carefully downstairs, thinking how, at this very moment, Elizabeth Shippen was waiting in a wagon a short distance from the house. And Lieutenant Frazor was making his way to our back door. I worried about him. In the bright moonlight, a red officer's coat would easily be seen.

In the downstairs hall, I saw candlelight spilling out of the library. Mr. Shippen *was* in there. They said he never slept until Peggy came home.

I closed the door to the warming kitchen carefully, set down the candle, and went to get some milk to put in a pan on the fire. Because of the large, uncovered windows, the room was like daylight.

I was trembling as I spooned some honey into the milk and swung the pan back over the flames next to a cauldron of soup that bubbled slowly. There was always a pot of soup on the fire here. Coxie believed in being ready for any emergency. It came to me then that it might be a good idea to put some in a bowl and have it ready for Frazor. So I fetched a wooden bowl from the table and spooned soup into it. Then I waited.

In a moment I heard the footsteps crunching on some old snow outside. They came closer and closer. I stood in the middle of the warming kitchen, arms folded across my middle, trying to steady myself.

Then came the soft knock on the door. Three raps, silence, then two, as Elizabeth had described it. I hesitated for one awful moment, then walked clumsily across the brick floor and lifted the latch.

In the moon-washed night, I could see him as

clearly as if it were day. He was tall and dressed in a shabby British officer's coat. The sleeves were too short on him. From under the tricorn hat, his face stared down at me, gaunt and unshaven, haggard, with sunken eyes.

There was no doubt about who he was. The man had the look of sickness about him. But I must be sure. "Yes?" I asked.

"I'm here to see Becca."

"I'm Becca. Come in."

He slipped inside, and I put a finger in front of my lips and gestured to the door to the hallway. I led him to the fire, where he extended his hands and warmed himself, gratefully. Then I handed him the bowl of soup and a pewter spoon.

"You're most kind. Do you have the clothes?"

"Yes." I scrambled to the cupboard and pulled out the bundle.

He nodded as I set it down at his feet. He was spooning the soup into his mouth as fast as he could, making little slurping sounds.

Why, I minded, *he's fair to starving!*

In a moment he was holding the wooden bowl up to his lips, draining the last of the liquid.

"Would you like more?"

"No time." He set the bowl down and took up the clothes. "I'd best be on my way. Kindest regards to you, miss. I hear tell you've a brother at Camp Valley Forge."

"Yes."

"I'm on my way there this night. Pray we get through." Then he started to cough. To muffle the sound he put the bundle of clothes in his face. When he was finished, he smiled at me. "Sorry, miss, it's my lungs. They got the sickness in prison. I'll be going now. I'll change in the necessary out back."

"But it's too cold."

"I'm accustomed to the cold, miss."

"No. Change here, in front of the fire. I'll step out into the hall and keep watch."

"Don't want to bring trouble down on you."

"Hurry! It'll only take you a minute. Call out softly if you need help."

I stepped into the hall, half closed the door, and stood waiting. I heard some movement from within the kitchen, and in a very short while he called out in a loud whisper.

I went back in. He was standing there in the Quaker dress, stuffing the British officer's clothes into a bundle. I helped him with the cloak Elizabeth had provided and in a moment he was ready. Another fit of coughing took him. Again he put the bundle in front of his face.

"You're very sick," I whispered.

He looked down at me. His face, I minded, was very young. He was no more than twenty. But his eyes had years of longing and knowledge in them. And, as he looked at me, they became filled with tears. "Times we went six days without food in prison. I'm dying, miss, that's the truth of it. I want to die with the army. At Camp Valley Forge. Besides, I've got information for Washington that could be useful."

Tears came into my own eyes. Men like him were starving and dying. And I was spending my time pouting because I would never go off in a coach, dressed in some ridiculous finery, to a ball with a British officer.

I felt ashamed. For not only myself, but for Peggy Shippen, her sisters, and all the other spoiled young women I had met this day, who had spent their time indulging themselves in frivolous pleasures while all around them people were dying for what they believed in.

"I'll be going now, miss. Thank you."

"Godspeed," I said.

He went out the door. I watched him go for a moment, watched him trying not to trip on the skirts of the dress as he made his way through the snow around the house to the side gate.

"God, take care of him," I prayed. It was so cold out there. But at least now he had the protection of the Quaker cloak.

I latched the door, put the wooden soup bowl and spoon into a bucket of water that sat near the hearth, took my mug of milk and honey, and tried to keep from trembling as I went back upstairs.

I trembled long after I had put another log on the burned-down cinders, drunk my warm milk and honey, and climbed back into my warm bed. For I was shaken to the bone. But not from the cold.

Chapter 12

 $\mathscr{T}$ he first thing Mama said when she fetched me the next morning was that we were going to see Blair at Camp Valley Forge.

The second thing was, "Tell me what you've learned."

I had to give an accounting. So I recited some French, told her about the watercolor I was working on and how the American rules for ladies at balls differed from the English. "Mrs. Shippen is teaching me to play the harpsichord. And Sarah is teaching me some dancing." I was extra careful with my diction. She was most pleased.

But I did not tell her everything. I did not say what I had learned about Henry Job. She would only deny it, keeper of secrets that she was. Well, I had my own secrets now, aplenty of them. For one thing I would not tell her I'd been in a theater.

For another I would not make mention of what I had done for Lieutenant Frazor last night. I felt very much a woman, keeping such matters to myself. They were the first proper secrets I had ever kept from my mother.

"Tell me more about these dresses I am to make," she said.

So I told her. She glanced at the sketches as we drove along. "I never thought the day would come when decent American girls would subscribe to such fashions."

"They're special. For the *Meschianza*, Mama."

"No gown is so special that it violates the rules of decency."

"Oh, Mama!"

"You've forgotten what we've taught you already?"

"No, Mama, I haven't forgotten anything." If she thought I was in the least bit corrupted, she would not make the dresses. No one could be as stubborn as Mama when the humour seized her. "I know the dresses are indecent. But I wouldn't want you to lose your job as mantua-maker for refusing. Don't you need the money?"

She sighed and did not answer for a moment. When she did her voice sounded very tired. "Yes, we need the money," she said. "I suppose I should not consider myself above others. All kinds of people are doing things in this war to survive that they would not be caught dead doing in peacetime. But don't let Papa Henry see those sketches. Heaven forbid!"

. . . . .

"Wagon coming! Wagon coming!" The cry of the men in the guard post up ahead rang across the forlorn expanse of snowy ground. As Mama pulled up on the reins, they ran out to meet us, muskets poised and ready.

"Halt!"

They were dressed in an assortment of rags that could not be described in any language. Yet they accosted us, one to each side of the wagon, in as threatening a manner as if they belonged to the fancified Queen's Rangers.

"For what purpose do you come?"

Mama surveyed them and took a deep breath. "To take the waters here. I heard it was a spa." Mama could be sarcastic when she felt the occasion warranted it.

"Don't try to flummox us," one of them said. He was considerably more ragged than his partner. And it was as if that qualified him to be in charge. "State your purpose or you'll be hauled before the authorities."

"I come to see my son."

"What's his name?"

"Captain Blair Syng. He's with the Pennsylvania Line. Under General Wayne."

"Ask for paper, Salem," the other man said. "Don't let her in lessen you see paper."

"I know what to do," said Salem. Then he looked sternly at Mama. "Do you have paper?"

Mama had it. She drew it out of her cloak. I do not know what it was, but they felt safer seeing it. "Pardon us, ma'am," the man called Salem apologized, "but 'Zexcellency has issued a new General Order to tighten restrictions and prevent any sudden attempts from the enemy."

"Do I look like the enemy?" Mama asked.

They allowed that she did not. "But the enemy never looks like the enemy," Salem said, handing the paper back to her. "Leastwise not when they try to come here."

"Who is 'Zexcellency?" she inquired.

Salem eyed her as if she were without benefit of the brains she was born with. "Why, General Washington, ma'am."

Mama nodded and looked around. Her gaze swept the bleak landscape. "Why would even the enemy want to come here? We've heard about the disease and desertion and death you have. You haven't enough to eat. You haven't enough guns. How can you hold here?"

They looked at one another. They raised their eyebrows. Salem shrugged as if to tell his companion, "Let's humour her." Then he put one hand and one foot on the wagon and looked up into Mama's eyes earnestly. "You ever met 'Zexcellency, ma'am?"

"No. I can't say I have had the honor."

Salem nodded, as if that explained it all. "If you did, you would know how we can hold on here," he said. There was a look in his eyes that reminded me of something, but I could not think what. Then he slapped Duke's rump and the wagon started off.

"Wait," Mama started to yell back but had to concentrate on the reins. "Of all the cheek." She did not like being so dismissed. "Indeed. Ruffians. If that's what we have in our army, we haven't a chance."

We drove on past artillery emplacements, past earthen walls that rose ten or twelve feet. Then we came into the open to drive by huts that were little more than shanties. In the distance beyond the huts hundreds of tree stumps stuck up out of the frozen ground. Wind, balmy as it had become, whipped across the vast openness, sometimes sending up little gusts of snow. Smoke struggled out of the meager chimneys of the huts.

An air of desolation lay over the land.

"All my life I've been wrong," Mama said grimly.

I hoped she wasn't coming down with something. She never admitted to being wrong. "Don't

let those sentries beleaguer you. They *were* ruffians," I said.

"All my life I thought hell was fire. Now I
know it is snow and cold and desolation. This is
hell, Becca. Right here."

Her words frightened me. Mama was not one
to be so put off. "What is it, Mama?" I asked.

"Look at this place. They don't have adequate
shelter. They don't have shoes, some of them. They
don't have enough to eat. And this is where my
son is. For what, Becca? Can someone tell me for
what?"

When she put it to me that way, I could not
tell her. I did not know myself, half the time. The
war we spoke of and lived in Philadelphia was far
removed from this.

Except for, what? And then it came to me, what
Salem's look had put me in mind of. It was the
same look Persifor Frazor had worn last night. All
the same longing and knowledge had been in Salem's eyes. *Longing for what,* I asked myself.
Knowledge of what? I felt cheated because I did
not know. And I said naught of it to Mama.

We drove past a group of men crowding around
what looked like an Indian, who was giving a dem-
onstration with his bow and arrow. We came upon
more men clad in rags. You could not call such
clothing uniforms. They were digging trenches.
Other men were fetching wood.

I could not help noticing that many of the soldiers were nigras.

Finally, as we came around the corner into what seemed like a commons or parade ground, we saw dozens of men in formation.

In front of them stood a short, rotund man in cape and tricorn, waving his arms and shouting at them. He was speaking French. Sometimes when he became angry, he would switch to German.

We waited in the wagon, watching. The man was instructing them in the use of the musket. Two officers stood at his side, and they would translate his commands. A little to the distance, but watching the instructor always, was a dog. A lean, sharp dog.

"There's Hamilton," Mama said.

Indeed, one officer was Alexander Hamilton, now Washington's senior aide-de-camp. He turned, saw us and bowed, and in a moment went to speak to another officer whom neither Mama nor I recognized, for his back was to us.

The other man turned, saw us, said something to Hamilton, and then came striding across the snow and the frozen ruts of the road.

"Blair is sick," Mama said. "I just know it. And this man is coming to tell us. I just feel it in my bones."

"Mama." The officer took off his hat. "What a pleasant surprise."

We stared. His hair was sprinkled with white. It was not a wig; it was his hair. And it was sprinkled with white. His face was thin, marking the bones. His eyes were bright, as with fever.

Mama leaned down to embrace him. I heard her sob.

"Mama, what is it? Is everything all right at home?" He looked over her head to me. "Hello, Becca."

"Hello, Blair."

"Tell me what's wrong."

"Your men are ruffians, that's what's wrong." Mama straightened up and wiped the tears from her face.

"What men?"

But she would not answer. She sat straight, staring ahead. I knew she was trying to compose herself. I smiled at Blair. "The sentries. We had trouble getting in."

Blair laughed. It was the same laugh he'd always had, the laugh that had driven me to distraction at home when he used to tease me. "Ruffians? The baron calls them bandits."

"The baron?" Mama asked. "First I hear about 'Zexcellency, then the baron. Is this the American army or the British?"

Blair laughed again. It was a good sound. "I speak of Von Steuben. He arrived the twenty-third of last month. He is from Prussia. He is teaching us the manual of arms in only ten motions. And to drill with simplicity. Seventy-five steps a minute. It suits the rough terrain. That's him over there."

"Is that his dog?" I asked Blair.

"Yes, that's Azor. I'm sorry the sentries were rude, Mama, but they were acting under orders."

She sniffed. "I brought supplies. Potatoes, a side of mutton, flour, eggs, turnips, onions."

The booty was uncovered. I saw tears film Blair's eyes as he looked at it.

"But, Mama, you shouldn't have come. The risk is too great."

"I can use a fowling piece." And she showed him the gun at her feet.

"A fowling piece! Zounds, Mama! In January Captain Henry Lee and his Light Horse were exploring the area and took refuge for the night in a farmhouse. Lee had sentries posted. Captain Banastre Tarleton came along with upwards of two hundred British dragoons. Only spirited use of firearms by Lee and eight men put down the assault."

She patted the side of his face. "Let this Banastre person come. I've the mettle to stand up to him. Now do you and your men want these provisions or not?"

Blair raised his eyes in despair. He knew better than to say more. "Yes, thank you."

In a moment he'd recruited two men to carry the provisions to one of the meager huts. "Gather more wood," he told them, "and when you've finished your other duties, get the stew pot. This will make a fine stew. Come along, Mama. You, too, Becca."

We went into a hut.

"And where do *you* live?" Mama asked.

We were standing in the middle of the hut. To one side were four bunks, to the other the hearth. There were two windows covered with oiled paper. On a rude table in the corner were a stack of Bibles. Blair had to duck his head when he'd come in the door. He brought forth some stools and we sat down. "This is my hut," he said.

Mama looked around. I could see the disappointment wrap itself around her. As if someone had put a wet blanket on her shoulders. "But you're an officer," she said.

"This is how we live, Mama."

She nodded. It was hard for her. This was not the stuff of which her dreams for Blair were made. To give her credit, she kept herself composed. "So this is the shelter you built."

"Yes. The roof is made of straw and evergreen branches. Washington offered a twelve-dollar prize for the best-constructed hut to be completed in each regiment. Our hut won."

"What's that smell?"

"We're burning a little powder from our musket cartridges to purify the air. Washington is worried about health."

"Do you believe in him like the sentries do?" Mama peered into Blair's face.

My brother got up to put a log on the fire. "Yes. If I didn't, I wouldn't be here. By now all the officers who don't believe in him have left."

"Officers have deserted?" Mama's eyes went wide.

"Resigned," Blair said. "Officers can resign. Some have. Many others have taken extended leave."

"And why, then, if this Washington is so excellent?"

Blair bristled. "Officers must keep themselves out of their own pockets. Enlisted men get provided for. Mama, Washington lived in a tent in the cold until he realized he couldn't run an army from such a shelter. On Christmas he invited the Marquis de Lafayette to his table. They had only the smallest portions of veal, mutton, potatoes, and cabbage. No need to worry, I'm keeping fine."

"Then why did I hear tales that you men ate dogs and rats, if you're keeping so fine."

"That was in the beginning when we first came into camp. We're better off now. Didn't I write you how I went on a foraging expedition with General Wayne in February? We rounded up cattle in southern Jersey. And the shad are running. We've had less smallpox than we feared. And Baron Von Steuben is turning us into proper soldiers. Must we talk about this?" Blair felt pushed. I knew my brother. He would eat dog and rat if necessary, but he would not talk about it. It was something he chose to do. But he did not choose to explain.

He kicked a log in the fire with his boot, turning his back to us.

Mama fell silent.

"Does anyone else in camp have a dog?" I asked Blair.

He turned, smiling, grateful for the turn I gave the conversation. "No, but General Howe has one. It wandered into our camp when we were at Whitemarsh. His name was Nimrod. Washington sent two men to return him to Howe under a flag of truce."

"He didn't!"

"Yes. He sent a note along with them. I saw it. 'General Washington's compliments to General Howe—does himself the pleasure to return to him a dog, which accidentally fell into his hands, and by the inscription on the collar, appears to belong to General Howe.' "

I laughed, delighted with the story. Mama didn't.

"How do men mark the difference in war where the games stop and the killing begins?" she asked.

"We know the difference, Mama," Blair said.

"Those who don't become savages. It's the little things like I've just made mention of that keep us from becoming savages."

She nodded. But I could see she did not understand. And the chasm between them was growing wider. If we did not leave soon, I thought, all three of us would fall into it.

"Well, at least you still read the Bible." She gestured to the pile of them in the corner.

"What?" Blair turned. "Oh, no, those aren't for reading."

"What are they for then?"

"For making cartridges, Mama."

"For what?"

"We need the paper. To make our cartridges. We don't have enough paper. So we foraged these from a local church."

Mama stood up. The visit was over.

"I'm sorry," Blair said.

"For what?" she asked.

"That things aren't as you expected. That I'm not as you expected."

For an awful moment Mama said nothing. Then she reached up and put her arms around him. "You are more than I ever expected," she said. "One of the sorrows of being a mother is that our children travel to places where we can never go. You've traveled far in this valley without a forge, Blair. But you are still my boy."

I breathed easier. Outside, Mama went to get

into the wagon. Blair dallied, so I knew he wanted to talk.

"How do you like working for the Shippens, Becca?"

"I like it fine."

"We had an escaped prisoner from the Walnut Street Jail come in this morning. An officer. He was on parole at the Golden Swan and disguised himself as a Quaker woman. Said he was given aid by a servant in a prominent Quaker household."

"Did he, now?"

Blair smiled down at me, a knowing warmth in his eyes. "If you're going to make a habit of this sort of thing, be careful."

"Likely I'll never do such again."

"Well, I'm glad you did this time. He had information for Washington. Aren't you going to ask after him?"

"How is he?"

"Sickly. They wanted to send him to a hospital in Reading or Bethlehem. But too many of our men have died in those places. So I convinced them to allow him to stay in our brigade hospital here. He felt a kinship with me, it seems. Asked for me. He'd heard the girl who gave him aid had a brother here."

"Do you think he'll mend?"

"With proper rest, yes. I take it Mama doesn't know."

"She doesn't."

"Well, your secret is safe with me. What's worrying at her, Becca?"

"She's as she always is, Blair."

"She was here before. She saw the suffering. Why does she act so angry today? Today she's more of what she always is."

I shrugged and looked past him to the desolate landscape. "I don't know as I can explain."

"Try."

"All right." I took a deep breath and looked into the thin face of my brother. I saw the brown eyes, so deep set and filled with the same longing and knowledge I'd seen in the others. I saw the white in his hair. I saw the mark of a man in the lines around his mouth. "She acts angry because she can't do anything about what she sees here. When she can't remedy things, it makes her angry. And you mean so much to her. 'Tis the memory of you, Blair, the hope of you, and the idea of you that keeps her going. I don't know how else to put it."

He nodded and looked at his tricorn hat, which he held in his hands. "You put it fair to middling," he said.

"It's the way of her. It always was."

"I lie to myself," he said. "You put it well. But I don't want her feeling that way about me, Becca."

"Well, you've got it, Blair, whether you want it or not."

He nodded again. "Talk to her, Becca. Tell her I'm keeping. I know it doesn't look it. All this—" He waved a hand and took it all in. "I know I don't look it. But I am keeping, Becca. You must tell her."

"I know you are," I said.

"Do you, now? And how is it you can see this when our mother can't?"

"By your laugh," I said. "It's still the same. I know by your laugh."

His eyes showed disbelief. "My laugh?"

"Yes. It's as it always was. Back home. When you teased me. It has the devil in it. I mind that if you weren't keeping, you couldn't laugh like that anymore."

He smiled. "Tell her then," he said. "And thank you again for what you did for Frazor."

He hugged me. The hug said more than words. Tears came to my eyes. I got back into the wagon feeling closer than I ever had to my brother. Whatever childhood rivalry we had was gone. His thanks for what I'd done for Frazor had been true. He saw me as a real person now. His respect warmed me. I no longer cared if he made up Mama's world more than I did. It was a heavy burden on him. I did not envy it.

We watched him cross the ice-rutted street in

long, confident strides. His cape was worn but sat his broad shoulders well. Its edges swung back, showing red lining as he walked. His tricorn, with the clay pipe secured in back, was cocked just right on his head. He went up to Hamilton and murmured something to him.

Hamilton turned, took off his own tricorn, and gave us a sweeping bow. His uniform, too, was in disrepair. But the picture they made—they and the bedraggled men, wrapped in every kind of cast-off, some with rags around their feet—was etched against the clear blue sky in bold, sure strokes, like some tapestry torn out of time, which I knew I would never forget.

Baron Von Steuben was screaming at the soldiers in German. He must have said something funny, for they roared with laughter. His shouts rang out. He was counting in German. "*Eins, zwei, drei, vier!*" he shouted.

The soldiers scrambled to obey. We heard the metallic clashing of steel as the soldiers removed the ramrods from their muskets and started loading the weapons in ten easy steps. We drove away with the sounds of the ramrods being shoved down the musket barrels and the baron's orders echoing in our ears.

I patted Mama's hand. "He's fine," I told her.

"Oh? And what revelation have you had to make you say such?"

"His laugh. It's still the same. Do you think it would be if he weren't fine?"

She said nothing. That in itself was a good sign.

.   .   .   .   .

For all my new revelations about Henry Job, I could not bring myself to regard him any differently. He was still clumsy. He stuffed his mouth with food, spoke while he chewed, and slopped his biscuits in gravy, which dripped down his shirtfront.

A spy for Washington? I watched him with new eyes at supper as he dug into the roast mutton, gulped his rum, and wiped his mouth with his shirtsleeve. Spies were heroes, weren't they? How could anyone with dirt under his fingernails be a hero?

And I could still see only darkness in him, no light.

I minded what Elizabeth had said. *Spies are just ordinary people who can't abide what the British are doing to us and have decided to make things right in their own little way.*

I could not fix it right in my head. I was confused.

"This *Meschianza*," he said. "We've heard of it." He rested his forearms on the table and regarded me with cool appraisal. "Are they having to do with it in the Shippen household?"

No reason to lie. "Three of the daughters are going."

One thing about Henry Job: His face never gave away his thoughts. For this reason, his face was still round and smooth, with no secrets written there.

"And so you volunteered your mama to make the gowns."

"Yes. I knew she could use the money."

He looked at Mama. "And you'll do it?"

"I'm their mantua-maker, Henry. I can ill afford to say no. Word will get around, and no one will want my services. And pray, why should I refuse to make them?"

"You went to visit your son at Camp Valley Forge today and you have to ask that?"

Mama did not answer.

"What I've heard about the *Meschianza*, it's not a good thing. Prisoners are coughing their lungs out in the Walnut Street Jail. And these fops are making a game of the war. It is not a game. Not a sport. When you get your face blown away by a musket ball, you die. You don't get up again and have the last dance with a pretty girl. They make a mockery of all the suffering."

It was the longest speech Henry Job had ever made. And it was exactly what Elizabeth had said. Mama's spoon paused, midair. My mouth fell open. No one said anything. Candles on the table sputtered. A clock ticked in the corner. Mama and I stared at him and then at each other.

After a moment, Mama spoke. "You are right, Henry," she allowed. "But making the dresses does not mean I give my blessing to them. Someone else would only sew them, if I refused."

"Then let someone else. They won't be as fine as yours."

"Thank you, Henry, but we need the money."

"Don't wash it away," he said.

"I'm not washing it away."

"Damn their money." And he threw down his napkin, got up, and went to the hearth, where he put another log on the fire. "We can do without their money. It's you who want it, Jane. You who need to rub shoulders with them. It's your needs that must be served." He poured himself some coffee from the pot and stood there sipping it. His heavy frame was laden with misery, with his own failure to put into words what was plaguing him. What *was* plaguing him of a sudden? I didn't know.

"Well, of course, I won't make the dresses if you don't approve, Henry," Mama said.

"It isn't for me to approve or disapprove. It's for you."

"Come finish your supper. I did not mean for this to trouble you."

He came back to sit down. "If I am troubled by it, Jane, it is because you are not. You blame me because I won't go to see the boy at Camp Valley Forge. I do not need to go to have a true anger in my heart for what the British are doing. You go, and you do not have the anger."

They had forgotten me. Or they would have kept up the pretense of being neutral. Mama would have come back with some remark about him delivering goods to the British.

She did not. She looked sad instead. I sat very quiet and still, making no move, scarcely even breathing.

"I have the anger, Henry," Mama said wearily. "But it is not like yours. People from Boston have a different anger."

"Don't make this a thing between Boston and Philadelphia."

"But that's what it is. You people from Boston must always make a grand show of your anger. Always it is better than everyone else's. Always it must explode all around you."

"If we weren't that way, we'd still be under the king's heel, serfs on our own land."

"We here in Philadelphia nurse our anger," Mama persisted. "We stir it and brew it. We taste it and age it. Then when we are sure, we make our move."

He stared at her dully. She was speaking in abstractions. He could not abide abstractions. When Mama talked like that, she had him whipped and he knew it. "Bah," he said. And he got up, waving her off. "Go and do your stirring and brewing. Make your dresses. You'll do it anyway." And he made to leave the room.

At the doorway, he paused. "Did you get payment first?"

"The Shippens are good for their word," Mama said.

"I hear his store of silver is depleting."

"One minute, Henry, you don't want me to do the dresses, and the next you're worrying about payment. Now which is it?"

"Make sure you get payment. I don't want to see you duped. All the merchants know that the British will soon be leaving the city. Many are demanding now that customers settle accounts."

"British customers," Mama said.

He shrugged. "British or Loyalist. There's no difference."

"The Shippens won't leave."

"Won't they? They're being watched by the independence men." He paused, opened his mouth to say more, saw me watching, and closed his mouth. He'd said too much already. He turned and left the room.

Mama gave a great sigh, put her elbows on the table, and rested her head in her hands. Then she raised her eyes and looked at me. "He's a good man," she said.

Chapter 13

I was rushing back to the Shippen house on a fine morning, the first day in May, when I spotted the small silver inkstand. There it was, in a pawn shop on Second Street, right in the window, between an ivory chess set and an old leather-bound copy of Plutarch's *Lives*.

I'd been glorying in the beautiful spring day, the warmth of the sun on my face, the embroidery of green buds on tree limbs, the daffodils and tulips budding all over. My spirit responded in kind. I was glad to be out, glad for Peggy's errands, thinking of nothing in particular. And then I saw the inkstand and stopped dead in my tracks, staring.

Something in its delicate curves, its rich patina gleaming in the sun made me feel a kinship with it. I went in and hesitantly asked the proprietor if I could look at it.

He was an elderly man and his shop was filled with items of value, obviously left here by families whose store of hard specie was running low like Mr. Shippen's.

I touched the inkstand lovingly, traced my fingers along its edges, turned it upside down. Underneath, as I had half suspected and half hoped, were my father's initials, P.S.—Phillip Syng.

Tears came to my eyes and a thrill went through me. My father had made this. With his own hands. I was hard put to give it back to the man. For I knew it, instantly, for what it was.

It was one of my missing pieces.

How wonderful if I could buy it for Mama! I asked the price.

"Ten pounds sterling," the man said. "Of course, it may go down in price after the British leave. And it's not likely anyone will be buying it these days. It'll be here for a while, I wager."

I left the shop with a mystical feeling. How strange and wonderful that I should come upon it like that. Surely it was meant that I should have it. I wondered who had owned it.

"Becca! Becca Syng! Is it thee?"

I turned. A few doors behind me stood Ann Darragh. She ran toward me, her Quaker bonnet kept from falling off her head of shining dark hair only by its strings. "It *is* thee! They told me thou were in town. I didn't believe it. What are thee about?"

"I've just come from the salon of Henri Du-marae, the French hairdresser. I work for the Shippens now, since early March."

"The Shippens, is it? Thee is a sly fox. They're quality." Ann used the traditional Quaker manner of speech, something the Shippens did not do, though I never found out why. And she wore Quaker clothing, too. Proper Quaker clothing of good homespun cotton, not of gray silk or taffeta as Mrs. Shippen wore. But she looked fetching nevertheless. The dress was molded to her body and, somehow, on her the prim white collar and cuffs stood out like jewels. Her round face with its sprinkling of freckles was saucy and cheerful. Her blue eyes sparkled.

Ann's mother and father had emigrated from Ireland. I envied her ready laughter, her lightness of manner and heart.

"I don't have to ask why thee hasn't come to call, then, do I? The Shippens have belabored their neutrality."

"Yes," I lied quickly. I did not want her to know it was my own parents who had forbidden me to see her. "But I've missed seeing you. I have no friends. I scarce ever go out. Today I was sent to fetch special soaps and perfume so Peggy can wash her hair. Monsieur Dumarae is coming over later to do it in the new style. She is attending a ball tonight."

Ann scowled. "Is it the one at Howe's headquarters? To celebrate the British rout of General Lacey's men at the Crooked Billet Tavern?"

"Yes." All spring Howe had been plagued by American militia on the perimeters of the city. He had sent out Hessian jägers, known for their fierceness, to determine American positions. For weeks they had played hide and seek with Daniel Morgan's riflemen. But the jägers could not pin them down. Word came back about what wonderful fighters the riflemen were. The jägers toasted them in taverns at night.

Howe sent men into Camden and Gloucester counties in the Jerseys, too. His soldiers were particularly plagued by Brigadier General John Lacey and his Rebel militia.

Then, two days ago, the town had been in an uproar. Lacey was near the city at Crooked Billet Tavern! Howe sent out a column, fourteen companies of light infantry. And dragoons. The best—Simcoe's Queen's Rangers.

Peggy and her sisters had stood outside their door waving and throwing flowers at the rangers as they passed by.

"My mother was on the committee of Friends who toured the battleground yesterday," Ann said. "They say they never saw such wanton carnage. Don't be surprised if Peggy Shippen doesn't get to go to that ball."

"Why?"

"Don't tell, but my mother and the committee are visiting the homes of all the girls invited whose parents are Quakers, to tell them of the atrocities visited upon Lacey's men. They say it was worse than Paoli."

I nodded. "Your mother is a brave woman, Ann. How is she? I always mind her stories about Ireland, especially the fairy stories she told us."

"She is well. And busy." Her blue eyes gazed, unblinking, into mine, filled with things discretion prevented her from saying.

"Are the British officers still in your house?"

"No, they say it was not commodious enough. They have moved out. When the British leave Philadelphia, thee must come and see me, Becca."

"Are they leaving? All we hear are rumors. That they will pull out before the gala on the eighteenth, that Howe's staff officers are refusing to serve under Sir Henry Clinton, and that the Rebel Light Horse is going to attack and ruin the *Meschianza* after dark."

She smiled. "Wouldn't that be fun?"

"Yes, I'm sick to the teeth of it, and it's still more than two weeks away. It's all I've heard for the last two months. Peggy and her sisters are completely taken up with it."

"I heard thy mother is sewing their dresses."

"Yes. She comes to the house twice a week to do fittings. All Peggy does is have hysterics. The waist on the dress is too low, the sleeves are not right, the neckline isn't flattering enough. I don't know how my mama abides it. I have to leave the room for fear of lashing out at Peggy."

"Has thy mother been paid for her labors?"

The way she said it made me pay mind. "Not yet, no."

"Tell her to settle her account."

"Why?"

She smiled, showing even white teeth. "Thee knows I can divulge no more. Thy mother is a good woman, Becca. Advise her to settle the account before the day of the *Meschianza* arrives. It is a ridiculous farce. Everyone with an ounce of sense knows it. The British will be leaving Philadelphia soon, and everyone who attends the *Meschianza* will be marked. The whisper of the day, heard from police chief Galloway, is that the people are afraid of the vengeance of the Rebels."

The words were not Ann's; she had heard them somewhere. But the solemnity and concern with which she uttered them were. I thanked her, and we parted. I hurried back to the Shippen household, head down, no longer conscious of the beautiful May morning.

Meschianza. The word was suddenly filled with foreboding for me. I had lived in the Shippen household for these past two months, and every sinew in me decried its excesses. But I had been forced to remain silent, betimes distrusting my own instincts.

Now Ann Darragh had given voice to my sentiments. I no longer felt like an oddity.

Mr. Shippen was hard put to stop the whole business, for once set in motion it was unstoppable. He just kept handing out money and growing quieter and quieter. Mrs. Shippen, of course, never had a voice to begin with. And Elizabeth had removed herself to Lancaster at the end of March to care for her grandmama, who was feeling poorly again.

I think Elizabeth used that as an excuse. Before she left she said, "If I don't get out of here, likely I'll do something terrible and disgrace the whole family. I can't abide the fuss over this stupid party."

Peggy and her sisters were all involved in helping Andre redecorate Walnut Grove, Joseph Wharton's confiscated mansion. There was to be a triumphal arch, 108 feet long, under which General Howe was to walk after he disembarked from galleys at the wharf.

It was Peggy's idea that those galleys be lined with green silk, as well as decorated with bunting. So there was a search all over town for green silk, as well as mirrors, carpets, candelabra, spermaceti candles, statuettes, military insignias, and fabric for blue-and-white turbans and sashes for the twenty-four nigras who would serve supper.

Andre came almost every day to confer with the Shippen girls. Peggy advised him about how best to use the fruit being brought from the West Indies, about the cornucopias of flowers being designed.

There would be a midnight supper. Peggy helped with the menu. There must be pyramids of jellies and sillabubs as well as chicken and lamb, puddings, buttered hams, sweetmeats, and Yorkshire pies. And spirits, of course.

Peggy and her sisters raided their mother's attic for fabric and china, platters and mirrors, ribbons and paintings. Then they had Pepy drive them about town to requisition from friends anything else that would serve to decorate the mansion.

Four hundred tickets were to be printed for the event. Peggy spent hours poring over Andre's design. She wanted a setting sun on the ticket, so Andre came up with a Latin motto: *Luceo descendes, aucto splendore resurgam*. It meant "I shine in setting; I shall rise again in greater splendor."

I opened the iron gate at the side of the house and went into the yard. My forays out of the house were limited to errands for Peggy. But I knew from overhearing whispered exchanges in shops this day that the people were angry over the *Meschianza*. Ann Darragh spoke no lies.

I went into the house, minding the words of Monsieur Dumarae to his assistant as he'd wrapped my packages in his salon. "A setting sun," he had said. "Let us hope that with the advent of the French alliance, it soon sets on the fortunes of the British army here in America."

· · · · ·

Coxie rolled her eyes at me as I came into the warming kitchen.

"What's wrong?" I asked.

"Trouble," she said. "You take warning. There be a committee of Friends behind the doors of the liberry wif the master."

Here already? I could not believe it! But I pretended innocence. "What for?"

"Doan know," Coxie said, "but it ain't good. You'd best be light on your feet an' keep your lips tight shut. The girls, they be out in the hall listenin'."

I thanked her and went into the hall to sit on the stairs with Peggy and her sisters.

We didn't have long to wait. After less than five minutes, the doors of the library opened and the committee filed out.

"The old crows," Peggy whispered savagely. She was seated on a step. I stood over her. As the gray-clad women and men walked down the hall to the front door, Mrs. Darragh sighted me. With her eyes she acknowledged my presence in such a subtle manner that the agitated Peggy never noticed it.

"Peggy! Sarah! Mary! Come in here!" Mr. Shippen called.

He left the library doors open. I waited in the hall. And it was as Ann Darragh had said it would be.

Mr. Shippen told his family solemnly that "the atrocities visited upon Lacey and his men were worse than at Paoli. The British butchered them with bayonets."

"Lies, Daddy," Peggy told him. "Andre said the Rebel scouts neglected their rounds during the night so it was a surprise attack. Our people had the upper hand."

"*Our* people?" Mr. Shippen said sternly. "*Our* people are not butchers, Peggy. These are not our people."

"Then who are? The Rebels?" Peggy threw at him. "Who *are* our people, Daddy? If I am confused, you must forgive me, but I don't know."

He ignored that. "Word has it the British threw the wounded into a field of straw and set the straw afire."

From where I stood, making myself as inconspicuous as possible, I saw father and daughter glare at each other.

"Andre says the fire was started by the gunpowder from American muskets." Peggy was near to crying.

"Andre has an answer for everything, doesn't he?" Mr. Shippen asked sarcastically.

"Not an answer, Daddy," Peggy chided. "He has *intelligence*. He is too good an officer to repeat rumor."

Mr. Shippen sighed and lowered his voice. "Members of the committee said the dead had dozens of bayonet wounds apiece. Near a hundred Americans were brutally murdered."

"Wayne's soldiers did the same at Germantown," Peggy said petulantly. She sounded like a child begging off some naughtiness because her sister had been forgiven the same prank.

Mrs. Shippen, who had been quiet, then spoke up. "Does this make it *right*?"

Silence. Peggy knew better than to sass her mother in her father's presence.

"I cannot let you go to a ball to celebrate such behavior," her father said.

"Oh, Daddy, please! Andre wasn't responsible. It was Simcoe's Queen's Rangers who did this. Why should we suffer?"

"Suffer?" her mother asked. "You call being kept from a ball *suffering*? What of those poor men burned alive in the fields? The committee is right, Peggy."

"Oh, bother the committee!" Peggy burst out.

"Peggy," her mother warned, "Mrs. Cooper has already stood up in Meeting and beseeched the mothers and fathers to keep their daughters from exchanging visits with the king's warriors."

"Warriors!" Peggy laughed. "Mrs. Cooper is jealous because her daughter wasn't asked to be a knight's lady!"

And then she had a thought. "You want to stay neutral, Daddy. You've ruined yourself to stay neutral. If you keep us from the ball now, you will be taking sides."

In the end she and her sisters went, of course. Monsieur Dumarae came that afternoon to do their hair in the latest of fashion, piled at least a foot high and festooned with ribbons and flowers.

But it wasn't the last we heard from the committee.

* * * * *

On the sixteenth of April, a frigate had arrived from England with an official peace offer for the Americans. It was dispatched to York, where Congress sat. For two weeks everyone waited. Then word came from Congress.

There could be no peace unless Great Britain recognized American independence.

On the fifth of May, just as that news came to us, I came downstairs to fetch some tea and cakes and bring them to Peggy's room. Her parents were out; she was expecting Captain Andre. The gowns were finished, and she was to display herself in hers for Andre's approval.

Mama had, with my urging, asked for her payment on her last visit. But she had not received it. It would be forthcoming, Peggy had said, as soon as the *Meschianza* was finished.

As I was setting some small iced cakes on a tray, the guns started to go off in the distance.

I stopped and looked at Coxie. "Cannon," I said. "They sound like they come from Camp Valley Forge."

We went to open the back door and listened.

We distinctly heard a thirteen-gun salute.

"What can it be?" I asked Coxie. "We saw no soldiers march out of town. Andre would not be coming today if there was an attack on the Americans." All the Loyalists in Philadelphia wanted Howe to attack Washington at Valley Forge. But he did not do it.

In the distance, the musketry rippled on the spring air. "It sounds like a *feu de joie,*" I told Coxie.

"What be that?"

"It's a firing of joy."

"Praise the Lord," Coxie said. "Let's hope there be good reason."

I went back upstairs with the tea and cakes to find Captain Andre lounging in a gilt-edged chair in Peggy's chamber, his legs outstretched languidly in polished boots.

I felt his eyes on me as I set the tray down on a small table. No woman of quality, Quaker or not, would entertain a gentleman in her private chamber. It was just not done. But Mr. and Mrs. Shippen were out; the servants were too afraid to tattle. And Sarah and Mary depended too much on Peggy to convince their father to allow them to continue their social schedule. I, of course, could be trusted.

"Where is your mistress?" Andre's voice was very cultured. There was a note of rich amusement in it.

"Likely in her sister's room, dressing, sir. So she can look fetching for you."

"And what am I to amuse myself with while I wait, then?"

"I can serve your tea, sir."

"Do, please."

He regarded me from beneath hooded lids as I performed the task. I had poured tea hundreds of times since I had become maidservant to Peggy, but for some reason I became clumsy. I missed the cup he was holding and the hot liquid fell on his hand.

"Damn!" He set the cup down and drew his hand away. "Clumsy oaf!" He reached for a handkerchief, but I was there with a linen napkin first. I had meant to offer it to him, but he smilingly held out his hand for my ministrations. I wiped the hand, apologizing again.

Then, as I was about to withdraw the napkin, his other hand came down on mine, holding my small hand captive between his. I blushed. "Please, sir."

"Please, what?" He caressed my wrist, my forearm. "You American girls are not as innocent as you look," he said. "Or so my brother officers say."

"Sir, I must ask you to release me, please!"

"And if I do not? What will you do? Tell Peggy? I shall say that you threw yourself at me in a most wanton manner. Whom do you think she will believe?"

For a terrible moment blood pounded in my ears. Or was it the cannon from Valley Forge? I did not know what to do. I was trapped. He was caressing my arm with his fingertips. One hand held my wrist, the fingertips of the other played up my sleeve to the fleshy part of my arm. And all the while he sat there at ease, smiling.

Never did I feel so put upon, so degraded. How could I ever have thought this man graceful or gallant? How could I have been drawn to him? Desperately, I cast my eyes around. And then they fell on the poker by the hearth. And I recollected what Coxie had told me the first day I had come here.

With a fierce strength born of resolve, I pulled

myself free, ran to the hearth, picked up the poker, and held it in front of me. "Perhaps you don't want tea, sir," I said. "Perhaps you are in need of something stronger. Like your flip."

He stared at me. I thrust the poker into the fire, then held it up. "Shall I go down and get the makings of flip, sir? I know how to do it. Coxie told me exactly what to do, should you require it."

His mouth opened. I saw disbelief in his eyes. But before he got the chance to reply, Peggy came through the door in her Turkish slave girl's costume.

"How do I look? Is it as you expected? Don't you think I'll be the prettiest girl there?"

"You are lovely, darling," he said. "Ravishing."

She pirouetted before him. And, in turning, saw me standing with the poker in my hands. "Why, whatever are you doing, Becca? You're supposed to be serving tea."

"I thought Captain Andre wanted some flip," I said.

"Do you?" Peggy asked him.

"Of course not. It's too early for flip, even for me. Wherever did the child get such a notion? Honestly, Peggy, how can you endure the poor quality of servants these days?"

"What are the cannon for? Do you hear them?" she asked.

He shrugged. "Our intelligence has it that the Rebels are going to have a formal observance of the Treaty of Alliance with France today."

He examined his fingernails as he said it. I thought he was straining to appear nonchalant. A surge of joy went through me. I could scarcely wait to tell Coxie.

•　•　•　•　•

But a few days later the British had another reason to celebrate. Washington decided to scuttle two frigates on the Delaware, rather than let them fall into British hands. The small galleys in his navy could offer little defense if the British moved upstream. Or so Andre told Peggy.

On May seventh Howe sent the Second Battalion of light infantry, two fieldpieces, eighteen flatboats, four galleys, two armed schooners, and four gunboats on the river to the Bordentown area in a show of force. They burned the Rebel frigates that hadn't been scuttled yet. They also burned a warehouse.

They were back in the city by the tenth. Another party to celebrate. Again, all three sisters were going. And again, the Quaker committee came to visit the Shippens. This time they stayed longer behind the library doors. Again I waited with the girls as they fretted out in the hall.

"I wonder what their objections are this time," Peggy whispered. "Old Mrs. Cooper likely owns part interest in the burned warehouse. She's as rich as God."

When they left, Mr. Shippen summoned his daughters. This time he looked grimmer than before. "Soldiers from the Second Battalion burned the private homes of some well-placed Americans in Bordentown," he told his girls. "It was wanton destruction of private property. I advised the committee to present their grievances to General Howe. Your mother is going to collect clothing and furnishings for the dispossessed."

"Can we go to the party?" Peggy asked.

Her father looked at her with a measure of disbelief. "Yes, Peggy, though I would have hoped you would show some sympathy for those who have been burned out. The committee approved your going only because I said you and your sisters would help with the collections."

"Approved?" Peggy went red in the face. "Now I have to have a committee approve my social life?"

"Mind your tongue," her father said sternly. "We are Quakers in good standing. And we shall stay that way."

Three days before the great event, a knock came at the front door just as they were at breakfast. It was a lovely spring day. Cecil ushered a ragged-looking man into the hall. Mr. Shippen went out to see what he wanted.

He came back into the dining room.

"What is it?" Mrs. Shippen asked.

"Not another committee!" Peggy's face had gone white.

Mr. Shippen sat down. "Nothing of importance."

"Tell us!" Peggy demanded.

"Very well. Word just came to me that the Frenchman Lafayette is twelve miles north of the city with a large detachment of Rebel troops."

A wave of moans erupted around the table from all three girls.

Mr. Shippen held up his hand. "The messenger told me that Howe has decided to let Lafayette stew for a while. He will be attended to after the party."

And there would be a party. Everything was in readiness. But Peggy was on edge, feverish with excitement and dread.

"A pox on the Rebels," she told me as I fixed her hair that morning. "I know your brother is a Rebel officer, Becca, but a pox on them all, I say, if they ruin our party."

"I wouldn't worry," I told her dryly. "My brother told me Howe is not one to allow any military maneuver to interfere with his festive moments or romantic liaisons."

Chapter 14

Of course there would be a party. Everything was in readiness.

I took a drive with Peggy the next day to Walnut Grove at the south end of town. She would see the decorated mansion. Two arches graced the lawns that sloped down to the water. On the top of one was a figurine of Neptune.

The front steps of the mansion were covered with red plush carpet. Hundreds of fine white candles waited to be lighted inside, where tables were laden in the mirrored banquet hall with food and spirits, enough for four hundred.

I had seen Andre's outfit. His vest was of white satin. The upper part of the sleeves, being puffed and pink, sported a row of white satin straps laced with silver. On his right shoulder he wore a large pink scarf with a white bow crossing the breast.

His sword belt was pink and white, laced with black and silver. He wore wide buff-leather boots. His horse's trimmings were in kind, with bows that tied around its chest and plumes on its head.

When I saw it, I thought of the men at Camp Valley Forge, who had worn rags as they practiced their maneuvers with Baron Von Steuben. I thought of Washington's army, which had suffered all winter for want of food and blankets, medicines and clothing.

But, of course, there would be a party. The bands had been practicing all week. The heralders and trumpeters were ready.

On a marble-topped table in Peggy Shippen's room was her ticket. On the back it said: *The Favor of Your meeting the Subscribers to the Meschianza at Knight's Wharf near Poole's Bridge to Morrow at half past Three is desired.*

Her dress lay on a gilt-edged chair in her room, all gauze and silk, a delicate confection.

Of course, there would be a party.

The seventeenth, the day before, it rained. Everyone in the house was sleeping when I crept downstairs. It was my day off. In the kitchen, Coxie was waiting. She handed me a napkin wrapped around something warm and fragrant. And a mug of tea. "Breakfast. You'd best be goin' afore that hellcat up there wakes up an' thinks of some errand fer you."

"Thank you, Coxie. I'll be back tonight."

I went outside. Henry Job was driving the wagon. "Where's Mama?"

"Feels poorly. I made her stay in bed. This dampness is bad for her bones."

We drove out of the city in silence. All along the waterfront, the houses and wharves were festooned with brightly colored bunting. Ten barges and four galleys rode at anchor, sporting streamers, flags, and buntings bedecked with flowers.

Henry Job held the reins, his old tricorn pulled down over his eyes to fend off the fine rain. He said nothing.

Finally, out on the Germantown Road, he spoke. "Did you get your mama's money?"

I could scarce answer. "No."

"What do you mean, no? It was promised."

"Mr. Shippen doesn't have it. He said . . ." Every week when I came home, it was the same thing. Henry Job would ask for the payment for the gowns. I knew Mr. Shippen did not have it. And I had been hard put to ask the poor man for payment. He did not look well these days. He spent all his time locked in his library going over his ledgers. Once I heard him tell his wife: "In a very short time there will be nothing left to us if this war doesn't end soon."

In truth, I had approached him three times but only asked for the money once. I could not bear to badger him. Mr. Shippen always had a kind word for me. His wife spent hours teaching me French, drawing, and needlework. Sarah was faithful in her dancing instructions.

"He said what?"

"Next month."

"Did your mama say 'next month' when they wanted those dresses? No! She sewed her eyes out. She kept her word! She stayed up nights, working by candlelight. Her fingers are pricked from the needles. Her head hurts. But she kept her word!"

"He doesn't have it." I had determined not to fight with Henry Job, but he was pushing me into it.

"He *has* it!" He spat the words out. "People like the Shippens always have it. The trouble is, people don't keep their word anymore. There's no honor. It went out the window when the king's men came. Now it's all frippery and fancy manners with nothing behind them."

"He's a good man," I said. "He doesn't like all this. But he can't say no. He can't go back now from what's been started."

"Is he master of his own house?"

"Yes."

"Then he can put a stop to it whenever he wishes. He doesn't wish to."

There was no sense arguing. I fell silent.

"There will *be* no next month," he growled.

"Loyalists and neutrals are scrambling to make arrangements to sail with the fleet."

"What fleet?"

He looked at me in cold disbelief. "Don't you keep your ears open, girl? The British will be pulling out. Next month. All ships under construction are under order to be burned. Your mother and others are already planning to ask Howe to leave the stores of food for the poor instead of destroying them."

I had not heard anything about this. I stared straight ahead, working it in my head.

"Likely the Shippens will be going with the others," he said. "Rather than risk the wrath of the independence men."

Going? I said nothing. What would happen to me if they went? I would have to go back to the farm. I felt desolation grip me. Henry Job would take satisfaction out of that. It was not true, I decided. He was saying it to punish me because I had not brought home Mama's money.

"Things are bad at home," he said. "Your mother gets headaches. If I could buy some coffee, it would help, but coffee is dear. And Howe has put an embargo on all apothecary items from New York."

We drove the rest of the way in silence.

* * * * *

"I don't have the money." I stood at the foot of Mama's bed in their small room. She was sitting up, leaning against the pillows. She looked tired. Her head ached and she had a rag on it that she had wrung out in a bowl of cold vinegar that sat on a small table.

"It's all right, Becca. Don't worry the matter."

"Papa Henry says you need money for coffee for your headaches."

"My headache will go away as soon as the weather clears."

But she looked white in the face and there were purple circles under her eyes. I pulled up a chair and sat next to the bed.

"I'm sorry, Mama. You've done so much for me. And I've failed you."

"Hush. It isn't your fault. None of my clients are paying. They're all begging off. Don't listen to Papa Henry. All I need is rest and to see my girl. Tell me now. Everything."

* * * * *

I left at the end of the day. I cooked for her and straightened the house. Mama was sitting up in bed, sipping some broth I'd made, when I said good-bye. I felt grievous hurt leaving her. My life in the Shippen household was so different from here that I felt guilty over it.

It was still daylight when we left. I watched Henry Job loading the wagon with butter, eggs, and fresh milk for a run. I knew that butter sold for over a dollar a pound in the city. Couldn't he buy Mama some coffee with his earnings?

He read my thoughts. "I don't get the proper price for produce anymore. I've stopped going to market myself. I deliver outside the city gates. Those who sell in the market get inflated prices and I get less."

"I can buy some coffee for Mama with the guineas you gave me," I offered. It was only right.

He scowled. "No," he said fiercely. "I told you to keep them! So you never have need of the begging words in your mouth."

On the outskirts of the city, he brought Duke to a halt. The rain had stopped. There was a sweetness in the evening air. Birds chirped their nightsongs. "You can walk the rest of the way," he said. "I have to meet my contacts. It's too dangerous for me to go farther. I took my chances fetching you."

I got out of the wagon. What had happened suddenly to make it too dangerous for him? I didn't ask.

"Go straight to the Shippens'. No loitering. You ask him for that money! He's got it. Act with strength. Like someone from Boston. Not like a poltroon from Philadelphia. If he doesn't give it to you, you leave his employ next week."

My whole being came alive. "What?"

"You heard me. I'll have no more shilly-shallying about the matter. You don't get that money, you pack your bags and come home. Speak up for yourself. And for what is right. Stop being so taken with those Shippens. You hear?"

I heard. He drove off. I turned and walked toward town.

· · · · ·

Tears stung my eyes. It was so unfair! It wasn't my fault that the Shippens couldn't pay Mama. Nobody was paying. She'd said so herself!

I was so angry at Henry Job that I didn't care whether or not he was getting information to Washington. The man was still a dolt. And he was mean, too.

I was happy at the Shippens', happier than I'd been in a long time. No, I had no love for Peggy. She was spoiled and vicious, shallow and false, all at the same time. But I was not there to like Peggy. I was there to find my missing pieces. To become finished.

And to learn. I *was* learning, too. I was making a beautiful crewel-worked petticoat, a surprise for Mama. Mrs. Shippen had provided me with the fabric and the colorful threads. I could understand French, though I could not yet speak it. Sarah had taught me all the dancing steps. And I was learning to do watercolors. But more than that were the things I was learning that could not be put into words.

Hadn't I decided all on my own to help Frazor escape? Hadn't I stood up to Peggy? And what about Andre? I'd fended him off, hadn't I? And hadn't I determined the right amount of fabric to purchase for the girls' dresses?

I liked my newfound powers. I considered them as much my missing pieces as the silver inkstand. And given half a chance, I knew I could find more of myself. So the point was moot. I simply could not go back to the farm.

But Henry Job had spoken with such authority. From whence did it come? Was Mama sicker than I was given to believe? And he in charge? Or was it just that he knew that Mama would give him his due if he demanded it?

Then I had another thought. Henry Job had told me again this morning that I should never allow the begging words in my mouth. Wouldn't I have to do that to get the money?

And then, of a sudden, I knew what I would do. And the knowing was undiluted revelation, so simple and pure that I wondered why I hadn't thought of it before.

At first I was pained by the thought. For it meant I would have to give the money back. Never before in my life had I had money of my own. The sensation was delightful. The idea that I could, if the humour seized me, buy myself a pretty furbelow was like a warm mug of tea on a cold day. Even though I had decided to save my money for the silver inkstand.

My five guineas could not buy it, of course. But they would help. Better yet, if things proceeded as I thought, the Shippens might be paying me for my services soon. Mrs. Shippen had hinted as much to me just last week. "You're doing so well. Soon there won't be anything more I can teach you. I shall have to speak to my husband about paying you. After all, you're not an indentured servant, dear."

She had called me "dear," like one of her own daughters. And Mr. Shippen was always so kind. No, I could not demand payment. And I could never make Henry Job understand. So I resolved what I must do.

No, the guineas would not make up Mama's payment. But they would stall Henry Job. They would buy me something more precious than anything right now. Time. The time I needed away from the farm to learn, to become finished, to earn money to buy back my father's silver inkwell.

Time to find the rest of my missing pieces.

• • • • •

The day of *Meschianza* dawned bright and blue and balmy. Birds twittered in the trees. Squirrels jumped from limb to limb. Flowers nodded their heads in the backyard. The air was like silk. Even if *Meschianza* never happened, the day was a celebration all of its own making.

Monsieur Dumarae was coming at ten in the morning to do Peggy's hair and that of her sisters. Everything went according to plan. At eight, Cecil brought the copper tub into Peggy's room. Dorothea fetched hot water until the tub was brim full. I put scented soap and special oils and flower petals into the water.

At eight-thirty, after Peggy was ensconced in the tub, I went downstairs to fetch her breakfast tray. The girls would be excused from dining with their parents because they must get themselves ready.

At eight-forty-five, the committee came.

I had just assembled Peggy's breakfast on the tray and was on my way back upstairs when the front door clapper sounded.

Cecil went to open it. Just then I turned.

The group of Friends stood there on the front stoop, like a cluster of grim birds of prey. Their gray clothing was in contrast to the brightness of the day.

I went up two more steps, so I would not be seen. Cecil went to fetch Mr. Shippen. There were six of them. I knew only Mrs. Darragh, but I recognized the others from their last visit. One, I was sure, was Mrs. Cooper.

They stood stock-still—serene, determined, waiting—saying nary a word to each other. Then Mrs. Darragh raised her eyes, saw me, and smiled ever so briefly. I smiled back and went up two more steps, out of their sight.

But I stood there listening.

Mr. Shippen came into the hall. "Good day to you," he said in his genteel manner. "My wife and I are just at breakfast. May we offer you some refreshment?"

"We are here on an unpleasant mission, Friend," said the man in front. "We would speak with thee. And thy wife. But we will take no refreshment."

As they followed Mr. Shippen down the wide, spacious hall, I set the tray down on a step and peered over the balustrade.

Mrs. Shippen came out of the dining room. There were brief greetings. Then I heard the words "heathenish costumes." And "indecent" and "unseemly for proper Quaker girls."

One woman's voice came through especially firm and clear. "In these frightful times, which we have earned through our sins . . ."

The doors of the parlor closed.

I sat on the steps, trembling. My mouth was dry. Oh, how sorry I felt for Mr. and Mrs. Shippen! To be visited once again by the committee. The shame of it! I was filled with foreboding as I picked up the tray and brought it to Peggy's room.

. . . . .

At nine o'clock Dorothea knocked on the door of Peggy's room and that of her sisters to say that their father wanted them downstairs. Now.

Peggy was still in the tub, luxuriating in the fragrant hot water. I was laying out her clothes, smoothing her bed.

My hands were shaking.

"Whatever is the matter?" she complained. "Get my wrap, Becca. Doesn't Daddy understand what it takes to get ready? If this is another lecture about money, I'll scream."

It was not a lecture on money.

Looking more solemn and stern than I ever recollected seeing him, Mr. Shippen told the girls the news.

The committee had contrived, somehow, to see the gowns they would be wearing.

"Why wasn't I told about the gowns!"

His voice reverberated in the paneled library. No one spoke. "Mrs. Shippen, did you know they are the gowns of Turkish slave girls?"

"No, Mr. Shippen, I did not. I was told they were"—she shrugged—"gowns made of silk. And gauze and ribbons. Gowns for knights' ladies. I have been remiss, I suppose, but I have been busy collecting for the burned-out victims in Borden-town."

He turned back to the girls, who stood clutching their morning wraps, their hair wrapped in great swathes of flannel, their faces oiled and creamed.

"I will have no more of it!" he bellowed. "Enough! How am I perceived by the Friends as head of this family when I did not even know that my girls are to be garbed as Turkish slaves! How did it look to them?"

"Daddy!" Peggy wailed.

"Keep a still tongue in your head! The committee is right. The costumes are indecent. And by agreeing to wear them, you make light of the shame these British officers visit upon you!"

Sarah started to cry softly. Mary followed suit. Peggy's face went sharp, as it did when she was plotting, rendering her older than her years.

"Daddy, if you will just listen!"

"I have listened, and I have kept my own good counsel. Now it is time to speak out. I will not suffer my girls to wear those dresses and bring admonishment down upon this house by the Friends."

"What are you saying?" Peggy's voice was unsteady.

"I am saying, daughter, that you are all to go back upstairs, get dressed in proper clothing, and tend to your knitting for the burned-out victims in Bordentown."

"No-oo-ooo," Peggy wailed.

"I am saying that you will not attend this celebration today. My girls are not going. That's what I am saying."

Peggy screamed one long, piercing scream. Servants came running.

"Go back to your work," Mr. Shippen ordered. They left.

Peggy was convulsed with racking sobs. She doubled over, clutching her stomach. "Mama, make him change his mind! Make him say we can go. Mama, *please.*"

Mrs. Shippen stood firm, white-faced beside her husband.

"What will I tell Captain Andre?" Peggy screamed it at him so that her throat was raspy. "What will I say?"

"That your father has come to his senses."

"Everyone will mock us! We will be the laughingstock of the town. Is *that* what you want?"

"I stand firm in the rightness of my decision. Let people laugh. They cannot hurt me."

"What about *us?* They can hurt *us!* Don't you care? You wretched man!"

"Peggy!" her mother admonished.

"I don't care! I hate him! I hate both of you! Allowing that stupid committee to push you around. To come in here and ruin our lives! Have you no backbone? No wonder you're losing money! Everyone else has profited with the British in town! But you"—she flung the words at her father—"you are such a milksop, you are afraid to stand up and take advantage of the moment and profit from it. You cower in here hiding, day after day, fearing the independence men, fearing the British, fearing *everybody*. And we suffer for it!"

It was then that her mother slapped her. She stepped forward quickly and without fuss, and simply slapped her daughter's face. "Don't speak to your father in such a manner! Go to your room! You bring shame on us!"

Peggy gasped, held her face with her hand, and ran screaming from the room. Sobbing quietly, Sarah and Mary embraced their mother, then their father, saying they were sorry.

Mr. Shippen looked at me then. I'd been standing just outside the door of the library. "Go and see to her, Becca."

"Yes, sir."

"I don't envy you the job."

I turned to go.

"Becca?"

I hesitated.

"You knew of the gowns. Your mother sewed them."

Here it was, then. At my feet. Where, I

suppose, it belonged. I met his eyes. "Yes, sir, I knew."

He gave me a long, sad look. "I don't blame you, Becca. The day I hired you, you told me you wouldn't tattle on your mistress. And I told you I'd rather you be circumspect. We had an agreement and you have honored it."

I bobbed a curtsy. "Thank you, sir." Then I went upstairs to attend to Peggy.

As I was going through the hall, the door clapper sounded again. Cecil opened it. There stood Monsieur Dumarae, laden with the tools of his trade.

"I am a bit earl*ee*. But there is so much to do. Are the young ladies ready to receive me?"

Five minutes later he left, after conferring with Mr. Shippen. It was nine-thirty.

At ten, I was crouching in a corner, taking shelter near a clothespress in Peggy's room. It looked like the battleground at Crooked Billet Tavern after the Queen's Rangers had surprised Lacey's men.

Peggy had overturned the copper tub. Water soaked the good Persian carpet. She had thrown all the items from her dressing table across the room, shattering a mirror. Oils and creams, powder and perfume lay all over the place.

She had torn the hangings from her bed. I had tried to stop her at first, but it was like stopping a hurricane. Her morning gown was open, half off, showing her naked body.

A knock came on the door. "Come in!" Peggy shouted.

The door opened. Dorothea stood there.

"What do you want?"

"An aide of Captain Andre's is here for the gowns. Your daddy says I'm to fetch them for him."

Peggy's eyes narrowed. Her face took on a look that made it hard for me to believe that someone so beautiful could twist her features into such a mask of hatred.

"You benighted fool!" As she reached behind her to pick a delicate figurine from a shelf, her morning gown fell open, revealing her full nakedness. But she did not care.

The figurine was a porcelain Venus. I saw Dorothea standing there—open-mouthed, frozen in horror—saw Peggy raise her hand and draw it back with the figurine in it.

At that moment I roused myself from my stupor where I was crouching, ran across the room, and dove at Peggy just as she was about to throw the porcelain Venus. It flew out of her hand and hit the doorjamb, inches to the right of Dorothea's head.

• • • • •

They say Peggy Shippen often had hysterics when she couldn't have her own way. So no one in the household thought anything of the disrepair and damage in the room. It was up to me to clean it up.

She fainted after she threw the porcelain figure. They say she frequently fainted, too. It was an aftermath to her hysteria. Her sisters and Dorothea and I got her into bed in Sarah's room and closed the curtains against the beautiful May morning. Then Sarah and Mary went down to help their mother work on clothing for the burned-out families of Bordentown.

I had fetched old rags from Coxie and was sopping up the water when Dorothea came into the room and without so much as a by-your-leave, knelt down on the floor to help me.

We worked together for a minute or two before she spoke. "I thank you for saving my life."

I wrung out my rag in the tub. "Did I do that?"

"If she'd hit me with that statue, I could have been killed."

I shrugged. "Anybody would have done the same."

"Yes, but you didn't have to. I haven't been exactly friendly to you since you arrived here. It was decent of you."

I nodded. We continued working. "From now on," she said, "consider me your friend. You poor wretch. Working for her, you need one."

Peggy stayed in bed all day. Because the weather was warm, all the windows were open and the sounds of the festivities drifted in on the spring breeze. In the distance we heard band music, thirteen-gun salutes from down at the waterfront, the distant shouting of cheering crowds.

Mr. Shippen stayed in his library, Mrs. Shippen and the girls in the parlor, knitting and sewing. The servants tiptoed around. Everyone spoke in whispers.

Just before noon, Elizabeth came home. She alighted from her carriage in the backyard and called for Pepy to carry in her bundles of greens and neck beef. She also brought two very large cast-iron kettles. "Make your broth, Coxie," she said. "I'll take it to the jail. Those poor wretches ought to take part in the festivities, too, don't you think?"

She was wearing her boys' clothing. "Who died?" she asked. "Ye gods, what long faces around here."

She laughed when I told her what had happened. "My sister Peggy never did know how to spend her passions," she said. "The Knights of the Burning Mountain are tomfools and the Knights of the Blended Rose are damned fools. I know of no other distinction between them."

Her profanity both shocked and delighted me. I didn't see her for the rest of the day. She went to her own room to rest. Dorothea and I set Peggy's room to rights again. At dusk the Shippens ate a cold supper in the dining room as candles eerily flickered in the sweet May evening air. I took a bowl of soup up to Peggy. As I passed Elizabeth's room, the door opened and she came into the hall, smiled at me, and put a cautioning finger to her lips.

Still dressed in boys' clothing, she had her hair tucked under her hat. She went down the servants' stairway to the warming kitchen. And I knew she had plans for this night.

Peggy was still in Sarah's room. It was on the side of the house that faced the waterfront. She was sitting up in her sister's bed, staring at nothing. Her beautiful corn silk–colored hair was listless and ragged. Her face seemed sunken. She would take no nourishment.

"I might as well be dead," she said.

I sat with her, working on the crewel petticoat for Mama. We did not speak. Outside, as the lovely May darkness wrapped itself around the house like a silken cocoon, we heard a drumroll in the distance. It sounded as if it were traveling all along the waterfront. Then came what sounded like musket shots popping off in the night. Peggy gave no indication that she heard anything. I got up and went to the window, pushed the curtains aside, and looked out.

The sky down near the waterfront was streaked with fireworks, like gigantic fireflies, exploding in the night. But between the shrieking sounds and the little explosions, I was sure I heard musket fire, too.

I went back to sit down. Peggy was asleep. I took the bowl of uneaten soup and went downstairs.

In the morning Coxie told me that a unit of Rebel Light Horse made a ruckus at the time of the fireworks display. She'd heard it from the fishmonger.

"Such a noise like you never heared, from the whale oil they set fire to in their iron kettles." And she laughed. "I heared the British forti'cations near Germantown went up in flames. Kept those Britishers on their toes, chasin' after 'em. The word be no harm come to *Meschianza*. But"—and she lowered her voice—"I also heared that there was a break outa the jail an' some 'merican prisoners escaped last night."

I could not believe it. I stared at Coxie as she arranged Peggy's breakfast on a tray. Were she and Elizabeth in on things together? Or was my mind fashioning fancies out of Elizabeth's bringing home iron kettles and having them filled with soup to take to the jail?

I would never know. I did not want to know. As I passed the dining room on my way upstairs

I saw Elizabeth at breakfast with her family, looking as fresh as if she'd slept soundly all night.

Two days later she went back to Lancaster.

. . . . .

Three days after that I stood in the parlor of our house. Mama was up and about again, putting supper on the table. I handed four guineas to my stepfather. "It's all I could get," I said.

He nodded glumly. I prayed he would not recognize the coins. I had taken great pains to scrape them on the cobblestones in the Shippens' yard and rub them in the sandy dirt when no one was looking. They were no longer shiny and new.

"Now, you see how you can speak up when you put your mind to it?" he asked.

"Yes, sir."

"Of course, this isn't enough. But he's been put on notice now, and he has to pay."

I knew Mr. Shippen would pay for the *Meschianza* dresses. Though they had been taken by the British and other girls had been found to wear them, he would consider himself honor bound to pay.

"You act now like someone from Boston," he said with pride. "And not like some poltroon from Philadelphia, where there is no honor. It gives you pride to act so, is this not true?"

I said yes again.

"I hope you have learned from all this. Your old stepfather, he knows what he's about after all, doesn't he?"

We went to supper. The old tomfool, I told myself. All I learned is that when you have money you can buy yourself out of any dolorous situation. It was a good feeling. Yet at the same time I hated myself for doing it. And I hated Henry Job even more for forcing me into it. I had one guinea left. Now I would never be able to buy the silver inkstand.

· · · · ·

Peggy stayed in bed the whole week following *Meschianza*. Andre came to see her two days after the gala, but she would not receive him. He gave me a note. She made me read it. It said he had pursued Lafayette the day after the party, but Lafayette, with all the true callowness of a Frenchman, had slipped away.

Peggy laughed at that. "Andre is half French," she said.

He came again and left flowers. She cried and would not have them in her room. He did not come back.

A little more than three weeks later, on June eighteenth, the British left Philadelphia.

During those three weeks the city was in chaos. Rumors spread like fire. Clinton would go to sea. No, he would march across the Jerseys. Or was it New York? Then rumor had it that he was going to burn Philadelphia before leaving.

On the twenty-fifth of May, Mr. Shippen attended a meeting at the Indian King Tavern on Market Street with other leading citizens and merchants. He came home that night, weary and discouraged, and called everyone—his wife, his daughters, his servants—into the library. "We have elected," he said dourly, "to ask Clinton's permission to treat with Washington. We must accommodate ourselves to the Rebel government or leave the city, as the Loyalists are doing."

"Leave? Where would we go?" his wife asked.

"Wherever the British fleet sails. Likely New York."

After much commotion and wailing and tears and talk, the family decided they wanted to stay and protect their property against the onslaught of Americans, who might think of them as Loyalists.

"But they may kill us," Sarah said.

"My brother Tench would do no such thing," Mrs. Shippen said.

"But he's aide-de-camp to Washington," Mary wailed. "What of the regular soldiers?"

"What say you, Becca?" Mr. Shippen asked. "Do you think the independence men will kill us?"

"No, my brother does not kill for no reason."

The Shippens decided to stay. But Clinton

would not give the Loyalists or those who had remained neutral permission to treat with Washington. He would not acknowledge that Washington was anything but a blackguard Rebel. No one should ever treat with the Rebels.

Meanwhile, Washington wrote to Congress asking for amnesty for Pennsylvania Loyalists and neutrals.

Elizabeth came home and told us about it. "I saw Uncle Tench." She did not say how, and they did not ask her. "He read me a copy of Washington's letter. It said, 'Many hundreds, nay thousands, of valuable artisans and their goods will leave with the departing British for fear of their property, honor, and fortune.' Not bad sentiments for a blackguard Rebel, are they?"

Many Loyalists did leave. We watched them go.

In early June, upward of three hundred British ships dropped anchor off Reedy Island. All you saw were carts and wagons, drays and carriages leaving the city, piled with goods. Those who couldn't get horses dragged their furniture and trunks, beds and tables in the streets to the wharves.

Henry Job, never one to miss an opportunity, offered his wagon and Duke to cart many a Loyalist family with their goods to the British fleet. He was paid handsomely for it.

We started seeing fires around the wharves. The British were burning shipyard stocks. Fires blossomed in the night, fearful in their intensity, in Southwark near Gloria Dei Church, in Northern Liberties, and in Kensington. Several houses belonging to poor folk burned with them.

Mrs. Shippen and her Quaker Friends went to attend to the poor who were left homeless. They found that barrels of pork and beef were thrown into the water at the wharves, when such provisions could have been used for the poor.

They went to see Clinton. He would not receive them. Then Elizabeth Drinker, a Friend, found out that the commissary had left seven hundred hogsheads of rum, ten of brandy, twenty of molasses, thirty-eight packages of medicines, and twelve thousand bushels of salt. On Peggy's eighteenth birthday, the eleventh of June, her mother and her Quaker Friends were retrieving these goods for the poor.

"I might as well be dead," Peggy told me. "My life is over."

On the eighteenth it seemed as if everyone in the city were dead. Mr. Shippen would not allow anyone out. The silence, as the sun beat down, was like a downward spiral into a nightmare. Only the birdsong could be heard outside.

The next morning the fishmonger came to the door. As usual, he had gossip for Coxie. It was my job to tell the family what she had learned.

They were at breakfast. I went into the dining room.

"Well?" Mr. Shippen asked.

"Some Americans who left before the British occupation are returning."

They waited. I went on. "The filth left in the houses occupied by the British is not to be borne. And piles of garbage are in the streets."

"We shall have disease," Mrs. Shippen said.

"Go on," her husband ordered.

I hesitated, twisting the corner of my apron. "I dasn't."

"Tell us," Mr. Shippen said. "We would know the worst."

I cast a sympathetic look at Peggy. "Captain Andre took boxes of Benjamin Franklin's personal things."

"It's a lie!" Peggy cried. "Coxie is a filthy liar!"

"Hush," her father ordered.

"Coxie has her informants," Elizabeth put in. "I would trust her with my life. What did he take?"

"China, musical instruments, books, and a portrait painted by Benjamin Wilson."

"Well," Elizabeth said. "And Andre's the one who said the British officers were setting a wonderful example for us provincial Americans."

"Shut your mouth," Peggy told her.

Elizabeth only smiled.

I went on. "Knyphausen, the Hessian commander, took nothing. He had his aide prepare an inventory of all possessions of General John Cad-walader's house, where he was staying. I paused to catch my breath, then continued. "He had it checked by the general's agent, even to the exact number of bottles of wine. Everything was left as he found it."

"Anything else?" Mr. Shippen asked.

"Yes, a man named Franks is riding through the city looking for suitable lodgings for the new American commander."

"What's his name?" Mr. Shippen asked.

"General Benedict Arnold."

"Trouble," Elizabeth murmured.

"My life is over." It was all Peggy could say.

Within a week the new commander had moved into Penn Mansion, where Howe had lived.

Peggy's life was not over. It was just beginning.

Chapter 15

He sought her out. And he found her.

He sought her out like a moth seeks a flame. And she was there burning for him, waiting for him, though she did not know it at first.

She knew it when she saw him. And she knew it at once. Something quickened in each of their spirits when they met. I was there at that first meeting, and I saw the something come alive between them.

It was the nearest thing I had ever seen to what they talked about in Philadelphia as being electricity from Benjamin Franklin's experiment with lightning and a kite.

She was the lightning. He was the kite.

When in his presence that first time, she played the coquette worse than she had ever played it with Andre. Even I could not believe the exaggeration of her mannerisms.

He was pleased by the performance.

He sought her out like a moth seeks a flame. And she burned brightly for him. Even as our own destruction does for us when we first sight it in the distance. And it seems to us, in the beginning, like the brightness of a star.

Chapter 16

General Arnold had not been in town a month when he came one day to call on Mr. Shippen. I was in the hall when Cecil admitted him. As Cecil opened the door, I caught a glimpse of Arnold's fancy coach, attended by four servants. The man himself was dressed like a gallant, with silken hose, a soft crimson sash, gold epaulets on the shoulders of his soft blue coat, a fancy sword knot, and breeches the color of butter.

As he swept into the hallway, I ducked back into the shadows, tea tray in hand, feeling a thrill. They were saying things about him already in Philadelphia. That he lived too high in the Penn Mansion, that he had too many servants, that he gave lavish entertainments.

He came to see Mr. Shippen about his daughters. I stood outside the parlor listening.

"I have a social problem, Mr. Shippen," Arnold said in his deep voice.

"Oh? And how may I be of assistance, General?"

"The ambassador from the Court of Louis XVI has arrived in honor of the French Alliance. He is staying with me. I feel impelled to give an entertainment."

"You don't sound at all taken with the idea," Mr. Shippen said.

Arnold laughed. It was a deep, rich sound. "I have never had any love for the French, Mr. Shippen. Not since I drove a French suitor of my sister Hannah's out of the house years ago. I hate the idea of being beholden to them."

"So do I." Mr. Shippen leaned forward, warming to Arnold.

"But this man must be feted. The trouble is we are short of accomplished ladies. The Patriot girls in their homespun are . . . not polished enough. Is one permitted to say?"

"One is permitted, General."

All the Patriot girls in Philadelphia were making a great show of wearing their virtuous homespun and clumsiest shoes. They dressed so to distinguish themselves from the fashionable set of young women who had cosied up to the British.

"I heard you had four pretty daughters. And three are available."

As if the words were connected to make an invisible rope that pulled at her, Peggy came down the stairs to stand beside me. She was dressed in her best green silk trimmed with ivory lace.

"Is that Arnold?" Peggy peeked in the half-open door. "Oh, he's handsome."

"He's thirty-seven," I said. "And he limps from an old wound. Word has it that one leg is two inches shorter than the other and his one boot must be built up."

Her eyes shone. "Word could have it that one leg is *six* inches shorter than the other and I'd forgive him for it. Did you see that coach-and-four out front?" She sighed. "I heard he's bent on showing the people of Philadelphia that the British aren't the only ones who know how to live. Give me that tray."

"What?"

"The tray, noodle-head. I'll bring in the tea."

"You?" I gaped.

"Yes."

"But it wouldn't be seemly. . . ."

She took the tray from me. "Not seemly? For an American girl to serve her own father tea? I heard that Arnold owns a privateer! And half interest in the schooner *Charming Nancy*. How does my hair look?"

It was swept up and tied with a bit of lace. Golden curls dangled and tendrils framed her face.

"Beautiful," I said. "But be careful. I heard that Arnold is a marked man already here in town."

She scowled. "How so?"

"There is talk he's speculating. He's given passes to three schooners loaded with European goods to sail from here to Wilmington. Even *before* Reed closed all the shops so the army could have first shot at everything. Reed and the Council are watching him."

"Then he is in need of a friend. I know what it means to be watched." She smiled and went into the room.

I knew she still smarted from what the Quaker committee had done to her. They had persecuted her, she said, nothing less. And she would never forgive it. I also knew that if she perceived that Joseph Reed and the Supreme Executive Council of Pennsylvania were persecuting Arnold, that would be all she needed to befriend him.

So I watched her prance into the room with the tea tray, kiss her father, and curtsy to Arnold. She had never served tea in her life, but she did so now, preening for Arnold. I felt repulsed. Thirty-seven was old. How could she?

She was acting. Andre would be proud of her. Why did it seem of a sudden that Andre was right here in the hall with me watching, too? Why had I thought of him?

There was more at work here than I could sort

out. Mr. Shippen and Arnold spoke of the victory of the Americans at Monmouth in the Jerseys the last week in June. They spoke of the return of Congress to Philadelphia on July second.

They spoke as friends, though Mr. Shippen was not a professed Patriot. "When are the three hundred Hessian prisoners due in the city?" Mr. Shippen asked.

"Not soon enough," Arnold said. "Clinton has ordered the American prisoners, who are to be exchanged, to board British ships at Penrose Wharf. I fear the Hessians they're to be exchanged for won't arrive in time to keep the Americans from being sent down river. But the Hessians are difficult to find. They are in three states. Many are working on farms and want to stay in America."

I knew about that. Henry Job was working for the Americans now, riding out in the countryside and visiting farms in Pennsylvania and New York, trying to round up Hessian prisoners. Mama complained that he had not been home in over a month.

"You have your problems, General," Mr. Shippen said. "I don't envy you."

"Yes, I do."

And all the while Arnold was exchanging glances with Peggy.

· · · · ·

If I was to come to despise Peggy Shippen for anything in my tenure with her, it was for how she treated her father. I came to accept everything else about her—her shallowness, her voracious hunger for every frippery, her selfish ways—but I could not forgive the way she badgered him for money.

By that hot summer of 1778, I had become accustomed to many things. Blair had gone to the White Plains encampment with Washington's army. I resigned myself to not seeing him soon again. The Americans who had come to town walked Philadelphia's streets in worn-out clothing. And many of their families were ragged and near starvation, yet there was a new class of "patroons" in Philadelphia.

The Quakers called them "crafty and designing." They had made money supplying Washington's army with inferior goods. They were engaged in smuggling. They made scarce goods available to the public at exorbitant prices. They had lavish supper parties, where betimes 160 different dishes were served.

Mama sewed for their wives and daughters. Things had changed with the coming of the Americans, and yet they also stayed the same. I became accustomed to it.

But the one thing I would never become accustomed to was Peggy's callous indifference to her father's troubles. Clearly, he was growing poorer by the day, not only in the state of his finances but in spirit.

Did no one else in the household see it? Elizabeth was away again at Lancaster, spending the summer with her grandmama. Was I the only one, then, to take note of Mr. Shippen's spells of vagueness? The way he ofttimes seemed hundreds of miles away when someone spoke to him? The way his hair was turning white and his hands had taken on a palsy? It seemed as if he were growing older in front of my eyes. Yet Peggy never stopped complaining. She needed new clothes. The cushions on the dining room chairs were becoming shabby. The parlor carpeting was worn.

Betimes I would bring Mr. Shippen tea of an afternoon. It was not my job to do so. But I felt that he needed some extra attention.

I brought tea the day Mama came to confer with Peggy about new fall gowns.

Mr. Shippen knew she was expected and told me to have her stop in his library before she went upstairs. He had a matter to discuss with her.

My hands shook as I prepared an extra-nice tea tray in the warming kitchen. He was going to speak to Mama about his inability to pay her yet for the *Meschianza* gowns. As far as Mama knew, she had been paid, in part at least.

What would I do when he disavowed paying her? My little deception would be uncovered. And then, I knew. I would blame his dementia. It was the perfect excuse.

When the door knocker sounded, I let Mama in.

"Don't pay mind if he acts strangely," I whispered. "Ofttimes he doesn't recollect things."

"Poor man," Mama said.

I ran to get the tea tray and made her wait in the hall. Mr. Shippen was bending over his ledgers at the desk. He looked up, and for an instant his mind *was* confused.

"I must sell my farm and my 370 acres and gristmill in New Jersey." He said it with a wonderment in his voice, as if the idea had just presented itself to him.

I stood stock-still. Never had he confided in me about anything. *He does not know who I am*, I told myself.

"It should bring nine thousand pounds. It takes four or five thousand pounds per annum to care for my family. That expense is unsupportable with no business coming in."

I ran my tongue along my lips and nodded.

"The taxes on this house are now three thousand pounds a year. And Elizabeth is marrying Neddy in December. I am allowing them to marry before the war ends, because of my affectionate regard for her, though people will say it is to lessen my monetary burden. I still must dower her and pay for the wedding."

"May I pour your tea, sir?"

He smiled at me. "Why yes, thank you, Becca."

"My mama is here."

He seemed himself again. "Is she? Show her in."

I went into the hall to get Mama. "He's having a difficult day," I told her.

"How nice you have time to stop in, Mrs. Claghorn." Mr. Shippen got to his feet and greeted Mama as if she were a great lady. "I am embarrassed to have to ask your forbearance about what monies I owe you. I simply cannot pay now."

I saw Mama draw herself up to her full elegance, glad to have this occasion to show her breeding. "What you have already given me is enough. We trust one another."

I was flooded with relief. Mr. Shippen thought Mama was talking about my lessons. She thought he knew about the guineas I had given Henry Job. There was no need to worry that my little contrivance would be exposed.

"When I sell my farm, I will pay you for the *Meschianza* dresses."

"That would be good, Mr. Shippen. My husband wants to plant more wheat this summer and ship it south."

"South?"

Mama blushed coyly. "We have a young helper on the farm now. He and my Henry put their heads together and decided that the people of Philadelphia never did make proper use of their ports. They hope to ship wheat to Baltimore. And sell some to our army."

"Sound thinking. My wife and I have put *our* heads together and decided it is time to start paying Becca for her services. She has learned all we have to teach. That is, unless you want her to return to the farm."

"No," Mama said. She smiled at me. "She is finished, then?"

"As far as we can take her," he said.

Finished? I thought. *Are they mad? There are days I feel I have more missing pieces than ever.*

"Who is the helper on the farm?" I asked Mama later, when she was leaving.

At first she wouldn't tell me. And I became suspicious. "A soldier who had to leave the army because of his health," was all she would say.

"Henry Job didn't bring home a Hessian? Not after the way they raided us!"

"No Hessian."

"Who then?"

"If you would come home to visit, you could see. You haven't visited since your stepfather came home."

"I'm busy." I didn't want to see Henry Job. I didn't want any more questions about the owed money.

"You could visit. What do you do on your day off?"

"I do my watercolors. And practice my music. Mrs. Shippen is teaching me to play the harpsichord. Are you going to sew the dresses for the wedding?"

"Yes."

"I'm not finished, Mama. No matter what Mr. Shippen says."

She said something strange then. "Who ever is?"

"I still have missing pieces."

"So do we all." She smiled at me, but there was no substance to it. She did not understand. "The new helper is staying in your room," she said.

"My room? And where do I stay if I come home?"

She got into the wagon. "Your winter room. It's summer. When you visit you stay in your summer room."

"What are you hiding from me, Mama?"

"You have your secrets," she said, "and I have mine."

I felt alarm. "What secrets do I have from you, Mama?"

But her smile was serene. "Come home soon; we miss you," she said. And she drove away.

But the weeks passed and I found it more convenient not to go home. For one thing, I saw Mama when she came weekly to work on the gowns for Elizabeth's wedding. For another, the Shippens had started to pay me. And I sometimes worked on my day off because now I was saving money. The silver inkstand was still in that pawn shop window. I still wanted it for Mama.

Money was very much on everyone's mind that summer. All Peggy talked about was how many servants Arnold had in Penn Mansion: a housekeeper, a groom, a coachman, and seven others. And how Arnold had paid one thousand pounds for two pipes of wine. And how Robert Morris, financier, or some other New York businessman, was coming to visit Arnold.

By September Peggy was being courted, unofficially, by the general. That was when Coxie and I were asked to work at the entertainment he was giving.

He had brought his sister Hannah and his three boys to Philadelphia and wanted to introduce them. But the real reason for the party was the execution of the two Quakers.

Everyone in Philadelphia was up in arms about it. The Pennsylvania Council ordered their execution because they had collaborated with the British.

Mr. Shippen was not happy about it. "The council is making an example of them because they are wealthy men. But we have brought this on ourselves. Too much revelry has been going on in this city. The rich are too rich, and the poor have no hope. Reed and his council must strike a blow, lest such a class structure become part of America."

What this had to do with Arnold's entertainment, I could not understand. Peggy did. She always understood such things. She explained it to me as I helped her dress for the party.

"Benedict is inviting only Loyalist ladies to this party. It is his way of taking a stand against the council. They've been plaguing him because he is making money. They say he is a lukewarm Patriot. Imagine! And he became near crippled in the cause of his country. He must take a stand against them."

In the mirror, she met my eyes. "I'm so glad Benedict has his wits about him. Why should patriotism mean a sacrifice of prosperity?"

I said nothing.

"The council hates him," she said, "like the committee hated me."

Members of the Pennsylvania Council were not the only ones who hated Benedict Arnold. Or so I found, as Coxie and I carried our bundles into Penn Mansion the day of Arnold's entertainment.

There was a guard of American militiamen around the house. Not one of them came forward to help us, not even when Coxie dropped a bundle. As we went in the back door, I heard one murmur: "Another party. My family's fair to starving, and he's living like an English lord."

"When the British raided Egg Harbor they did

damage to his lordship's *Charming Nancy*," another said. "Word is his lordship used twelve government wagons to salvage the cargo, and he's bringin' it here to sell. Loaf sugar, tea, wool, linen, glass, and nails. Word is . . ."

The back door slammed behind me, and I came into the cool dimness of the kitchen, where servants were preparing the evening's refreshments. We were there because Peggy wanted special cakes and sillibub that only Coxie could make. And, of course, I was to assist Peggy in dressing.

I was whipping up eggs for the cake batter a bit later and gazing out the multipaned kitchen windows. The bottom sashes were open because of the warm weather. Three or four militiamen had started up a game of bases. Blair told me the soldiers had played it at Camp Valley Forge. It borrowed from the British game of cricket, but it had some American touches.

Of a sudden, Arnold's carriage clattered into the drive in back, obscuring my vision. But I could hear his voice bawling out the militiamen. It crackled in the summer air with the true timbre of command. The coachman moved his carriage, and Arnold went in the side entrance of the house. I saw the militiamen set down their balls and bats, pick up their muskets, and resume their guard duty. I could not help noticing how ragged they were in comparison to their dashing general.

Silence reigned again in the yard, except for the chirping of birds and cicadas. The afternoon hung heavy with heat and hatred. You could feel it in the air, pouring in the open windows.

A bad business, I minded. His own men do not like him.

I felt troubled being part of the whole thing. As the sun rose high in the sky I wanted to bring cold cider out to the militiamen, but Coxie wouldn't let me. I wanted to tell them I was one of *them*, not one of the upper classes inside the house.

For the first time since I'd worked with the Shippens, I wanted to mark the difference between myself and the wealthy.

I did not know why. The sentiment was new to me. Coxie said it was because bad feeling was growing in the city against the rich.

"This war be turnin'," she said. "People say the Rebels gonna win. If'n that happen, the old order gotta be changed. No more the money people gonna be runnin' things. The regular people wanna know they gonna have a say, too. That's what the Declaration was about, wasn't it?"

Coxie still believed in her Declaration. And she kept up with things to know what was going on.

That evening, under hundreds of blazing candles set in silver candelabra, the Loyalist ladies came to meet Arnold's sister Hannah and his three children, who were allowed to stay briefly before being taken to bed. All the *Meschianza* ladies were there, as Peggy and her circle of friends were now called. They were in their finest silks and flounces, laces and ribbons—gowns they had not had occasion to wear since the British had left. They danced with the French ambassador and Arnold's New York business friends.

It was more grand than any of Andre's parties. Peggy acted as hostess. She laughed, flirted, and danced.

As for Arnold, the old wound in his leg must have been plaguing him. He sat to the side in a great chair, his leg propped up on a stool. He was never alone. A bevy of pretty girls surrounded him like a cluster of flowers in their pink, yellow, lavender, green, and white gowns. They listened wide-eyed to his stories, *oohing* and *aahing* over the hero of Fort Ticonderoga and Saratoga.

The food, if not equaling the despised "160 servings" the people were complaining about, came close to that approximation. The tables near groaned under the sumptuous dishes. As I rushed back and forth attending to the wants of Peggy and her friends, I caught whiffs of the food, and it near drove me mad. For I hadn't had time to eat. The night was warm; Peggy's demands were many; Coxie was afraid there wasn't enough ice to keep the sillibub from melting. And then there was the additional annoyance of Becky Franks.

She was the woman of the hour. That day there was a report in the *Pennsylvania Gazette* that she had mocked the poor clothing being worn by the American soldiers. Copies of the *Gazette* were being circulated at the party. All the girls of the *Meschianza* set were squealing in delight over it.

More than ever I wanted to go into the yard and feed the hungry militiamen. Coxie had to stop me. "They ain't gonna take dat food, chile. Leave it be."

"Why does General Arnold stand for it?" I asked Coxie. "Why does he let those little noodle-head women carry on so? They're his soldiers, aren't they?"

"Not from what I hears," Coxie said.

"What?"

She sighed heavily. "More an' more what I hears in the street is that he be leanin' to bein' a Tory. An' that our Miz Peggy be the cause of it."

Coxie had waited for the independence men to come to Philadelphia. Now they were here. Howe and his jackanape officers were gone. Now we had Arnold. And things were no different, it seemed. I know Coxie was having misgivings. She had thrown her lot in with the independence men. But she said little of the matter. I was brooding on it, having cold cider in the kitchen, when I heard the commotion. The musicians in the grand ballroom had stopped of a sudden.

"General, how can you dally here like this when I am being put out of my home!"

The guests had come to a full stop, too. I went to look in the ballroom. And once again what I saw before me was like a tableau, something one would do in needlepoint.

A ragged militiaman, musket in hand, stood just behind an interloper. She was a woman of obvious breeding, though her clothes were in disarray. She was my mother's age and very agitated. She stood in the center of the ballroom, on the polished parquet floor under the blazing chandelier, and confronted Arnold. The pretty girls surrounding him fell back like discarded flower petals as he stood up.

"Madam, I have awarded you every courtesy!"

"Courtesy! General, I was one of the richest women in this city. And this night I leave it. I drive off to live on the charity of friends!"

"You have brought this on yourself, madam."

"Have I, General? And why? Because my husband was General Howe's chief of police?"

"Because he cooperated with the British and then absconded, leaving you to face the music."

Her husband was Howe's chief of police? Then she must be Mrs. Galloway. She stepped closer to Arnold. The militiaman behind her made as if to intercede, but Arnold waved him back.

"What of these girls?" she demanded with a grand sweep of her arm. "Did they and their families not cooperate with the British? And you give parties for them!"

A terrible silence settled over the large ballroom.

"You surround yourself with them. Because it pleases your vanity to do so! There!"—and she pointed to Becky Franks. "There is one who made public sport in the press of your soldiers' poor attire. And you fawn over her. Yet you allow a woman of my station to be evicted from her own house!"

"Madam, I have tried to help you," Arnold said wearily. "I sent my housekeeper to assist you in moving. I lent you my carriage to take you this night from the city."

"Yes, you would be rid of me. Because I am too old for your frivolity. Because I am not sixteen anymore." A great sob escaped from her.

"In heaven's name, madam," Arnold said, "act according to your station."

For a moment it looked as if she would set herself upon Arnold and rake his face with her fingernails. She did step forward. Some young girls tried to restrain her, but she shook them free and composed herself.

"General Arnold," she said, "do you know what they say of you in the street?"

"I care not, madam."

"You should, General. You should give a care. They say you are a Tory!"

His face went white. "Kindly leave," he said, "before I have you removed." With a gesture of his head, he signaled to the ragged militiaman, who came to stand beside her. Holding his musket across his chest, he escorted her to the door.

There she paused to look back at Arnold. "I know what I am, General," she said with a great measure of dignity and sadness. "I made my choice and stood by it. But you shilly-shally between both sides. You do not even have the courage to be what you are. Whatever it is."

Then she left.

Arnold lowered himself into his chair rather shakily. The musicians commenced playing. The chatter resumed. But a pall seemed cast on the entertainment for the rest of the night.

Chapter 17

"You don't like him, do you?" Peggy asked me one day when I was fixing her hair.

It brought me up short. Of course she was speaking of Arnold. He was all she spoke of these days.

"I don't dislike him," I said.

"Then what is it? You stammer and get red in the face like a country bumpkin when he even looks at you."

"Mayhap that's because I am a country bumpkin."

"You?" She laughed. "I've never seen anyone so adapt herself to city life. Well, out with it? Why don't you like him?"

"I'm afraid of him," I admitted.

In the mirror I saw amusement come into her eyes. "Why?"

"I don't know. There's a melancholy about him. He broods and appears angry so much of the time."

"He has much to brood about. Do you know how many times he's been passed over for promotion, while fools were given honors over his head?"

I shook my head no and struggled to keep a curl in place.

"He has been a fearless and dedicated officer, one of Washington's best," she said fervently. "He was wounded twice. He had his horse shot from under him at Saratoga. And who did the idiots in Congress strike a gold medal for in honor of that victory? Horatio Gates, the idiot under whom he served!"

There was more than a melancholy about Arnold, I decided, reaching for a fancy comb. Like Peggy, he put me in mind of Henry Job. There was that darkness about him. But again with a difference. Arnold took refuge in the darkness. He nursed it like his war wounds.

"Then," Peggy went on, "to add insult to injury, Washington made him wait months before he signed the papers to make Benedict a major general. And it was Benedict who carried the day at Fort Ticonderoga, but Ethan Allen got credit for it. Why, Benedict even took 440 pounds from his own pocket to supply his troops. Then when he presented the bill to Congress, they refused to pay. Started asking him about records. Was he supposed to keep records in the middle of battle?"

I did not know. But she had drawn me into the conversation so she could defend Arnold. Not for my sake. She didn't care if I had no love for the man.

"Then Congress shilly-shallied in Quebec and didn't reinforce him, and America lost its chance to take Canada. Congress and the army are full of dunderheads."

I kept a still tongue in my head.

"Then the following October, what happened on Lake Champlain? He managed to delay the British invasion. No mean feat, considering that his little homemade fleet was outnumbered by the British. Was it appreciated? No! John Brown, one of the Green Mountain boys, charged him with misconduct of the Continental fleet. Brown was out to get him. You say he broods?"

"I meant no disrespect."

"Well, the list of wrongs is long and requires much brooding. And now he has the Pennsylvania Council after him. But worst of all is his past. His father lost the family money and took refuge in drink. Benedict still minds the shame of being pulled out of school because his father couldn't meet the bills. And of having to fetch him home, always in his cups, from the tavern. Benedict has risen above it. He has much to recommend him."

There were tears in her blue eyes. And it was then that I became sensible of two things. She had entered into this conversation with me to defend her loving Arnold. Because she knew her love for him was wrong.

The other thing I knew was that she and Arnold would become soulmates, forever.

That fall, even as plans were being made for the marriage of Elizabeth to Neddy in December, Arnold wrote Mr. Shippen asking for Peggy's hand.

My fortune, sir, as you know, is not large, though it is sufficient. And I hope to increase it even more. Knowing how the war has decimated your own wealth, I ask for no dowry. My public character is well known, my private one is, I hope, irreproachable. Our difference in political sentiments will, I hope, be no bar to my happiness.

Peggy showed me the letter. I thought it cruel of him to remind Mr. Shippen of what the war had done to his fortune. Mr. Shippen may have thought so, too. He refused.

He did not like Arnold. Why should he, I heard him ask his wife. The man was thirty-seven! He had three children! He had mysterious dealings with strange men who came and went at Penn Mansion. Hadn't he played host to Silas Deane, Congress's commercial agent to France? And hadn't a fellow purchasing agent accused Deane of cheating Congress? Why did Arnold associate with such people?

What about the talk concerning Arnold's business dealings with Robert Livingston and other New York business patroons?

No!

In the rushed and frantic weeks before Elizabeth was to marry, Mr. Shippen brooded about the house in the manner of a father who was sparing no expense for a beloved daughter's wedding yet fearing the holes it was causing in his pocketbook.

He seemed torn with opposing feelings. And the one person he could vent his anger on was Arnold.

"No! He shall not marry you!"

It may seem strange, but Peggy took none of this blustery behavior seriously. Nor did she argue the point. Instead, she luxuriated in the promise of the future.

She clung to Arnold's written proposal. She pored over it. She giggled. She seemed taken with a lovely secret.

One day weeks before Elizabeth's wedding, Peggy smiled at me from the middle of her featherbed as I was putting away the dress Mama had made that she would wear as a bridesmaid.

"Will you stay with me after I marry Arnold?"

I was taken aback. I folded the dress carefully

in the clothespress. "What of your father? He hasn't given permission."

"He will."

"How can you be sure?"

Her smile deepened. "This wedding is costing him a fortune. He is running out of money. Why do you think he is carrying on so about Arnold?"

I shrugged, waiting.

"Because Benedict can support me. And he no longer can."

Our eyes met. I saw the triumph in hers. She was gloating over her father's failure.

"And he won't give in without a fuss. Well? Will you come with me when I marry and be my personal maid?"

I was struck dumb. But I managed a reply. "I'll have to ask Mama," I said.

"I'll pay you well. We can afford to. My parents are paying you now, are they not?"

"Since September."

"I'll double the amount."

"I'll have to ask Mama," I said again.

Chapter 18

I had not been home all summer and it was now October. The trees were in the fullness of their splendor, flaunting the colors that Mama attempted to duplicate in her dyeing shed. The sky was the color blue of the dresses Mama had made for Peggy, Sarah, and Mary to wear to their sister's wedding.

But it was the farm that I found most pleasing to my eye as our wagon approached. All around, fields of golden wheat waved in the sun. Never had I seen such fields of wheat! No matter what direction one looked it grew, where before the fields had been fallow.

There was a new fence around the front yard of the house, and the bells of two more cows made music in the pasture where they grazed with Opal. A team of mules was hitched to a wagon where two men worked in the fields. A fresh coat of whitewash was on the barn.

The whole place was as bright and saucy as a painting. The apple trees were laden with fruit. Mama's kitchen garden boasted crisp rows of herbs, pumpkins, squash, and potatoes. Piles of wood were neatly stacked. The corncrib was full to overflowing.

In the kitchen I set my things down and looked around. Here, too, there was a crisp sort of order, where before mayhem had reigned. A turkey was roasting on the spit. Soup bubbled. When I went with Mama to the springhouse, I found crocks and jars and barrels of preserved foods.

"I thought Henry Job was out rounding up Hessians all summer," I said.

"He was." She poured two mugs of cider. "But he was also visiting many farms in both New Jersey and Pennsylvania. And talking with the farmers. And learning."

"But if he was away, who did all this work?"

"Our soldier," she said. "And with him doing all the outside work, it gave me time to make candles and soap and put up preserves. They're harvesting the wheat now, he and Papa Henry. Mayhap you would like to take them some refreshment and visit."

I looked around. With all the improvements, something was missing. I felt a sense of dread. "Where's Merlin?"

"Out in the fields with them. He gets on well with our soldier. They're good friends."

•　•　•　•　•

I walked through the fields with my basket of bread and meat in one hand and a crock of cold cider in the other. Overhead birds swooped and circled in the wind currents. I felt the warm sun on my face, breathed in the familiar farm smells. They mingled in my brain and brought back a hundred memories. It was good to be home.

As I crossed a small wooden bridge over the stream, Merlin sighted me in the distance and came bounding.

"Here, Merlin! Here, boy!"

I set my things down and knelt on the ground as he rushed into my arms. "Oh, Merlin, I'm so glad to see you!"

He licked my face. He whined and barked. I hugged him. Oh, it was so wonderful to hug him! Without realizing it, I'd missed him so. I'd missed this whole place. Coming home was like a gift, I minded. It was like being given a gift to open, and though you knew what was inside the wrapping, your fingers trembled anyway. Because when you opened it, everything that you'd always known and taken for granted was there. Only it was being given to you all over again. And it was new to your eyes. As if you'd never seen it before.

I suppose if anybody asked me, as I picked up

my basket and crock of cider and walked toward the two figures working in the field, that I would have to say I hated Mama's "soldier" before I met him. She'd been so smug, so secretive about him, bragging about his accomplishments, displaying the farm today for me to see and praise. Certainly everything that been done was his doing. So why, then, did I resent him so?

Henry Job saw me first. He waved and jumped down from the wagon where he was guiding the team of mules. Henry Job had never before been this glad to see me. I supposed he was putting on a display for Mama's soldier.

He took off his hat as I approached. "Well, and so welcome home at long last. It's about time you've come, girl."

Merlin ran around and around barking. Henry Job took the basket from me. And the crock of cider.

"Come," he called to his helper. "Come and meet our girl. Here is Becca."

The man set down his scythe, took off his hat, and wiped his face with a kerchief. He wore plain homespun breeches and shirt. He was tall and well built, and his hair was tied behind him, military fashion. He walked toward us until he was a few feet from me.

"This is our Becca," said Henry Job. He was smiling. His eyes twinkled as I'd never seen before.

Something in the back of my mind stirred. I felt a quickening in my head, though I did not know why. I looked up into the bluest eyes I had ever seen. The stranger smiled, showing even, white teeth. A lock of brown hair fell over his forehead. His face was at once impudent with youth and health, vanity, and good looks, and at the same time it struck some chord inside me that I could not name. I felt annoyed.

"Hello," I said.

"Becca, please to meet Persifor," my stepfather said, "the man who's done such wonders with the farm."

Persifor was looking down at me with a mixture of pleasure and bemusement. "We've met," he said.

. . . . .

I was furious with Mama. Standing out in that field with the eyes of Henry Job and his Persifor on me, I had been hard put to know who this stranger was who seemed to know me.

Henry Job had to tell me. "This is Persifor Frazor. The soldier you helped escape."

I had not recognized him. My eyes widened in amazement. The sickly soldier I had handed the bundle of Quaker woman's clothing to that night so long ago in the warming kitchen appeared before me now as a strong, capable young man.

They laughed, he and Henry Job, at my dismay. Then Persifor apologized. "How could you be expected to know me? I don't know myself these days."

"You could have told me," I whispered savagely to Mama later in the kitchen as I helped her put the food on the table.

She would not acknowledge my anger. Neither would my stepfather. They thought the whole secret great sport. Truth to tell, I could not understand my anger myself. Or my resentment at Persifor, who was most courtly.

"I was mustered out at Camp Valley Forge," he told me at supper. "My lungs were so bad. They were going to send me to a hospital in Reading. Your brother intervened and perhaps saved my life. So many of the soldiers who were sent to hospitals in Reading or Bethlehem died. Your brother asked your parents to take me in. They did. And they saved my life. I owe them a great deal."

"Posh," Mama said.

"Are you going to rejoin the army now that you're well again?" I asked.

"They won't have me," he said. "My lungs are still not strong."

"You look strong to me."

"Becca!" Mama was horrified. "He's been serving since Bunker Hill! He's been wounded twice. He's of more use here raising food for the army!"

"Is this what living in the fancy Shippen house has done for you?" Henry Job asked. "Made you a saucy wench?" But he was not angry, as the old Henry Job would have been. I marked some difference in him. He no longer seemed encumbered by his shortcomings. He was inordinately pleased with himself.

"Henry Job seems happier," I told Mama. The men had gone outside to smoke their clay pipes and have some rum. We were cleaning up.

"For the first time, the farm is working," she said. "We have a good harvest, a full corncrib, fat livestock, good markets for our wheat, a spring-house fair to bursting. That's no mean feat in these times."

"Where did Henry Job get the money?"

She shrugged. "He's been working hard. And saving. I told you he was a good man."

I could not tally the cost of making a successful farm out of a failing one. But I'd learned about money working for the Shippens. And it seemed unlikely that Henry Job could have accomplished all this. Had Mama sold her silver coffee service?

"Persifor has made all the difference. You should be grateful to him instead of laying blame. You don't like him because I found out your little secret. What did you think, that we'd be angry because you helped him?"

"I just thought I had a right to a secret, Mama.

You have them all the time. You didn't tell me he was your soldier all these months. Why?"

"You're not home a day and we're fighting. Is this what working in the Shippen house has done to you?"

"I'm sorry, Mama." I was. I looked at her. She was getting grayer than ever. Why had I never noticed it before?

"You're getting prickly," she said.

"I'm not prickly."

"You'll never get a man to pay mind to you if you're prickly."

"I don't want a man paying mind to me. Are you talking about Persifor? Is this what the two of you have in mind?"

"Don't be silly," she said. "You think I sent you to the Shippens to learn to dance and do watercolors and play the harpsichord, just to be paired off with Persifor? No. He's a fine person, but I want better for you than living on this farm, Becca."

What *did* she want? What did she think I was capable of doing? It frightened me.

"What do *you* want?" she asked.

Henry Job, I decided. He wanted Persifor for me. "Oh, I don't know, Mama. Arnold has asked for Peggy's hand. Her father refused, but she says she'll marry him. She's asked me to work for them. I said I'd ask you."

She set down a large platter. I picked it up to dry. "Do you want this?" she asked.

"Yes, I think I'd like to work for them. Do you think Henry Job will allow it?"

"He won't like it. He's been wanting you to come home. And he doesn't like Arnold."

I shrugged. "Not many do. But it's a good opportunity, Mama. I'll be able to save some money."

"For what?" she asked.

"For what?" I stared at her. "Why, for anything, Mama. Don't you think I have a right to earn some money? I've never *had* any. Didn't you ever think I might want things?"

"What kind of things? What don't you have now?"

She was testing me, so I knew what answer to give, what she wanted to hear. And I said the words. "Well, for a dowry. Mayhap I'd like to start my dowry."

She had no argument for that. And I felt guilty because a dowry was the furthest thing from my mind. She nodded, pleased. "He will give me an argument," she said, "but he will allow it." Then she took the piece of flannel from me. "But you were still rude to Persifor. So why don't you go outside and make it up to him? Here comes Henry Job now. I'll talk to him about it. Go on, go along."

I went along as she directed. No sooner was the kitchen door closed behind me than I heard them arguing. I walked down the path from the house with their words ringing in my ears.

"No!" Henry Job was shouting. "No Arnold. I don't want her with Arnold. Don't you hear the things they're saying about him in the city?"

"They say things about everyone in the city," Mama yelled back. "This is Philadelphia, not Boston. If they don't have someone to gossip about they'll find someone! When the British were here it was Howe and Mrs. Loring. Then Andre. And now it's Arnold."

"Don't make this a thing between Boston and Philadelphia!"

"But that's what it is again, Henry! You just don't understand Philadelphia. You never will!"

．　．　．　．　．

Mama's dyeing supplies were now in an outbuilding. I found Persifor there, moving things around, straightening.

"What are you doing?"

"Tidying up. Nobody uses these things anymore. The doctor said the smells were causing your mother's headaches. Your stepfather asked me to throw it all out. But I thought that rather a shame. It all comes dear."

"How do you know about such things?"

He gave me that impish smile. "I'm from New England."

"Oh."

He gestured with his head up to the house. "Another argument about Boston and Philadelphia, is it?"

"You've heard them before, I take it."

"Yes, often." He moved the indigo pot and wiped his hands with a rag. "What brought it on this time?"

"What has New England to do with knowing about dyestuffs?" I asked.

"My mother weaves and dyes. My father built a room onto the house for her loom. She has six girls working for her. She makes a respectable living from it. Of course, my father didn't leave her barefoot."

"Your father is dead?"

"He died last year. He was a doctor."

"Don't throw anything out."

"I beg your pardon?"

"It took my mother a while to assemble all this. I know a thing or two about dyeing myself."

He smiled. "Are you coming home then?"

Something about the way he said it annoyed me. "Why is everyone so concerned about my coming home?"

"Your stepfather wants you to."

"He never wanted me to go to work for the

Shippens in the first place. He wanted me to stay here and be a farm girl."

"It's a beautiful farm."

"It wasn't always. You've made it so," I allowed.

He gave a little bow. "Thank you." Then he smiled. "That wasn't so difficult now, was it?"

My face flamed. "You're a cheeky sort."

His eyes twinkled. "Are you sorry you helped me that night?"

"I'm beginning to be."

"What's there in Philadelphia for you? I hated the town when I was there."

"You were in jail."

"That's so. But I still don't see . . . well, no mind."

"I need to find my missing pieces, if you must know," I told him.

He took my measure with that level gaze of his. "I see."

"No, you don't. There's pieces of me missing. Always was." How could I explain it to him? And why did I want to try? "You know about weaving," I said, "about cloth and how it must look when it is finished. Well, there are pieces of me out of the whole cloth. I'm not finished."

He nodded. "Everyone feels so at times."

"Do you?"

"I never did, until the war. Then I started looking for more meaning to my life, if that's what you mean. A man has a lot of time to think in prison. I was searching, too. Thought the army was the answer for me. For all I know, it was, but I couldn't serve anymore. When they mustered me out, I thought I'd die."

"But you didn't."

He smiled. "I've done my share of it."

"And now?"

"I've found my missing pieces, as you would call them, right here on this farm."

I nodded and we shared a moment of silence, gazing out over the peaceful fields.

"Sometimes a person has to go away to find what's right inside him. I suspect it's the case with you. Upheaval ofttimes makes us look at things differently. Things that were right in front of us before, we start to see with new eyes."

"Well, I don't see anything around here with new eyes," I said.

"That being the case with you, I don't suppose you are ready to come home yet."

"I never will be."

"You will," he said.

His quiet certainty had an air of superiority about it that annoyed me. "I hate this place, if you must know. I belong in the city. So I'm going to work for Peggy Shippen when she marries General Arnold."

He raised his eyebrows. "Well, so that's what your stepfather is yelling about. He hates Arnold."

"Why?"

"Doesn't everyone?" He laughed. "That'll provide you with all the upheaval you'll need for a while."

"Oh? You know about farming, about weaving and dyeing, and now you're telling me you know about Peggy Shippen, too?"

"No, I know about General Arnold."

The way he said it, so quiet and plain, brought me up short. This was more than gossip. "What do you know?"

He shrugged and stared out the window. "He was at Camp Valley Forge for a while before I came there. Long enough for the soldiers to get to know him. They told me things. He's ambitious and self-seeking. He gave illicit passes permitting schooners to leave Philadelphia loaded with goods that would bring high prices in Patriot-held territory. They say his partners in the scheme were Tories. He's speculating. That means he's making money on the war."

"I know what it means." I gave a little laugh. "Do you think Washington would have given him command of Philadelphia if he knew such?" But I felt a sense of dread. I had heard such tales about Arnold before.

"Just mind yourself," he said.

I sniffed. "Do you think I don't know how?"

"I know you do, Becca Syng," he said. "Or I wouldn't be standing here now. I never thanked you properly for helping me that night. I'm beholden to you. I'll keep everything here in order. For when you come back. I can even collect peach leaves, goldenrod, and other supplies for you. I used to help my mother. Weaving and dyeing can be a lucrative business."

"Thank you," I said, "but I won't be coming back. I'm going to work for Peggy and Arnold."

He looked at me long and hard. There was sadness in the look, too. "I wish you luck, Becca Syng," he said. "If there's ever anything you need, feel free to call on me."

I wanted to laugh in his face, to ask him what he could ever do for me. And why I would ever have need of him. But I kept a still tongue in my head, bade him good night, and went into the house.

Chapter 19

In December Elizabeth Shippen married her Neddy. The wedding was held on the first Thursday evening of the month.

There were twenty-five bridesmaids. All but the Shippen girls wore their very best dresses. Sarah, Peggy, and Mary wore the blue gowns Mama had made. Elizabeth was embarrassed by all the fuss. She stayed most of the time with her grandmama, coming home only occasionally for fittings of her wedding dress.

It was rose-colored silk trimmed with silk gauze. The sides were looped up *à la polonaise*. She wore it over a pink silk-satin quilted petticoat.

"Shameless girl," her cousin Elizabeth Tilghman wrote. "How is it with your highness? How can you be so naughty as to have so many witnesses to your actions?"

"I'm mortified," Elizabeth told me and Mama. It was the day before the wedding. Mama was there for a final fitting. Elizabeth had shooed everyone else out of her room except me and Mama. I brought a tray of tea and sweet buns and the note from her cousin.

Elizabeth read it, threw it on the floor, and burst into tears. "It's because I'm the oldest and the first to marry," she moaned. "This wedding must be lavish so Daddy can put everyone on notice that he hasn't been ruined by the war. I wish I weren't marrying first. This wedding would suit Peggy more than me."

"Peggy will have her moment," Mama said. "Enjoy yours." She stepped back and fluffed out the pale pink quilted underskirt of the gown. "There."

"I want to elope," Elizabeth whispered. Her face was very white.

"You will not elope." Mama stood with her hands folded over her middle. "Not after the labor I put into this dress. You will hold your head high and marry your Neddy tomorrow and do everyone proud. And, after all, your husband is an important man. You have your position to keep."

The revolutionary government of Pennsylvania had appointed Neddy prothonotary of the Supreme Court. I did not know exactly what it meant. But it was important. Neddy's Uncle

Edward had held the position in the years before the war.

The dress was pronounced finished. Elizabeth dried her tears. Mama left. I poured Elizabeth a second cup of tea and folded the dress away. She had tied a silk robe around herself. She eyed me carefully.

"You must think me a noodle-head."

"I don't."

"It's important to me what you think. Is this wedding silly?"

"No. Your mama and daddy want it. You must do it for them. It's your duty as the first daughter to marry."

"Has Daddy given permission yet for Peggy to marry Arnold?"

"No," I said, "but Arnold is pressing his suit. He's had new boots made with one heel built up even higher, so he doesn't limp. And he's let your father know, at least six times, that the legislature in New York has offered him a large tract of land in appreciation for his war services."

"Do you know what I heard?" Elizabeth whispered.

I closed up the clothespress and waited.

"The Pennsylvania Council is planning to bring charges against him."

"For what?"

"I don't know. They say they have a whole list

of abuses. I have no proof, so I can't say anything to Daddy yet. And even if I did, how could I ruin my sister's happiness when I'm about to enjoy my own?"

We looked at each other. "Don't worry the matter, Elizabeth," I said. "Peggy can always take care of herself."

"I hate the thought of her being married to that man. I thought Andre was bad." She shuddered. "Oh, Becca, do you think I'll get through this dreadful wedding? I have quakes and tremblings and a thousand other quirks."

"Yes," I said. "You're a woman of courage, Elizabeth. Look at some of the things you've done."

"Adventures," she said. "I was having sport."

"You were doing more than that."

"All right. I suppose I was. I was trying to do what you said you'd come here to do. I was trying to find some of my missing pieces."

Tears came to my eyes. "And did you?"

"I think so, yes. But looking back on it all now, I fear it was just selfishness on my part. Has any of it come to anything?"

So I told her about Frazor then, and how he was running my stepfather's farm and loving every moment of it. It brought her around. We laughed over it together as we had tea. "He sounds quite taken with you," she said.

"Don't be silly." But I blushed.

"You could do worse. He comes from a fine New England family. Promise me, Becca, that if things get bad when you're working for Peggy and Arnold, you'll get out. Promise me, you'll go home to the farm."

My eyes went wide. "What could go bad?"

"I don't know. But I have the blue devils about him marrying her. I can't help it. Promise."

So I did.

"You've helped me," she said, finishing her tea. "Now make me another promise."

I said I would.

"Will you help me dress tomorrow? I need your courage. I know I'll faint dead away and disgrace everybody."

So I said I would do that, too. And I did.

The next day Elizabeth married her Neddy. The house was full to overflowing with people. And Elizabeth did not faint dead away or disgrace anybody. She looked lovely and graceful and proud. And before she and Neddy left on their wedding trip, she grasped my hand and kissed me. "I couldn't have done it without you," she said.

. . . . .

I had stayed up half the night writing the letter to Blair by a single candle on the table in the warming kitchen. I labored over it, making sure it had just the right tone. I told him about Frazor and the farm and how the harvest had been such a financial success. I told him about Elizabeth's wedding and how she and Neddy were now visiting with their Uncle Joseph at his farm in Chester County. Mama and Henry Job were well, I wrote. Of course, I hadn't been home since Christmas, but I saw Mama regularly. Even when she wasn't sewing for the Shippens, she stopped by when in town.

Then I told him how I would likely be working soon for Peggy and General Arnold, if Mr. Shippen ever gave his permission for their betrothal. And that I was dispatching this letter with General Arnold on the morrow when he left for Kingston, New York, on his way to see the legislature. He would be stopping off first at Middlebrook in the Jerseys to see General Washington.

"It is snowing dreadfully as I write this," I penned. "I must go to bed now. Arnold is coming early in the morning to breakfast."

I sent my most devoted sisterly affections. Then I put the date. February 2, 1779.

· · · · ·

"Doan give it to him," Coxie said to me the next morning when I went down to fetch Peggy's chocolate and showed her the letter to Blair.

I was having second thoughts about asking

Arnold to deliver it to the Middlebrook encampment. For as often as he came to the house, I could never bring myself to speak to the man.

He was very imposing to me. A general. He dressed like one and acted like one, never relaxing his guard for a moment. But it wasn't that as much as the fact that he frightened me more than ever these days.

I was never at ease in his presence. He was not in the least friendly. He brooded more than ever. And the air of mystery about him seemed to be gathering darker clouds these days.

"Why shouldn't I?" I asked Coxie. "Why shouldn't he take the note for me? My brother is a captain in the same army."

She shook her head and wiped her hands on her apron. "Doan do it," she said. "Doan send no paper wif that man. Never send no paper wif him."

Coxie could read and write. Elizabeth had taught her. But enlightened as she was, paper with writing on it held terrors for her. Written words bound you, pointed fingers at you. You could never escape them once they were down on paper. It was with great trepidation that she read the notes that Elizabeth sent to her these days.

"Send the letter by post," she said.

"You know how awful the mails are with this war."

"Doan do it, chile."

I put the letter in the pocket I wore around my waist and brought Peggy's tray of chocolate upstairs. Did Coxie know something? She had been so determined. Was Elizabeth writing something in those notes that Coxie told no one? She destroyed all such correspondence instantly. By Elizabeth's direction?

Later on that morning, I stood in the shadows of the far reaches of the center hallway as General Arnold said good-bye to Peggy before leaving on his trip. The snow was still coming down steadily. Outside his coach-and-four, his servants waited. I fingered my letter to Blair in my crewel-worked pocket.

I watched them embrace. The silk of her gown made swishing noises. Candles in wall sconces threw shadows. I heard her whimper, then go quiet.

He was kissing her. It was an intimate moment. I shouldn't be watching. No one else was about. Sarah and Mary were in Lancaster, visiting their grandmama, who had taken ill again. Mr. Shippen was in his library, and Mrs. Shippen in bed with a cold.

"I wish you didn't have to go," Peggy murmured.

"I must, Love. I must see the legislature and claim my land."

"The roads are dangerous."

He laughed, a deep, rich sound. "The danger is here."

"What do you mean?"

"I hate to tell you, but you must be prepared. Reed and his council are going to issue a proclamation with charges against me. Once it's issued, I won't be able to leave. One of my aides found out about it last week. That's why I must go today."

"Charges?" Her voice cracked.

"Yes. Eight of them. That's why I must see Washington."

"But . . ."

So Elizabeth had been right about the council bringing charges. What else did she know?

"Don't worry the matter." Arnold kissed Peggy again. "I shall write to you. Take heart."

He was leaving! Should I run though the hall now and ask him to take the letter? Something held me back. The memory of the look in Coxie's eyes when she had said, "Doan do it. Doan send no paper wif that man."

He went out the door. Peggy stood there leaning against it and crying. I moved back, deeper into the shadows.

. . . . .

It is difficult to recollect how quickly things went bad before the end of the week. I don't hold with superstitions, but I almost came to believe in the "blue devils" that Elizabeth felt when contemplating the union of Peggy and General Arnold.

He'd left on a Monday. By Wednesday morning the council had distributed its proclamation against him to the newspapers and governmental bodies in Philadelphia.

By Wednesday evening his name was on the tongue of everyone in Philadelphia. And the eight charges were listed in the *Gazette*, the *Pennsylvania Evening Post*, the *Ledger*, and the *Packet*.

Thursday afternoon Peggy was determined to go out. I was to accompany her. Pepy waited in the carriage out front.

"Do you think it's wise?" Her father stood there in the hall with a copy of the *Packet* in his hands while we got into our wraps.

"And why not?" Peggy asked. "I'm bored to death."

"The snow is high," her father said.

"Pepy can manage the carriage." She glared at him, lips trembling, but determined. "And I can manage anyone who has a disparaging word to say about Arnold."

We went to Robert Bell's Bookshop on Third Street. The place had been the scene of many cultural diversions when the British were here, and Bell was one shopowner who had survived the occupation of both armies. I loved the bookshop, although the lecture on experimental philosophy was out of my ken. It was out of Peggy's, too, but she had heard several of her friends would be there.

I amused myself browsing amongst the books while the voice of the lecturer droned on and Peggy and Becky Franks and two other girls kept up a whispered conversation in the back row.

The lecture ended. Tea was served. Of a sudden, a well-dressed gentleman came over to Peggy and her friends.

"Have you heard from Arnold?" he asked.

It was the merchant Barnabas Higgins, who had the emporium on the Chestnut Street Wharf.

"No," Peggy said.

"The news of the day is that General Arnold has left Philadelphia and gone over to the enemy."

All the pleasant chatter of those who had attended the lecture stopped. Everyone looked at Peggy. I saw her face go white.

"Have *you* heard the news of the day?" she asked him.

He leaned forward, over his teacup, waiting. Everyone else in the shop waited, too, straining their ears.

"The news of the day is that you gossip like an old woman," Peggy said. "Come, Becca, we have more important things to do." And she lifted her skirts and sailed out of the shop.

* * * * *

But once home again behind the protective brick walls of her father's house, it was as if someone pulled a thread in the fabric of her reserve and her whole being came unraveled.

She threw off her cloak, stamped her feet, lashed out at Dorothea who brought tea, pronounced it cold, and demanded to know why her lazy mother was still in bed. "What right do they have to persecute him! He crippled himself in the Patriot cause. And this is how they repay him. They will push him into the arms of the enemy."

The tantrum promised to be almost as bad as the day her father refused to let her go to Andre's party. She stood in the front parlor about to dash a silver candlestick against the wall when the terrified Dorothea reappeared.

"Miss Peggy . . ."

"What is it?" She whirled on the girl. "Can't you see I'm busy? The stupid tea you brought is cold. And the cornbread is stale. You mean this household can't produce a better repast than this? Worthless servants, no wonder my father's fortune has diminished. We pay you for nothing. Bring some hot tea!"

The girl cowered, clutching something in her hand. "This note came for you."

"Well, give it to me. Don't stand there like a jackass in the rain!"

But Dorothea remained benumbed. I crossed the room, took the note gently from her. "You have duties in the kitchen," I said. "I'll get the fresh tea."

She ran her tongue along her lips and nodded her thanks and fled the room. I gave the folded and sealed vellum to Peggy and went to fetch tea.

Ten minutes later I came back into the parlor with a tray of leftover breakfast ham, cheese, dried fruit, and steaming tea. She was languishing in a chair. Tears ran down her face.

"What is it?" I asked.

She looked at me as if she did not know who I was. "The council sent a man after him with the proclamation. He has been to see Washington, who was most courteous and advised him to have Congress hear the charges. But he wants a military court-martial. He wants to be heard by his fellow soldiers."

I waited. She bowed her head, then went on.

"Listen to this:

My dearest life. Never did I so ardently long to see or hear from you as at this instant. I am all impatience and anxiety to know how you do. Just three days' absence from you is intolerable. Heav-

ens! What must I have suffered had I continued on to New York: the loss of happiness for a few dirty acres. I can almost bless the villainous roads and the more villainous men who oblige me to return. I am heartily tired with my journey and almost so with human nature. I daily discover so much baseness and ingratitude among mankind that I almost blush at being of the same species and could quit the stage without regret were it not for my dear Peggy. Let me beg of you not to suffer the rude attacks on me or give one moment's uneasiness. I hope to be made happy by your smiles on Friday evening; till then, all nature smiles in vain, for you alone—heard, felt, and seen—possess my every thought, fill every sense and pant in every vein."

I blushed hearing the words. She did not. She raised her lovely eyes to me and smiled. "Where is my father?" she asked.

"In the library."

"I must see him."

"I brought your tea."

She walked out of the room, went down the hall, and without knocking went into the library. I followed. She'd left the door partly open. I could see Mr. Shippen sitting behind his desk. The snow had started to fall again. It was mixed with sleet and sounded against the windows. A fire burned in the hearth. He looked up. "Yes, Peggy."

"I am going to marry Benedict Arnold," she

told him. "As soon as it is seemly and possible."

He nodded, slowly. "Do you think that wise? In light of what is happening?"

"I think it not only wise, I think it fitting and proper."

"I see." But apparently he did not.

She stepped forward and dropped the note on the desk. He took a few moments to read it. The fire crackled. The clock ticked.

Time stretched like worn fabric, forced to endure too much weight. I thought I heard something tear, but it was only the sound of the snow on the windows. Then, having read the note, Mr. Shippen set it down, leaned back in his chair, took off his spectacles, and ran a hand over his eyes.

"Are you going to give your permission?" Peggy asked. "I won't require a fancy wedding like Elizabeth had. I think it was vulgar. And Benedict is not asking for a dowry. I am sure you can afford it."

The sarcasm in her voice was lost on Mr. Shippen. He seemed befuddled. "In light of the tone of this note, I think it only fitting and proper that you should wed. Yes," he said, "I shall speak to your mother about it this day."

Chapter 20

I stood in the warming kitchen one morning two months later, facing the servants of the Shippen household across the old scrubbed oaken table. Their faces were all dear and familiar to me by now.

I had been in this house a month and a year. And it was time to say good-bye. Outside, Mr. Shippen's carriage waited. Pepy would take me this fine April day to Penn Mansion to begin my service with Peggy and Arnold.

They had been married last evening. The house was crowded with wedding guests who were still sleeping. As was the family. The wedding had been small but elegant.

Peggy had been radiant. Arnold, looking older than his years, had to be supported by a soldier aide. The last two months had taken their toll.

He had demanded a military court-martial to

clear his name of the charges that Reed and the Philadelphia Council brought against him. He did not trust Congress.

As it turned out, Congress could not back up the charges. The newspapers put the business on everyone's lips, of course, brought it down to the level of the tradespeople and even the servants who shopped in the markets.

Should Arnold be tried by the civilian court or the military? It made for lively discourse wherever two or more people gathered. People took sides. You would think they were betting on the horses or the cock fights. There were "Arnold people" and "Reed people." And they became downright ornery over the matter, whichever side they took.

Peggy and I had been in William Gardner's shop on Second Street one afternoon before the wedding. She'd gone for a ruffled shirt for Arnold. As luck would have it, that was the day the council dismissed the militia at Lebanon and Lancaster. They vowed they would not replace the militia until Arnold was removed from command.

A fistfight broke out right in the shop. A display of stationery was knocked over. Then one man recognized Peggy.

Unfortunately, he was not one of the "Arnold people."

"There she is, that Shippen girl who's to marry the traitor." The crowd was ugly. Mr. Gardner had to sneak us out the back door.

Peggy made me swear not to tell Arnold. "He'll rush into a duel on the slightest provocation these days," she said.

I didn't think it was the slightest provocation. But then, I did not speak to Arnold under normal circumstances. I would, however, have told Mr. Shippen. But she would not let me.

In spite of all the bad feeling, Arnold rallied. He was a soldier after all, and this was a fight. He loved fights. So while Peggy was caught in the whirlwind of preparations for the wedding, he prepared his own defense and gathered evidence to give to the special committee the council had appointed to hear him on March fifth.

In early March that committee exonerated him of six of the eight charges. The rest, they said, were up to Washington himself. Arnold had no fear of Washington. He was vindicated.

He celebrated by buying the most elegant house in Pennsylvania, Mount Pleasant, on the Schuylkill. But he and Peggy would not live there. He was renting it. He needed the money.

Last evening, after the wedding, they had gone to Penn Mansion. He would wait for a military court-martial. He looked forward to it. I'd overheard him at the wedding celebration saying he wanted to clear his name and get on with the business of being a great soldier. The war was not over, though many in Philadelphia acted as if it were.

There were battles to be fought yet. Commands

to be had. He felt destined for greatness. Surely he would achieve something wonderful so his name would be remembered forever.

His court-martial was supposed to be on the first of May.

I was not looking forward to serving them until then. But I was going.

Across the old scrubbed oaken table, Coxie smiled at me. "You look nervous as the cat that stole the fish heads," she told me. "You look like you just jumped the broom instead of Miz Peggy."

"Jumping the broom" was the nigra term for getting married.

"I don't want to leave here," I said.

"Well, you'd best be goin'." She held out her arms. "Come on, say your good-byes."

I'd said good-bye to the Shippens last night. It had been easier than what I was about to do now. I hugged Dorothea, who had to wipe tears from her face and handed me a folded linen apron with my initials embroidered on the edge. I could scarce speak. Then came Ellyn. I'd not had much to do with Ellyn. She was older than Dorothea and not very friendly. But to my surprise she put her hands on my shoulders and said, "You're too good for the job." That was all. Then she gave me a finely hemmed neck kerchief. Lettice gave me two candles she'd made.

Brilliana had baked a loaf of gingerbread. Baking was not one of Brilliana's strong points. So it had special meaning.

By the time I got to Coxie, tears blinded my eyes. She had her own gift for me. It was a dog-eared copy of Tom Paine's *Common Sense*, the pamphlet that had tipped the scales in the people's minds in favor of independence.

"Doan need it no more," she said. "I gots it all here." And she pointed to her head.

Cecil gave me a small square of Irish linen. "Belonged to my wife," he said. "She died afore you came."

"Cecil, I can't take this from you."

"Got no daughter to give it to."

All this had me sore afflicted, to say the least. They had become closer than family. I had been home for two days at Christmas and it had been terrible. Persifor was away, getting contracts from the American army for wheat. Mama kept busy sewing. And Henry Job refused to speak to me.

"Why are you like sour milk to me?" I had demanded finally.

He sipped his plum brandy. "I'm hard driven to know what compensation they give that makes it worth working for *him*," was all he would say.

It made me think that Henry Job knew something he wasn't telling. How could he know Arnold well enough to hate him so?

"I work for *her*," I told him.

"Bah." And he waved a disgusted hand at me.

He and Mama scarcely spoke. *The fault is mine,* I minded. And I could not wait to leave. The farm in winter was a dismal place in the best of circumstances. I had not been back since.

Coxie went with me now to the door. "We always here if'n you want us," she said.

I looked back, saw them staring at me. *They are part of me,* I minded. *They are some of my missing pieces.* It was the first time I understood that you can lose some pieces after you've found them.

. . . . .

People change. I was to learn that over the next month. But did Peggy Shippen change after she married Benedict Arnold? Or did she simply become more so of what she'd already been? I was to ponder that question for years to come.

Words don't do justice to the telling.

Betimes I think that Peggy had missing pieces, too. And that she found her most important one in Arnold. That he made her whole.

But that was frightening to me, that you could work so hard to find your missing pieces, then when you finally became whole, the result could be so dreadful.

What would I become when I found all my missing pieces? Would I be sorry once I became whole? I would not think on the matter.

One evening in April, they were dining late. The air was as warm and fresh as silk, rippling in the open windows of the dining room. The parquet floors shone. Birds were nesting down for the night with little chirping noises. Candles flickered in the gathering dusk.

For once they were alone at the table, without guests. I was across the hall in the parlor, playing the harpsichord as Peggy liked me to do whenever they took supper. I had just finished a tune when a knock came on the door and one of the servants admitted an aide. He rushed into the dining room, then in a moment or two rushed back out.

"What does the letter say?" Peggy asked.

I heard Arnold curse. Then I heard his chair pushed back and his boots sound on the parquet floor. "It's from Washington. He's postponing the court-martial!"

"Why?" she asked.

"The Pennsylvania Council needs more time to gather evidence! Reed again, damn him. Likely he's threatened to withdraw Pennsylvania's cooperation on future matters if Washington doesn't postpone it. Is there no resource in this country, by God, that will not fail me?"

I heard Peggy murmuring. I sipped some tea.

"Where is my music?" Arnold bellowed from across the hall. "Can I at least have music?"

I commenced to play an English ballad. Dusk deepened. I finished the ballad and took up a taper to light the candles in the wall sconces. As I moved around the parlor, I heard their low conversation.

"I thought Washington had more guts," Arnold growled. "The benighted fool, allowing Reed to push him around. After how well I've served him! He's no friend."

"He was the last friend you had," Peggy said.

"I've nowhere to turn now."

"Darling, a prophet is never honored in his own country," Peggy told him.

"My Peggy, I'm no prophet. I'm a tired old soldier who's been too often wounded and is being sent out to pasture. What devilish bargain have you made marrying me?"

"You will rally. You have greatness in you. I see you on a fine horse galloping to British lines."

He laughed, a deep, rich sound. "Under the fire of both armies."

"Yes! Of course!" Her resolve grew stronger. "But only until the British find out why you have come."

A silence in the room. "And why have I come?" he asked.

"To bring this torn, bleeding country back under the rule of the Crown. And bring back peace and prosperity to everyone."

"The Crown?"

"Yes, my love. A chastened Crown that has learned its lesson well. And will lovingly rule so that America returns to the proper class structure. Where the rabble are kept in line and the superior classes rule. Mayhap that is your true mission in all of this, Benedict."

The silence stretched out into eternity before he answered. And when he did his voice feigned disinterest, even amusement.

"My true mission?"

"What do you owe Washington now?"

"Nothing."

"You could be like George Monk."

"Monk?"

"Yes, darling. Cromwell's general who brought about the restoration of Charles II during the English Civil War a hundred years ago. I recollect having to study about him."

"Tell me what you learned."

"You're a famous general. Surely you studied it, too."

"Tell me," he insisted. He was teasing her.

She gave a little nervous laugh and recited like a schoolgirl. "Very well, he changed sides. And by doing so, he brought peace to England. He became a hero. And he was made Duke of Albemarle for his courage."

"Duke, is it?"

"Yes, darling."

"Are you proposing then to be a duchess?"

She giggled again. "No, I'd be Lady Arnold.

And you would be Lord Arnold. It has a wondrous ring to it, don't you think?"

Silence again. I heard the pouring of wine. "You little minx," he said. "You're joking, of course. How could I turn on the brave boys I fought with?"

She gave a throaty laugh. "What makes them fight?"

"They want independence."

"Nonsense. You don't believe that. You wrote your boys' tutor in Maryland that you wanted their education to be useful rather than learned. That life is too uncertain to throw away in speculation on subjects that perhaps one man in ten thousand has a genius to make a figure in."

"I wrote that, did I?"

"Yes, and more."

"What more?"

"You said that self-preservation is the first principle of the human race." ·

Something in the very shade of light changed. Was it just night settling over the house? No, it was more. What more, I did not know. Do we truly know the moment when evil creeps through the doors and windows and takes hold? Can we sense its presence? Or do we just think a chill has come over us and reach for a shawl, because it is more convenient to do so?

That is what I did—decided I was chilled. I

reached for a shawl and stood in the door of the parlor, looking through the hall to the dining room. He was sitting again. I saw their heads close, his gray, hers blond. They each had one elbow on the table, hands intertwined.

"Your brave boys don't fight for independence," she purred. "You yourself said they fight for the back pay and land they will receive should independence be realized."

"That's so," he agreed.

"What if"—and she ran her free hand through his hair—"what if you convinced the British government to make up these things to them if they lose?"

To his credit, he released her hand and got up. He pushed back his chair, leaned down, and kissed her. "I know now why I love you, Peggy."

"You agree with me, then?"

"No, but life is never dull with you. And you make seduction by the royal cause as interesting as seduction by you."

Then he bellowed again. "Music! I want music! Are you alive in there? And no ballads. Give me something lively!"

I commenced to play.

Chapter 21

*I*t was not an amiable house to work in. The servants were not friendly, to me or to each other. They quarreled; they snitched on each other; they stole food. I missed Coxie and the refuge of the warming kitchen. And since Peggy was married now, I did not sleep in her room anymore.

I slept in the dependency behind the house with the other servants. Peggy had wanted me on a small bed in her dressing room, which adjoined their bedroom. Arnold had said no. He needed his privacy. Servants had big ears, he said. They were always lurking about, listening. There was no trust in that house.

The dependency was cold in winter, the other servants said. They said it grimly, as if it would pleasure them to see me suffer.

I said nothing and went about my business. It

was not winter, it was spring. The way things were going, mayhap I wouldn't be here in winter.

Hannah didn't like me. She was Arnold's sister, older than him by a year, which put her at thirty-eight. But she looked fifty.

Benedict, she called him. And it was Benedict this and Benedict that. Of course she made sure I knew right off that she had been caring for him since he was eighteen, when their mother died. He was her whole life.

Of course he was. He had to be. She did not know that Peggy had told me how Benedict had, with a revolver, run off the only suitor Hannah'd ever had. On general principle. Because he'd been a Frenchman.

Hannah had no reason for not liking me. It was just on general principle. Which is the worst way, I have found, to be disliked. Because the person doing the disliking then constantly picks at you until they find firm ground for their hatred. And then when they finally light on a good reason for hating you, they are twice as smug about it. They get downright righteous, as a matter of fact.

Whenever Hannah saw me idle, she would dream up some errand. Fetch her tea. Light a fresh candle. Get a footstool for her sore feet. Did no one around here mind how tired she was? And while I was so employed, she would tell me about Benedict.

They had been the most well-placed family in Norwich, Connecticut, before their father lost his money. Benedict had been sent to an exclusive school in Canterbury. When he was fourteen their circumstances had been reduced and he'd had to come home.

Then he'd been apprenticed to his cousins who were apothecaries. "Benedict was smart," she told me. "He opened his own apothecary shop. And he did well. He even had his own Latin motto. *Sibi totique*. Do you know what that means?"

"No, ma'am."

"Don't you know Latin?" She clucked. "Such a shame. It means 'For self and all.' Get me more tea."

"Yes, ma'am."

It was Hannah who saw to her brother's clothes, who looked after and tutored his youngest child, Henry. Hannah planned his meals, made sure his boots were polished and his house clean.

And it was Hannah who caught me listening at the door one night to Peggy and Arnold's conversation.

• • • • •

Peggy had just finished dressing for supper. Guests were coming, as usual. Arnold had wandered in from his own dressing room, and I had been dismissed. Not by word from Peggy. But by Arnold's look.

What made me linger outside the door I do not know. I suppose I wanted to hear what disgruntled words he would say to her about me. He was always complaining.

They were living in extravagant style, entertaining Philadelphia's wealthiest. And from his mumblings I learned that his business ventures were not successful, that his court-martial was again postponed, and that he was still after Congress for the money it owed him.

And he started limping again. There were days he could not walk but would sit and stare morosely in silence. The other servants could stay out of his way. But I was always underfoot. He took his chagrin out on me.

Listening at the door, I suppose I just wanted to hear what his latest complaint about me was. What I heard was nothing new.

It was *the* argument, again. The one that went on constantly between them. It was so much a part of them by now that they picked it up, like Hannah picked up her crewel work, whenever they had an idle moment together. One of them would pick up the thread where they had last left off and the other the needle.

"Cannot you see?" she asked him. "They have wronged you. You owe them nothing."

"Others have been wronged, too."

"Not like you."

" 'Tis a grim business what you ask of me, Love."

"And what they are doing—postponing the court-martial like this, making you live in limbo—is this not grimmer?"

"It is still my country. I cannot abandon it."

"It has abandoned *you*, Benedict. It has abandoned *you*. Look what the council says about you, that you massacred an entire Canadian village. And plundered Montreal. That you are taking endless supplies from the public stores. You have a *right* to such rations. You are a major general. It is your duty to entertain."

"What are you doing there? Listening? How dare you?"

I straightened up. My heart fair stopped. I turned to see Hannah. I opened my mouth to speak, reached for words, but they were off somewhere with my breath, with my thoughts, not within my grasp. Quickly I gathered myself, then spoke.

"I was waiting to see if my mistress needed me. I feared she might call."

Her eyes narrowed. "Be careful, missy. Benedict does not hold you in high esteem. He is paying too many worthless servants and is after Peggy to dismiss some." Then she walked off. My heart was beating like a rabbit being chased by Merlin through the fields.

. . . . .

As spring bloomed and the days became lovelier, Arnold's moods and his leg worsened. Hannah purchased him a microscope and an electrical machine. He would busy himself with some experiments. Benjamin Franklin had so distinguished himself, hadn't he? Wasn't he as clever as Franklin?

He was holed-up in his laboratory one morning early in May. It was a room on the first floor that Hannah had equipped for him. She came upon me in the yard where I was taking breakfast and thrust some shillings into my lap.

"Go to Robert Bell's Bookshop. Fetch a pamphlet. It is by Benjamin Franklin. It is called *The Properties and Effects of the Electrical Matter.* Can you remember that?"

"Yes, ma'am."

"Ask Bell what else he has by Franklin. Don't loiter. There is a meeting this morning of the Republican Society at James Wilson's mansion down the street. There could be trouble."

"Trouble?"

"Don't ask so many questions. The Republican Society is composed of the merchants sympathetic to Benedict. The militia has threatened to break up their meeting. They accuse the merchants and Benedict of driving up prices."

The words exploded like fireworks in the peaceful air. I knew Arnold was speculating and in league with some merchants doing the same. He made excuses for himself, saying he could see no reason why civilians who had contributed naught to the cause should profit and he should not. He was only making up for what Congress had refused to reimburse him.

I took the money and went.

I purchased the pamphlet and two more by Franklin and was returning home, coming around the corner from Arnold's house, when I heard the sound of smashing windows and shouting men. Then of a sudden came running feet behind me. I turned.

Militia. Holding forth their muskets. They near knocked me down. "What's wrong?" I shouted.

They ran by. One turned. "Best not come any closer, miss. You'll be in the line of some spirited musket fire."

"Musket fire?" I became fear-quickened. Then as he said that I heard the loud reports of muskets. I had heard musket fire before, at Camp Valley Forge and the time Henry Job had fired his fowling piece at the Hessians.

But musket fire in the streets was different. It

echoed off the buildings with a sound twice as ominous.

"Who's firing?" I called after the soldier.

"Militia. Though we didn't start it. Them inside Wilson's mansion fired first. All's we set out to do to them merchants inside Wilson's mansion was beset 'em a little. Break up their meetin'. Put 'em on notice for drivin' up prices. But some of 'em started firin' on us. So we're reinforcin' our fellow soldiers."

I was aghast. The militia was going to attack citizens! "You're going to fire on them?"

"Only returnin' their fire, miss." And he ran on.

People were coming out of their houses. More militia came by then, urging them inside. "Off the streets, miss," a militiaman said sternly.

"Yes," I promised. But I lingered in the distance as they went around the corner. Then I, too, went around.

The air in front of Wilson's mansion was filled with smoke and shouting men. A small crowd had gathered to watch the exchange and were cheering on the militiamen. Then a tall civilian came rushing through the mob. He ordered the militia to cease firing. They obeyed him.

"Put down your arms and come out," he ordered the men inside the mansion.

"Call off your men!" came the reply. "We've

got a man in here wounded and bleeding. They attacked us."

"These men say you fired first!" the civilian yelled back.

"They set upon us," came the answer, "jeering."

"Jeering is not musket fire," the civilian returned. "Now will you set down your muskets and come out?"

For a moment no one moved. The militiamen were still kneeling, ready to fire. I heard more breaking glass from the mansion. I stood, cowering behind a stone post in front of a house across the street. A woman rapped on the window, gesturing that I should come inside. But I shook my head no. Then I forgot everything for what I saw.

A terrible roar went up from the militiamen. For they'd seen him, too. Their attention was diverted from the mansion house to a figure hobbling toward them in the distance.

"Hold your fire! Men, hear me! I've led you into battle! This is General Arnold. Hold your fire, I say. We can't have civil war in Philadelphia!"

The militiamen hissed and booed. They jeered. They picked up stones and threw them at him. They shouted things, terrible things. "Speculator!" they shouted. And "Tory! Go home, Tory!" And "Be off with you, before we fix it so's you can't walk at all anymore!"

They waved their hats at him and threw more stones.

He stood for a moment, his own hat in his hands, for he'd taken it off and waved it to attract their attention. He stood leaning on a cane. He'd put on his fancy coat with the gold epaulets. I could not see that well for the smoke, but I knew the outfit would include his crimson officer's sash and his sword.

He must have run out of the house, I minded, to stop them, thinking they would obey him as they had in the past. He was their general.

But they did not. They would not. He stood there amid the smoke and clutter while their jeers pelted him worse than any stones. Two militiamen started toward him.

He drew his pistols. "Benighted fools! Stay back! Stay back, I say! I'll have you all court-martialed."

The civilian leader stood tall, coming out of the smoke then. "Sampson! Rawls! Leave him be."

The men obeyed. They saluted. "Yes, Mr. Reed."

For an awful few seconds, while the rotten egg smell of musket powder clogged my nostrils and stung my eyes, I minded then who the leader was. No militiaman but Joseph Reed, Arnold's arch-enemy. I stood transfixed as the two men stared each other down in the smoke-laden air. Then

Arnold turned away and hobbled back to his own house, head bent.

The smoke was clearing. The tension had broken. Joseph Reed gave quiet orders and the spectators dispersed. The militiamen were edging up to the front door of the mansion. The door opened. A wounded man was being carried out. He was bleeding.

It was over. The militia took charge. People opened their doors and started coming out. I picked my way up the street through the stones and broken glass, past the militiamen who were laughing and talking now that it was all over.

Past Mr. Joseph Reed. He was plainly dressed and he had a deep voice. He reached out and put a hand under my elbow so I wouldn't fall on the broken glass. "Careful, miss. Sorry about all this."

I met his eyes for a moment. They were blue and honest. He took off his tricorn and gave a little bow. I smiled. *He does not know that I work for Arnold,* I thought. I did not want him to know. I was ashamed of it of a sudden. The militiamen were all young and badly dressed. They joked and slapped each other on the back. I was hard put to keep from stopping to linger, from telling them that I had a brother with Washington's army. That I was one of them. One of the people. And not with Arnold. But I did not. I continued on home.

Chapter 22

After that it was as if we took a turn in that house from which there was no going back. The militia had not only refused to obey Arnold; they had attacked him.

The old soldier was no longer honored by his men. They had obeyed Reed instead.

This was worse to Arnold than the impending court-martial, worse than the council's charges, worse than the unfeeling citizenry in Philadelphia who blamed him for causing prices to go sky-high with his speculating.

It broke his spirit. For he was a soldier first and foremost. He barricaded the doors and windows of the house against the lovely weather. He waited, his pistols always loaded, for an attack. He complained to Congress. He read the letter to Peggy while I did her hair.

"An honest man can expect no protection from the Pennsylvania authorites. I want a guard of Continental troops. I do not trust the local militia. They have other loyalties."

The army could not spare Continentals. Congress sent the letter to Reed. Reed sent a Pennsylvania guard. Militiamen. They walked up and down in front of his house.

Arnold hated them. And they hated him.

Outside it was the most beautiful spring in years. My thoughts turned to the farm. It was in the second week of May that we took our turn for the worse. I say *we* because I became part of it simply by virtue of not having the courage to get out.

Leave. It was such a simple solution. Why did it not occur to me? Because I did not want to believe what was really happening.

It came to me only to stay. I clung to the staying. Because I knew Hannah and Arnold did not like me, and it became a challenge to stay. And because going home would be an admission of failure. Not only to my family. But to myself. I did not want to admit that I had thrown my lot in with the wrong people.

That second week in May three things happened. I was told by Peggy that she was expecting a child. Mama came to confer with Peggy about new gowns. And I found that Peggy was communicating with her old friend Andre.

Mama had been to Penn Mansion once before, and Arnold might well have been out that day, as I recollect.

But this time he was not. And this was unfortunate.

Mama and Peggy had finished their conference. The session had exhausted Peggy, and she was resting. Mama lingered in the kitchen to visit with me. I made her tea. We sat at the table, catching up.

"What have you heard from Blair?"

"He's with Washington in the Jersey highlands."

"How is the spring planting?"

"We will grow more acres of wheat than last year."

"And Persifor's labors are still pleasing to you?"

"We could not do without him."

"Is Henry Job still angry with me?"

"You should come home. He isn't angry."

"Mama, don't take up for him. Why do you always do that?"

"I take up for you with him. It causes arguments between us. Do you think I like being in the middle like this? He thinks you consider yourself too good for us anymore. He's a plain man. He feels put off by all this." She waved a hand around. "He says you put on airs."

"Mama, I don't. You know I don't. And I can't come home. What would I do there?" I was becoming agitated. There was no common ground for us to meet on anymore. And I felt both the strain and the sadness of the visit.

At that moment Arnold came into the kitchen, which was separated from the house by a dogtrot. It was a warm afternoon and he stood there in his shirt and breeches scowling at us.

"Where are the other servants?"

I stood up. "At chores. Can I help you, sir?"

"Where's Hannah?"

"Tutoring Henry."

"Cider. I require cold cider."

I went to fetch some. Mama sipped her tea. I felt the strain in the air. He was still scowling at Mama. "How did the session go with my wife?"

"We are planning her whole summer and fall wardrobe," Mama said.

"Spare no expense. She's worried she will no longer be pretty with the coming of the child."

Mama nodded. "This is when a woman is most beautiful."

He grunted. "Please to convince her of that." He took the cider from me. "How is your husband keeping these days?"

It surprised me that he should ask after Henry Job, that he even knew him.

"He is well," Mama said.

"Is he still looking to make extra money?"

Over the rim of his mug, he exchanged a special look with Mama. And it came to me then. *Of course he knows Henry Job. My stepfather spied for the Americans.* The revelation near made me swoon. But then, why did Henry Job hate him so? And object so to my working here?

"He's devoting himself to farming." Mama's words were filled with meaning.

Arnold took the meaning. "Ask him to wait on me in the near future. It will profit him. My wife and I will be interviewing some people for certain work we need done."

"He is much taken with the spring planting." Mama was putting him off.

"Ask," he said. Then he turned to go, sighted me standing there openmouthed, looked from me to Mama, then back to me again. "You two seem well acquainted."

"This is my daughter," Mama said.

He scowled. "But she has a different name."

"My first husband passed on."

His scowl deepened. For some reason he was not pleased. He was not at all pleased. "Your stepfather is Henry Job Claghorn? Why was I not told such?"

My mind was still reeling. "I thought you knew, sir."

"Well, I didn't. Why does no one tell me these

things?" He shook his head in weariness. "No mind," he told Mama. "I won't be needing Henry Job's services after all." And he strode off.

"I'm sorry, Mama," I said. "It's me. He can't abide me."

She was inspecting the tea leaves in the bottom of her cup. "No matter. I shall tell Henry Job that General Arnold asked after him. But that I said he was too busy in the fields."

I stayed confused. Why had Arnold abruptly decided he didn't want to see Henry Job when he found out the man was my stepfather? And if Henry Job knew Arnold from his spying, why did he hate him so?

Mama left and I went upstairs to check on my mistress. The day had darkened. Raindrops started to fall. A strong westerly had started blowing.

I walked quietly across Peggy's bedroom to close the window. Then I stooped to retrieve a letter that had blown onto the floor.

The signature leapt out at me.

My dear Peggy:

I am in receipt of your favor of the second and am most pleasured to extend to you my best wishes for your recent marriage and coming motherhood. I recollect with fondness our days of Meschianza. And am yet in memory of the little society of Third and Fourth Street.

Yes, I may be able to oblige you with the list of goods you wish me to find here in New York. Do send it along with the proper messenger. As for the designs of headdresses, well I must decline. From occupation as well as ill health, I have been obliged to abandon the pleasing study of what relates to the ladies. I should, however, be happy to resume it had I the same inducements as when I had the pleasure of frequenting your home in the old days. But with this war, I am afraid that is impossible.

Yes, it is true what you heard. As of the 30th of April I have been put in direct charge of British intelligence and of encouraging disaffection among the Rebels. . . .

"Who gave you the right to read that letter?"

She was sitting on the edge of the bed, roused from sleep. I turned. The missive dropped from my hand.

"I'm sorry, ma'am, I just . . ."

"You just what? You're snooping! What right have you to snoop in my things?"

"I wasn't reading it. I just closed the window sash. It's started to rain. A gust of wind must have blown it on the floor, and I picked it up."

I was a poor liar. I never had learned the art of it. I made a miserable failure of it every time I tried.

She reached out her hand for the letter, and I

gave it to her. She folded it over. "It's from Andre," she said.

"Yes, ma'am."

"Dear Andre. How I long to see him. How I long for the old days. Life has become so complicated." She looked up at me. "But you know it's from him. You read it; don't lie to me."

I said nothing. My hands were sweating. Andre had written in response to her. He had said he would be glad to resume the relationship if he had the same inducements he'd had in the old days. But of course with the war . . .

With the war and being put in direct charge of British intelligence, the letter implied, he would expect more inducement.

Inducement. He meant he needed a good reason to resume the relationship.

Dear God! She had known Andre was in charge of British intelligence! She had known he was in charge of encouraging disaffection among the Rebels. *She had written to him because she knew this!*

"Well, what are you staring at?" she demanded.

"I . . . nothing," I said. "I didn't read the letter. I speak true, ma'am."

"You speak true," she said scornfully. "My husband told me you were a little sneak. So did Hannah. I took up for you, begging him to allow me to keep you. Now what do I do?"

I said nothing.

"I'll have to tell him this," she said.

"Oh please, ma'am, don't. It means naught to me."

She yawned, stretching, the letter still in one hand. "Where is he?"

"In his laboratory."

"Tell me the truth—did you read it? Be truthful with me, and mayhap I won't see the need to tell him."

I swallowed and nodded yes, miserably.

She nodded and sighed. "I thought you did. Well, and what will you do now?"

"Now?" I asked, sounding like an idiot.

"Yes. Do you intend to tell people I am corresponding with him? When he has the ear of British General Clinton?"

Thank heaven, I found some inner resolve to draw upon. "I don't see why it would be wrong for him to send you some goods, ma'am," I said dully.

She took my measure carefully. "You are either too stupid for words, Becca Syng, or too wise," she said. "Right now I don't know which would plague me more. I only know that I want tea and something to eat. I can't bear the idea of training a new maid right now in my condition. That's the only reason I don't go right to my husband about this. But mind yourself; I'll be watching you. I'll be testing your loyalty. I know you listen at doors. I didn't know you read other people's correspondence."

Hannah, I thought, *Hannah's told her I listen at doors.* I went to get the tea.

Chapter 23

I waited for the ax to fall. It didn't. Peggy said naught to me about the incident. Arnold never spoke to me to begin with. The occasion in the kitchen had been unusual. But I was so anxious, nevertheless, that I could not eat, waiting for one of them to pounce on me like a cat pounces on a mouse.

Though she said nothing, I caught Peggy watching me cautiously several times. It was as if she were looking at me with new eyes. This made me clumsy and bumbling. She knew it, and she enjoyed my discomfort. Everything I did in the next day or so fell just short of pleasing her.

Then on the second day of her cat-and-mouse game, her attentions fell elsewhere.

People started coming to the house, all kinds of people. One at a time, a steady stream of them came. Those from a higher station in life came to the front door. One was the crockery dealer Joseph Stansbury. Others, from the inferior sort, came to the back door. But they came.

All were ushered into Arnold's laboratory instead of the parlor like proper guests. There they would stay, sequestered with both Peggy and Arnold for at least half an hour.

I was to bring a tray of tea. I was instructed to knock twice, set the tray on the floor, and not linger.

I wondered, was this the position Arnold had briefly considered Henry Job for?

On the third day after I read the note from Andre, Peggy summoned me to the laboratory. It was right after a visitor had left.

"The general would speak with you," she said.

I trembled as I knocked on the door.

"Enter."

He was seated in a chair in front of a large window. On a table in front of him were books and papers. His microscope and electrical machinery were there, too. He motioned that I should sit.

"We require an errand of you," he said.

They were both in my line of my vision. She was standing just behind him. They have become as one, I minded. They think alike and feel the same things. They read each other's minds. They were even wearing the same grave look for the occasion.

"Yes, sir."

"Do you know the shop of Joseph Stansbury? The crockery dealer?"

"Yes, sir." Something warned me not to add that I had seen Stansbury here yesterday.

"Good. We wish you to go there this afternoon. Tell him General Arnold orders him to wait upon him."

They both eyed me. I waited, pondering the soberness of the occasion. Stansbury. I searched about in my mind but could recollect nothing. Then I did. Wasn't he the dapper social climber who fussed and fawned so over anyone he thought to be wealthy? But why was I so worried? They simply wanted to order new china. Likely Arnold was humoring Peggy because she was in circumstances, trying to make her happy. I felt both relieved and disappointed.

"Tell him to come at four this afternoon," Arnold said.

I curtsied. "Yes, sir."

"One more thing. Give him this." He reached through some papers on his desk, found a list, and consulted Peggy. "Are you sure everything is here now?"

She read it quickly. "Exactly as I told you. I

only want the china in blue and white. And settings for two dozen."

"Good. I'll just add a note and ask him to bring a sample bowl." He picked up a pen, scribbled a note, and then signed it with a flourish.

My heart fair to stopped beating when I saw what signature he scrawled. I had all I could do to keep my feelings from showing on my face.

He folded the list and handed it to me. "Tell him to bring this list back with him. So we can go over it again together."

It wasn't until I was on my way, a good distance from the house, that I dared open the note and make sure my eyes had not deceived me.

They hadn't. There at the bottom of the list of china was the signature. "Monk."

My mind was churning with thoughts, all tumbling about and trying to find their right place.

I knew who Monk was only because I'd overheard their conversation. They didn't know I knew, unschooled as I was. But why did he have to sign it that way? Then I recollected all the people who had come through the house in the last few days to be handpicked for this job they had.

Likely the only way Stansbury was to know he'd been selected was by that signature. Which was why he was to return this very afternoon with the same paper. No doubt so Arnold could destroy it.

What to do? I did not know. I should go to someone, I thought, someone in a position of authority. But who? I, a servant girl, should take this list of china and go to someone in a position of authority and say that General Arnold and his wife were . . . doing what? Even I didn't know what. All I had was snatches of overheard conversation, a lively mind, and a signature on a list of china for a china merchant.

Mayhap the signature was a nickname. Who could prove anything else?

Pieces, I groaned, as I walked along in the fine May sunshine. All I have is pieces. And most of them missing. I don't even have my own missing pieces. I don't even know what I'm about half the time.

Why would anyone listen to me?

What would Elizabeth do, I asked myself. Oh, how I longed to see Elizabeth. She would know what to do. She would do something wonderful, something fine and sure and clever. Elizabeth would know what she was about.

But Elizabeth and Neddy had set up house-keeping in Reading. I could talk to Coxie, of course. But she was a slave. Henry Job? He'd been a spy for the Americans. He would understand. But I hadn't spoken to him in months. And what did I have to tell him, truly?

My friend Ann Darragh's mother came to

mind. There, too, I hadn't seen Ann in months. I was not even sure if she and her family were still in town. And Mrs. Darragh was a woman of action. She would do something, yes, but what? Suppose all my fears were fanciful? All I would do was succeed in losing my position.

All at once I came to a halt, looked up, and saw the sign overhead. Joseph Stansbury, Fine China.

It hung above me all lettered in gold, swinging in the fine May breeze. I hesitated. Either I went in and delivered my message, or I could not go back and work for Peggy this day.

Then another thought occurred to me. Mayhap Peggy was testing me with this errand. Hadn't she warned me about that? That was why they had both been so solemn about sending me to deliver a list of china. A simple errand. Mayhap Arnold signed it Monk because they knew I'd overhead them that night. And now they were testing me. Mayhap they wanted rid of me, so they could go about their foul work, whatever it was.

Well, I would show them. I would deliver the message. And say nothing to anybody. If they dismissed me, how could I truly find out what they were about? If I stayed, I would be in a position to discover more.

I went into the shop.

It was empty. Stansbury sat on a high stool

behind the counter scribbling. And then it came back to me, too late. Too late to turn and leave, for the bell on the door had already tinkled and he looked up and smiled.

Seeing his long, thin face, I recollected him. He wrote comic verses. He had been at the Shippen house one time, delivering some samples of china, and Peggy had introduced him to Andre, who was a fine hand at writing poetry. Stansbury and Andre had gotten on, amusing a bevy of Peggy's friends with their recitations.

Stansbury had been born and educated in England.

He hid his papers under the counter. "May I be of assistance?"

I stood there like our cow Opal, not moving.

"Well, miss? Do you require help?"

I walked across the floorboards and handed him the note. He read it and smiled. "Tell Mrs. Arnold she has made a most elegant and dependable selection," he said. "Tell the general I shall be there at four."

I nodded. My throat was dry. *He knows Andre,* was all I could think. I stared at him dumbly, then remembered the rest of my mission. "General Arnold says you are to return the note to him."

"I shall do it." He smiled and stood up. He was enormously gratified, as if he had won some game of chance. "Tell the general I shall be there."

I said I would and went out the door.

I went home and was told by Peggy to put her room in order, to dust and polish, change the linens on her bed. "It's a pigsty," she said. "And dust my curio shelves."

There was a bad feeling in my innards. And something was eating away at the back of my mind like a mouse gnawing at a piece of cheese.

The world was off center. Somehow, somewhere along the line in the last few months, it was as if it had tilted on its axis, so gently that it was scarcely perceptible.

But I knew something was wrong. It was as if the cast in the sunlight itself had changed.

For one thing, at the moment the house was too quiet. Even Hannah was out with little Henry; making calls, Peggy had said. Hannah hated making calls. Peggy had also said most of the servants had been given the afternoon off. Two were preparing supper in the kitchen.

"We don't wish to be disturbed," Peggy said.

I was dusting the curios on the shelves in her bedroom when I heard the front door clapper. I went into the upstairs hall and heard Peggy's quick footsteps downstairs, heard the door open, heard her greet Stansbury, then lead him to the back of the house to the laboratory.

I was not thinking. My thoughts had failed me. I no longer trusted them. I was going on instinct.

I took off my shoes and crept downstairs.

The carpeting on the hall floor had been picked up with the spring weather and was outside being aired out. Arnold was especially protective of the parquet floors. I could say that's why I'd taken my shoes off if the servants asked. I went quickly out back to the kitchen and, as I'd done so many times in the last two days, prepared a tray of tea and cakes. The water was boiling on the hearth. It took only a minute. The servants were not suspicious. They didn't ask why I was not wearing shoes.

But I had to cover myself. Peggy had not told me *not* to bring tea.

I hovered, my heart beating rapidly, my palms sweating, listening to the voices behind the laboratory door.

They were talking about matters in general, the beautiful weather, Peggy's selection of china. Then there was a silence.

"Mr. Stansbury." General Arnold dropped his deep voice into the silence like stones into a well. "I know you signed an oath of allegiance to Pennsylvania. I also know this was done simply to keep you from being sent into exile. Am I right, sir, in thinking your sentiments are with your mother country?"

"You are right, General."

Like stones into a well Arnold's words made ripples that reached wider and wider. "I can't tell you how I abhor this separation of America from Great Britain. It is a measure that is ruinous to us both. May I have your solemn oath of secrecy, sir, for what I am about to say?"

"You have it, sir."

"Very well. I intend to offer my services to the commander in chief of the British forces in any way that would most effectively restore the former government and destroy the usurped authority of Congress, either by immediately joining the British army or by cooperating on some concerted plan with Sir Henry Clinton."

"I congratulate you, General, on your clear thinking."

"I need more than congratulations from you. I . . . we need help."

"And how may I be of assistance?"

"We need someone to slip through the American and British lines and call on Captain Andre. He is in charge of British intelligence. But we need your assurance that nothing will be put in writing. And if you are questioned, you are to swear you are on a simple business mission."

I closed my eyes. I felt myself swoon. I clutched the tray, which was getting heavy in my hands, and leaned against the wall. My stockinged foot slipped on the polished parquet floor and I near fell. I recovered myself, but not before the lid from the silver sugar bowl fell onto the tray.

I gasped and started moving away. Too late. The door opened.

Peggy stood there. I was a distance from the door by then, in the middle of the hall.

"I told you we were not to be disturbed!"

"I brought tea, ma'am. As I always do when you interview people."

"You were told to stay upstairs." Her voice was like ice.

Arnold came to stand behind her. "What is it?"

"Becca. She was bringing tea. I told her we were not to be disturbed."

He stepped in front of Peggy and came into the hall. He towered over me, though he was not that tall. "Can't you learn to obey your mistress?"

"I'm sorry, sir. I meant no harm."

"My sister Hannah told me you listen at doors." He whirled on Peggy. "I told you to get rid of this girl, didn't I?" He looked stricken. He whirled back to me. He ran his hand through his hair. Then he pointed to the dining room. "Go in there and wait for us," he ordered. "Don't move from that room. Don't go out of this house."

"Yes, sir." I bobbed a little curtsy, tea tray and all, and went down the hall to the dining room.

"She's such a little simpleton," I heard Peggy say as they headed back in the laboratory. "I don't think she heard anything, Benedict, honestly."

"I don't care. She goes. This afternoon," he said angrily.

"But how can we sleep nights then, if she *did* hear anything?"

The door closed. But not before I heard him say something about her not worrying. He would see to me. Proper.

Chapter 24

*I*t was such a lovely May afternoon. The air that drifted in the windows was filled with the sounds and scents of spring. How could anything so dolorous be going on in this house?

I sat at the polished dining room table. Sunshine shone on the silver candlesticks, danced on the glass face of the tall case clock that quietly ticked away the minutes of my life.

What would Arnold do to me? What would I do? What would I say?

I thought they would never come out. I wanted it over with. The man could be vile when he chose to. I had heard the way he dealt with servants who displeased him. I trembled, waiting.

No doubt he will dismiss me, I thought. That was the least of my worries. Surely he could do more. He was still a general, after all.

And then the whole dark truth of the matter came over me, wave after buffeting wave, assaulting my senses.

Arnold was going to go over to the other side! All the signs had been there for weeks now. I had chosen to ignore them. I had chosen not to believe them. But they stood out now, clear as signposts.

Arnold was going to be a turncoat. I had heard it with my own ears. What would I do? I had to do something!

And then it came to me. First I would swear that I had heard nothing. They could torture me and I would not admit I'd heard a word. Then I'd ask to go home.

Once home, I'd go to Henry Job and tell him everything. Never mind that we hadn't been speaking. This problem would wash all that away. He would know the right way to get the information to Washington. Yes, that was what I would do. I breathed a sigh of relief and waited.

* * * * *

"What did you hear?"

"Nothing."

He stood across the long polished table from me. Peggy sank down in a chair. She looked spent. She poured herself tea from the pot on the tray. It was cold, but she seemed not to care.

"You weren't listening at the door?"

"I was bringing tea, sir. I was not at the door.

I was in the hall." They could put hot coals on my eyelids, or whatever they did to spies, and I would not tell.

"That's true, Benedict," Peggy said wearily.

"If you weren't skulking at the door, why aren't you wearing shoes?"

"The carpet was picked up. I know how you don't like scratches on the floor."

His eyes narrowed. Oh, his look could wither the leaves from a tree! My heart was beating so. I felt as if he could see it through the thin cotton of my summer chemise.

"My sister caught you listening at doors before."

"Only to see if my mistress needed me, sir."

"I don't believe you."

I said nothing.

"You will leave here this day. You are to pack your things and go."

"Yes, sir." I moved to walk away.

"Just a minute!" His voice cracked at me like a whip.

I froze.

"Do you know who your stepfather is?"

I ran my tongue along my lips. They were dry, as if I'd been crossing some desert without water for days. "Sir?"

"Your stepfather, Henry Job. How do you think I made his acquaintance?"

"I haven't any notion, sir."

"He's a spy. Did you know that?"

"I know nothing about that, sir." Something warned me not to admit to the knowing.

"He has spied for Washington. And . . . others. I met him at Camp Valley Forge."

Something was coming. I could feel it, awful in its power, a rushing darkness.

"He spied for Washington. But he did more than that. Shall I tell you what he did?"

"You're going to tell me anyway, sir."

"Don't be saucy. This is not the time, miss. Your stepfather is a double agent. Do you know what that is?"

Where had I heard the word? I could not recollect. So many words I had heard over the years. All to do with this grievous war. New words. They made them up as they went along, it seemed, to cover over the awful things people were doing to one another. As if giving names to the terrible things made them familiar to us. I had heard of a double agent, yes. But it had never had meaning for me.

"Answer me!" Arnold slapped the table with an open palm.

I jumped. "No, sir, I don't know what it is."

"A double agent spies for both sides. For money. Lots of money. We have strong suspicions that is what he's been doing. Washington let him keep spying because he could use him to plant false papers."

We, I thought. Does he still think himself an independence man, then? Doesn't the man mind what he's about to do?

Arnold was enormously pleased with himself now. He clasped his hands behind his back and commenced to pace up and down, limping as he did so. I am sure he was acting as if he were reprimanding a disorderly soldier who served under him.

"Henry Job Claghorn." He laughed. "We all knew what he was. If you're sensible of what they're about, you can use them to your advantage, these scurrilous dogs. Why do you think your mama said he wouldn't come when I asked for him?"

"I'm sure Mama knows nothing about his activities, sir," I pleaded. "My brother is with Washington. Mama would never countenance such."

Then another thought came to him. "How did he allow you to work here? In this house? Did he plant you here?"

My heart thumped. "No, sir. He didn't want me here. He argued with Mama over it. We still don't speak about the matter. It's why I haven't been home in months. He hates you, sir." There, let him chew on that for a while.

"Hates me, does he?" He laughed, throwing back his head. "I wager he hates me. He *fears* me! Do you know why? Because as a general in Washington's army, I can search him out and bring him in anytime I wish. And have him hanged for what he is!"

Hanged. The awful word lingered in the room. I saw it made Peggy uncomfortable.

"If you repeat anything you heard in this house, nothing you say will be believed. Because you are Henry Job's stepdaughter. There is a taint on you. But try"—and he whirled on me—"try and I will hang him." He stopped pacing to peer at me hard. "Do you understand?"

"Yes, sir." I looked across the small distance that separated us, and I did understand. I looked into the man's face, into his eyes. And I saw evil there. I felt evil in the room, something cold and damp slithering around my ankles. And I knew then that this was a house of evil. A bad place, an unholy place. Why hadn't I been sensible of it before? I needed to get out. Now.

"May I go now, sir?"

"No. There is more. You are to go straight home. I will ask my man to drive you there. And you are to stay there on that farm. And not come back into this city for a year. I am putting a parole on you, like the British put on Peggy's father. If you are seen in the city, you will be arrested. Do you hear?"

"Yes, sir."

"And if you tell a soul anything, Henry Job will not only be brought to the gallows, his farm will be confiscated. Do you understand the conditions?"

I said I did.

"Have you anything to add, Peggy?" he asked.

She stood up, slowly, laboriously. "You have brought this on yourself, Becca. I will be sorry to lose you. You have served me well."

For a moment I wanted to cry. I wished she would not be kind to me now. I preferred Arnold's anger.

"Be mindful of what my husband says. He is nobody's fool. And he will always be in a position to carry out his threats."

"Yes, ma'am," I said. I knew what she was telling me. That it didn't matter what side Arnold came down on. Henry Job was a double agent. Even if Arnold went with the British, Arnold could get him.

Both sides wanted to hang him.

"My husband will pay you your wages." She walked to the door and turned. "Well, you've finished yourself now, Becca," she said, "haven't you?"

Chapter 25

*B*efore I left, Arnold did two things. He counted out the silver he owed me. Some of it was payment for Mama. "Tell her that her services will no longer be needed," he said.

I felt struck in the face. I'd ruined things for Mama.

"Wait." For I'd turned to go. He was writing out a paper. He finished, signed it with a flourish, and handed it to me. "Your parole papers. Keep them. Study them. You are under surveillance. Be mindful of it, always."

Tears blinded my eyes as I tried to read the paper. My mind was numb. But I saw his signature on the bottom. "Major General Benedict Arnold, Military Commander of Philadelphia, under the Commander in Chief of the Army of the United States, General George Washington."

I felt ashamed. Somehow I found my way out of the house.

I stayed benumbed as we drove out of the city. Then as we made our way down Second Street, I sighted the pawnshop. "Stop, please," I said to Arnold's nigra. His name was Clayton.

He did so, and I jumped down and ran to the pawnshop, praying it wasn't closed. The door was locked. I peered inside. The man was there. I rapped on the door sharply.

He shot the bolt free. "Please, sir. I'm on my way out of the city. I won't be back for a year. It'll just take a moment. I know what it is that I want."

He let me in. "The silver inkstand? You had it in the window. It has the initials P.S. on it. Did you sell it?"

He searched my face. He was an elderly man, and I could see he did not always have a clear recollection of things.

"You're the lass 'twas here months ago."

"Yes, did you sell it?"

"No. It's over here." He went behind the counter and fumbled around. *Oh please*, I prayed, *find it. Please!*

He found it, lifted it from a dark place, brushed it off, and held it in his hands. "Handsome, isn't it, lass?"

"Yes. Wrap it, please. I wish to take it."

"Ah, you have excellent taste." He went about finding wrappings. I counted my money out, ten pounds sterling. I had it in the little drawstring bag I always kept my money in.

I'd been saving my pay since last September. I had more than enough. I gave it to the man.

"This will grace a fine home," he said.

"Yes."

"Bless you."

"Thank you, sir." I ran out to get into the wagon.

. . . . .

Merlin saw me first. He was in the field with Persifor. And he came bounding out to the road to meet the wagon.

I jumped down. "Merlin!"

He was getting old. He did not jump quite so high anymore. But his kisses were still as wet and friendly. I greeted him and stood looking around.

Everything was so green. It fair hurt to look. Stretches of green fields lay shimmering in the sun. The soil was so rich and lustrous, the barns so stark in their whiteness, and the house newly painted, white too, its shutters a rusty red. Everything shone. I had forgotten how beautiful it was. I heaved a great sigh.

"You's home," Clayton said.

"Yes."

He helped me down with my trunk. I invited him in for a cup of cool cider. He declined but looked longingly at the well. I told him to help himself to some water. And his horse.

"Can I offer you some food before the drive back?" I asked.

"No."

I stood watching him sip the water.

"This be a nice place," he said, looking around.

"Yes."

"You be lucky. Ain't so nice back there. Heard you ain't gonna be 'round no more."

"How did you hear?"

"Alla servants know. They knows everythin'." He met my eyes and nodded his head. "You better off outa there," he said. "Doan come back if'n you kin help it."

How much did they know? I stiffened. "Thank you, Clayton. Thank you for your concern. You'd best be going so's you can get back before dark."

He carried my trunk down the path to the house, set it on the ground, bowed, and left. I stood looking around. It was so quiet. Off in the distance I saw Opal in the fields with the other cows. And it came to me then that something was wrong.

It was too quiet.

The quietness was eerie, and it had a warning about it. "Mama?" I called out. "Papa Henry?"

"Hello." Persifor came around the corner of the house from the barn. He took off his hat and wiped his face with a kerchief. "We weren't expecting you."

"Well, I'm home."

He looked at the trunk at my feet. "I see. For good?"

I colored. "For now, if it's any of your business."

"Still full of vinegar, I see."

"Where's my mother and Henry Job?"

He scowled and looked at some chickens scratching around his feet. "Your mama is off in the city. Will be home shortly. Understand she had a fitting at the Shippens' this afternoon."

I felt something bittersweet in back of my throat. "And Henry Job?"

He raised his eyes to me. "Oh, that's right, your mother didn't have time to tell you."

"Tell me what? What's going on around here, Persifor Frazor? What's to tell?"

He said it plain and soft. "Henry Job lit off a few days ago."

"What do you mean 'lit off'?"

He shrugged. "He just up and left. Packed some things. Wouldn't tell your mama or me where he was off to. Said it was business. Said I should tend to the planting."

"When did he go?"

"Let's see." And quietly, he counted back. "Three days ago. That's right. Nigh onto three days."

Three days ago. Though it seemed like a year by now, it had only been three days since I'd sat with Mama in Arnold's kitchen and taken tea. And he'd come in and asked her to have Henry Job wait on him. Then changed his mind.

"Do you have any idea where he went?" I asked Persifor.

"No, and that's what's so strange," he said. "We've become close. He confides in me. But he said nary a word this time. Was downright close-mouthed, matter of fact. I speculate it's something urgent."

"Urgent?"

"Yes. He gave me instructions about the farm. Asked me to look out for your mother. It sounded to me—though mind you, I haven't told your mother anything—it sounded to me like he wasn't going to be back for a long time."

I went upstairs to my commodious summer bedroom. It was sparkling clean. A neat quilt was on the bed, the linen was fresh. A bowl of flowers was on the small stand. The curtains were crisp and white and lifted with the slight breeze. The floorboards, wide and uneven, were spotless.

My china bowl and pitcher sat shining clean with a piece of scented soap and a clean piece of flannel next to them. I looked around at the stark whitewashed walls, the blanket folded across the chest at the foot of the bed, the framed sampler I'd done as a child on the wall, the bright rag rugs on the floor.

The peace of the place wrapped itself around me. And I minded the first day I'd walked into the Shippen house so long ago. And how the house had seemed to embrace me. How elegant it had seemed. What a child I had been!

I knew now that houses didn't make you elegant. Elegance was something you built inside yourself. Inside, where no one could touch you, you built commodious rooms, stairways that reached up. You built shining windows to let in the sunlight. And to look out on the world. And you furnished those rooms as you went along with strong pieces of yourself. Only first you had to find the pieces.

I sat down on the edge of the bed thinking.

Henry Job had run away. Mama did not know it. Persifor suspected something, but he could not possibly perceive the truth. Only I knew the truth.

Mama had told Henry Job that General Arnold asked after him. That was all my stepfather needed to put the fear of the Lord into him. He'd thought Arnold had caught up with him and he would be hanged as a double agent.

I fell back on the bed, sorting it out. Henry

Job, who had warned me not to dishonor myself, had done just that. Don't sell pieces of yourself off, he'd told me. Yet he did. What brought him to it? He'd hated the British—I know he did. But what brought anybody to do anything? Look at Arnold. He'd been an American hero.

Arnold and Henry Job were alike, then. Money had ruined the high-placed and the lowly. I lay staring at the beams that crisscrossed the low ceiling. Henry Job was gone. For a moment, I took heart. He would not return; I was sure of it. So there was no danger to him then. So couldn't I tell someone now what I knew? Persifor? Or Blair? Or Elizabeth? I could write to Elizabeth. Or what about Joseph Reed? He'd looked at me so kindly in the street that day.

Then a darkness fell over me. I could not tell. It went further than Henry Job. Arnold had said they would confiscate the farm. But even were I willing to sacrifice the farm, Arnold had said no one would believe me. Because I was the step-daughter of a double agent. I felt the dread, the shame of it.

Arnold, for all his talk of treason, was still a general in Washington's army. Anything I tried would have to be done *before* he committed his act of treason, to prevent it.

And before, he was still a general in Washington's army. And he could discredit me.

Oh, dear God. I rolled over and gazed out the open windows at the endless stretches of green, which had seemed so beautiful to me only a few minutes before. It was so quiet here. No city sounds, no arguing servants, no voices below the windows. I started to cry. I cried out all the fear that had gripped me for the last three days. I cried for Philadelphia, for what I had lost—my position, earning money, being on my own. *How can I ever live here again,* I asked myself. *What will I do all day? This place is my prison now.*

Then I heard Peggy's voice. "Well, you've finished yourself now, Becca, haven't you?"

Epilogue

*M*ove over, Opal, move over. It's cold and I want to get this milking over with." I set my pail down and blew on my hands. Persifor milked the other cows, but I always milked Opal. She'd hit Persifor in the head with her tail too many times. He was glad to have me do it.

I started milking, talking to her at the same time. "Today I'm going to finish telling you the story about General Arnold and Major John Andre, Opal. I've been saving it up to tell you. Wanted to see how it would turn out. Now stop that moving and settle down."

My voice becalmed her. "I've told you everything else that happened to me in Philadelphia. And why I came home. But we just found out the other day that Peggy and Benedict Arnold sailed for London on the fifteenth of last month. Picture it! Peggy Shippen Arnold in London!

"Here's the way it went, Opal. You mind, I told you how Arnold wanted to go over to the British? Well, nothing happened for a year after he got Stansbury to call on Andre. And then everything happened at once.

"First off, Arnold finally got his court-martial. In December of '79. At Morristown in the Jerseys. Blair was there, and he wrote to us how Arnold was acquitted on all counts but two. And for those two Washington wrote him a formal letter of reprimand. You ask me, Opal, I think Washington was too good to that man.

"Well, it isn't for me to say, is it? Anyway, the spring of '80 was bad for the independence people. The British were winning all kinds of victories in the south. You recollect how Persifor brooded over that. It was about the time I commenced milking you. He said he couldn't abide how you plagued him with your tail. But I think he was ornery because of the British winning all those battles.

"Never mind. It's better this way, with me milking you. You and I get on like Andre, Arnold, and Peggy got on. They were sending messages back and forth all along. After it was all over, Blair wrote that they had code books and invisible ink and everything.

"You know what else, Opal? Blair knew Henry Job was spying for the Americans. Saw him in Camp Valley Forge. Only after the war ended did Blair find out he was a double agent. And Blair said one of the things Henry Job did was to tell the British the Americans finally had invisible ink to write their spy messages with.

"But listen, in the summer of '80, Arnold asked Washington for a new command. Washington gave him the whole left wing of the army. Well, Arnold didn't fancy that. He wanted command of West Point. So there goes old Washington giving it to him.

"Then in fall of '80 I guess Arnold decided it was time to give Andre the plans to West Point. So they set up a meeting. But it didn't work. You have to be careful, I suppose, doing things like that. It's not the kind of thing you do lightly. It's no mean feat. Andre was a major by then.

"Well, finally they got Andre on this British sloop of war. That's a boat, Opal. They got it on the Hudson. And Arnold was supposed to get somebody to row him out to it to meet Andre and give him the plans. But things didn't go right. Do they ever? Look at the way Persifor and I planned to marry for the last year. And something always happened, what with Mama sickly and Henry Job never coming back, and then us hearing he was dead, and Persifor having to go and fetch him.

"But that's yesterday's kettle of fish, as Mama says. We'll be married in the spring. But don't you worry, Opal, I'll still be milking you. I won't let him do it.

"Where was I? You see what you did? Got me

all off course. Oh yes, Andre was on that boat. Don't ask me what all happened, but Arnold couldn't get out to him, so they rowed Andre ashore. And they met in some farmhouse. Arnold gave Andre the plans for West Point. Blair said Andre put them inside his hose.

"Then some nervous Nellie of an officer fired from shore on the sloop and Andre couldn't get back to his lines. So he had to go on horseback. That meant he had to wear a disguise. And you know what that means, Opal. That if he got caught, he'd be taken as a spy.

"Well, Opal, Andre got caught. By some New York militiamen. They were sharp and smart and didn't believe he was John Anderson or whatever he called himself, and they made him take off his clothes and searched him. They found those plans, Opal. Good for us. They arrested him, too.

"They say it broke Washington's heart that Arnold betrayed him, Opal. You know how Mama's heart was broken when Henry Job never came home? And she thought he left her? That happens to people sometimes.

"Well, there was Washington on his way to West Point to inspect fortifications and to meet with the Arnolds. You know Blair was with him. An aide to Washington now, fancy that, Opal. Blair said that Washington got to the place and Arnold wasn't there. His aide said he had to rush away on business.

"Business! With Washington coming! What could be more important business? Well, he had business, all right. They found out later that when he was at breakfast, a messenger came and told him Andre was captured. What does he do? Runs upstairs to tell Peggy what happened, is what. Then jumps on a horse, rides to the river, gets on a barge, and runs off, leaving Peggy to face the music.

"Washington comes to the mansion—oh yes, it was a mansion, Opal, what else did you expect? He's told Peggy is indisposed. And he and his aides inspect the fortifications all day. And Blair said the place wasn't in such good repair, I can tell you that, Opal. Then, as Washington is getting dressed for supper, Hamilton—you recollect him, he was here once—Hamilton and Lafayette rush in and tell him they've just learned that Arnold betrayed them.

"What does Washington do, then? Goes up to Peggy's private chamber. Because she was holed up in there. Took Hamilton and Blair with him so it would be properlike. And there is Peggy, still in bed, her gown *half-open,* Blair wrote, in hysterics. Blair wanted to know if we would believe such a thing. Well, I'd believe it! She's screaming and yelling and saying that the spirits carried her husband away and put hot irons in his head. And that Washington and his men wanted to kill her little Edward. He was six months old then.

"Poor Washington. Blair said he didn't know

what all to do. I could have told him. I've seen those hysterics of hers. I wonder if she threw things at them. Do you suppose?

"Well, anyway, they were taken in by her. Hamilton said she exhibited all the sweetness of beauty, all the loveliness of innocence, and all the tenderness of a wife and mother. Do you believe it, Opal? I could have just spit when I read that in Blair's letter. Although, of course, I can never tell him what I know about her.

"Old Washington said any woman who got herself in such a state surely must be innocent. Which just goes to show you what a passel of fools all men are, Opal, be they generals or not. If you ask me, somebody ought to see to it they get some women officers in that army. So Washington allows her to go back to Philadelphia to her family.

"Arnold? He joined the British army under Clinton. They hanged Andre. Blair was there, too. He said Andre behaved with the utmost gentility. That he was suave and debonair and kind to his captors. You know what he did on the morning he was hanged? Ate his breakfast and drew a sketch of himself. That's right, Opal. Did you ever hear of such?

"Blair said he went to the gallows dressed like a gallant. I recollect how he used to dress. Blair said he had white ruffles at his throat and that he bowed to the officers and unbuttoned his own shirt collar and handed his hat to his servant. And that all the men who got to know him and were in attendance cried for him.

"Blair didn't say so, but I think he cried, too, Opal. He said they weren't angry at Andre. He was doing his duty. They wanted Arnold. But they couldn't catch him."

I picked up the pail of milk. "I'm going on in now. Oh yes, one more thing I forgot to tell you. Before they hanged Andre, he blindfolded himself. Wouldn't take any help. Doesn't that beat all? Kind of gives me the shivers. Being that I knew him and all. All right, Opal, you've been a good girl. I'm going to write to Blair and tell him so."

I carried the pail of milk to the springhouse. Persifor was there, pouring the milk from the other cows into containers to take to Philadelphia. He would go this day to market, with eggs and butter and cheese.

He kissed my cheek lightly. "Want to come with me today?"

I marveled at the pleasure I got just from the sight of him. He was the sun in a room. And when he went away, the place was dark. "No, I've work to do." A year ago it was a lie. I could never tell him why for a year I refused to go back to the city. He suspected something, I know. Even after my parole was up last summer, I declined to go to the city. Too hot, I told him and Mama.

"Mayhap someday you'll tell me the real reason," Persifor had said. But he never pushed me.

I only started going back to the city in the fall of '80, when word came to us of Arnold's treason. Strange, that was about the time Peggy came home to her family. But I never saw her. I still have my parole papers well hidden away. I don't know why I keep them.

"How did you sleep?" Persifor asked.

"Well. But I'd sleep better knowing you were as snug in the house as I."

An old argument. Ever since Henry Job had left he'd removed himself to a log cabin addition he'd built onto the barn.

"I'm perfectly comfortable in the cabin with Samuel." Samuel was our hired man now. As Persifor had been Henry Job's. "That place is warm. I built it myself. Chinked those logs good."

"Still, I wish you'd sleep in the house. The log cabin puts me in mind too much of a dependency. And you're nobody's servant."

"Where we sleep doesn't make us a servant. It didn't make you one. I don't sleep in the house because it wouldn't be seemly."

"How can you worry about seemly? Nothing's been seemly since the war."

"In New England, we abide by it. Even with the war. Of course, I know they don't in Philadelphia."

Our eyes met. "Don't make this a New England and Philadelphia thing," I said.

"But that's what it is, don't you see?"

We both burst into laughter. Then I sighed. Were we to become, then, like Henry Job and Mama? No. Persifor had faith in himself. And there was no darkness about him. He had built plenty of large windows inside himself, so he could not only look out at the world but let the light in. And I had no pretensions of elegance.

Still, for all the faith he had in himself and what he'd accomplished with the farm, he did not put himself forward. "We'll have to consult with Blair on that," he would say when Mama or I suggested some new method of farming, some new venture for bringing in money. "Now that Henry Job is gone, we'll ask what Blair wants done."

He wrote to Blair often, keeping him advised of things. He kept strict accounts to show him. The funny thing was, Blair had never liked farming. He gave Persifor a free hand. Blair wrote that when he does come home he'd like to give Persifor a major share in the farm. That he's saved his back pay and bought shares in a merchant ship. He said that if we're going to ship wheat and other produce out of the port of Philadelphia, he might as well be the merchant doing the shipping.

Blair is still with Washington. The fighting ended last fall, when Cornwallis surrendered to

Washington at Yorktown. But Blair is not yet mustered out. The peace has not been signed.

"I'd better go and make breakfast for Mama," I said.

A round sun was polishing the grayness in the east with red as I walked on the frozen path to the house. And I minded a day, so long ago, when I'd walked to the house after milking to have Mama tell me I was going to the city that day to meet a girl named Peggy Shippen.

So long ago! Near four years now. How things had changed. Not only with Peggy, but with us.

In the months after Henry Job left, Mama gave in to her sore bones and took to her bed. Her rheumatism was just besting her, she'd said. But I knew it was because she couldn't abide the shame.

She thought Henry Job had left her for good.

Times I wanted to tell her the truth. How many nights I lay awake, pondering on whether it would cause her more shame to know that he'd left for good or that he had spied against the army her son was serving in.

I could have told her the truth, leaving my own part in it out. But I decided not to. Every once in a while she had a faint glimmer of hope. "He may still come home yet," she would say. And I would say yes, of course. That was before he was found dead on a deserted road just outside Philadelphia in October of '80.

Right after Arnold's treason came to light.

After that her hope took another form. "I'm sure he was coming home to me when he was killed," she'd say.

I gave her that, too. "I'm sure he was, Mama." I knew he was coming home, yes, but only because Arnold had now gone over to the British. And the British were far from Philadelphia.

I know she harbored the secret belief that he was killed on a spying mission for Washington. Though she never confided to me about his being an American spy.

We both had secrets from one another, me and Mama. And we kept our secrets well. One thing I've learned, and I didn't have to go into the city to learn it.

Mothers and daughters have to have secrets from one another, once the daughter is grown. Because they are of two different times. And they can no more understand each other, acting out of the influence of those times, than the times can mesh. But that doesn't mean they can't love one another.

Sometimes it comes hard to me that the farm is beautiful because of what Henry Job did, because he got the money to improve it from being a double agent. I'd always known there was some darkness in the man. Even when Elizabeth told me he was a spy for the Americans, I couldn't find the light in him. But I'll never tell anyone what he did. The way I see it, the dead are dead. And their secrets should go with them to the grave.

Besides, I've enough to dwell on. I do the cooking and keep house. Mama still does a little sewing. Betimes a fancy dress for a special client. I do the consultations. Her sewing keeps her going.

I do weaving, too. Persifor set up a large loom for me in Henry Job's old room. I weave and dye my own fabric and sell it in the city.

When I came home from Philadelphia, near three years ago now, I found that Persifor had collected all the things from the wild I needed for dyeing. He had pails of bloodroot, madder, and cranberry for red; goldenrod and sunflowers for yellow; bittersweet and alder for orange; adder's tongue, mint, and copperas for green; huckleberry for purple; spruce bark and toadflax for brown. I think it was the sight of everything in the dyeing shed that made me know I loved him.

I went into the house to make Mama's breakfast. And then I couldn't stop thinking about Andre. I suppose talking to Opal about him brought it all back. I could see him, clear as yesterday, the way he'd looked the first time I'd seen him, that morning he came to the bottom of the stairs to take Peggy's hand.

Where do the dead go? What do they leave us? Do we learn from them? I minded Mama's first commandment: Nothing we learn is lost to us.

What had I learned? Mama made arrangements for me to go to the Shippens' so I could become finished.

I scowled, laying strips of bacon in the pan over the hearth.

I learned that we all have missing pieces. Some people just look in the wrong places for them. Like Henry Job. And Arnold. I learned that the parts of us that are missing are not things. No, not even my silver inkstand that Mama so loves was one of my missing pieces.

They aren't people either, though we can find them by knowing some people. They are *parts of ourselves* that we must find and make strong and use to furnish that elegant house inside us.

I learned that, as happened with Peggy, what we become when we find our missing pieces is not always so nice.

I learned that if you have money you can buy yourself out of almost any dolorous situation, as I did with Henry Job. But that sometimes, even if you have the money, as Andre did, you can't.

I turned the bacon in the pan, reached for some eggs. Was that enough learning for a while?

No, there was one more thing. I learned it is best not to listen at doors. Best not to know some things. For the knowing, betimes, can hurt you.

I don't listen at doors anymore.

But every day in my life, though I'm not listening, I hear Arnold talking. I hear his deep voice dropping into my silence, like stones into a well.

"I intend to offer my services to the commander in chief of the British forces in any way that would most effectively restore the former government and destroy the usurped authority of Congress."

I suppose I shall hear it until I die.

And at night, just before I close my eyes, when I am in that limbo of half sleep, I see Peggy. I hear her gown rustling. And I hear her voice. "Well, you've finished yourself now, Becca, haven't you?"

And even half asleep, I murmur, "No, Peggy, no. Because there's one thing I've learned above all. No one is ever finished. Are you?"

Author's Note

$\mathcal{F}$inishing *Becca* is based on the story of Peggy Shippen and Benedict Arnold. For me, it is a story worth telling—the teenaged Philadelphia beauty and the twice-wounded Revolutionary War hero who was nineteen years her senior and who, upon meeting and marrying her, decided to betray his country.

There are many, of course, who proclaim Peggy Shippen's innocence in Arnold's treason. In doing research I came upon voices from both camps. In Lewis Burd Walker's article in *The Pennsylvania Magazine of History and Biography* entitled "Life of Margaret Shippen, Wife of Benedict Arnold," written in 1900, Walker paints Peggy as demure, loving, industrious, and long-suffering. He seems to establish her loyalty to the American cause simply by stating that none of the Shippen girls attended the *Meschianza*. As if that mere fact could establish loyalty.

They did not attend because the Quaker committee (the Society of Friends) visited their father and, as Walker admits in his article, "persuaded him that it would be by no means seemly that his daughters should appear in public in the Turkish dresses designed for the occasion."

In doing research one must consider the source. Lewis *Burd* Walker? Wasn't Elizabeth's Neddy's last name *Burd*? Likely Walker is a descendant, and as such has the family honor to uphold. Or it could be simply that the evidence of Peggy's complicity hadn't yet come to light.

In the October 1967 issue of *American Heritage*, an article by James Thomas Flexner entitled "Benedict Arnold: How the Traitor Was Unmasked" tells us: "That Peggy had been in the plot from the start and may even have instigated it was, indeed, to remain a secret until the relevant British headquarters' papers were made public in the 1930s."

Most of my other sources also lay blame at Peggy's feet for this horrendous act of treason, which was hatched within a month of their marriage.

In Flexner's *The Traitor and the Spy*, he lays the story out for us: "Now that Benedict Arnold and Peggy Shippen were together, treason flowered almost instantly; the bride was in the plot from the first."

Whenever there is controversy in historical matters, historical novelists have to come down on one side or the other. We novelists take risks when we make such decisions. We incur the wrath of some. But I consider this my job.

I also consider it my obligation to be as historically accurate as possible. In that vein, I always try to separate, in my author's note, what is real from what I made up.

I tried to depict Peggy Shippen's family as faithfully as I could. I did take liberties with the character of Elizabeth, her older sister. Elizabeth was engaged to her cousin Neddy Burd and did marry him in the time frame of my book, with all those bridesmaids. But in my imagination, Elizabeth kept surfacing as "different."

When I did the scenes about Becca's first day in the Shippen household, I didn't realize until they were done that Elizabeth wasn't in them. "I've forgotten Elizabeth!" I told myself, when those scenes were finished. "How could I forget her?" My research told me she was the older sister Peggy so looked up to.

The reason was simple. Elizabeth wanted to make her own entrance, late and dramatically. Elizabeth was demanding special consideration. And so, as frequently happens, I had to let her have her own "walk-on." I had to let her emerge as she wished.

She emerged as a rebel, though research does not tell us this. She emerged as someone who came and went as she pleased, dressed in men's clothing, going about her mysterious missions.

This quite often happens. A character walks in on me, and without so much as a by-your-leave takes on a life of her own. I know enough by now to give those characters free rein. Elizabeth played her role in my novel, and with a purpose. She brought into the house Persifor Frazor, the American parolee who escaped from the Golden Swan, who later assumes such an important part in Becca's life. And I did not think it farfetched, given the way the Shippen family was split down the middle over the war, to have a strong female character be for independence.

There was a Persifor Frazor (or Frazer) in Philadelphia at the time. He was a lieutenant colonel in the American army who was captured by a British patrol on 16 September 1777, near his Chester County home. He signed a parole promising to "do nothing sacredly, or say nothing directly or indirectly to the prejudice of the King's Service or bear arms against His Majesty, until exchanged."

He was sent to the jail on Walnut Street, contracted lung illness, was paroled, and like my character secured lodgings in the Golden Swan on Third

Street. He succeeded in escaping. His manner of escape, dressing in Quaker women's clothing, was carried out by many prisoners in Philadelphia at the time.

When I introduced Frazor, I had no intention of having him show up at the farm later in the book. But I decided there would be a soldier helping Henry Job at the farm. I just "saw him there" when Becca went home to visit.

Perhaps I was looking from a distance, as Becca did at first. Perhaps I did not recognize him immediately. But when I got up closer, I saw that it was Frazor.

Everything about the *Meschianza* is true, including the fact that the British officers did not consider the American girls ladies in the true sense of the word and so decided to have them dress in the costumes of Turkish slave girls.

Peggy and her sisters Sarah and Mary were invited and planned to go. The costumes were made, much to the dismay of their father, who could not afford the expense. (Becca's mother is their dressmaker only for the sake of fiction.)

Then, at the last minute, the committee from the Society of Friends came to call, strongly advising Mr. Shippen against allowing his daughters to wear such costumes. Mr. Shippen complied. And according to everyone's research (except Lewis Burd Walker's), "Peggy had hysterics."

That same committee of Friends did tour the battlefield the day after the battle at Crooked Billet Tavern, but their visiting Mr. Shippen to voice objections to his daughters going to a party to celebrate the British victory is of my making. I did this for the sake of building tension for the final visit of the committee.

Lydia Darragh (or Darrah), mother of Becca's friend Ann, was a spy for General George Washington during the British occupation of Philadelphia. She did listen in on the conference the British officers were holding in her house, then slipped off to inform Washington of their intended attack on him at Whitemarsh.

Washington had quite an intelligence network by this time in the war, so it was not unlikely that someone as ordinary and plodding as Henry Job Claghorn, Becca's stepfather, would be spying for him on his "runs" into Philadelphia with provisions. Nor is it unlikely that Henry Job would be a double agent. Both the British and the Americans had them. In their book *Spies of the Revolution*, Katherine and John Bakeless write: "Not all double agents are loyal spies whose work for one side is just a pose to cover their real work for the other. Often a double agent is really a traitor to both sides, a contemptible rascal with no loyalty to anything, interested only in self and money."

So I envisioned Henry Job. I played him against

Arnold, who was doing, for all intents and purposes, the same thing. Working for his own interests. Henry Job is, in my mind, the flip side of Arnold—the poor man who wants to get ahead and hasn't the means to do so but follows the same course. Of course, Washington did not meet all his spies. Half the time he didn't know who they were.

Henry Job, his wife, Becca, and her brother, Blair, are all fictitious. But there *was* a Phillip Syng, a silversmith, in Philadelphia. Edward Shippen, Peggy's grandfather, purchased a silver tankard from him in 1771 for fourteen pounds sterling. I made this Phillip Syng Becca's deceased father.

The only historical fact I toyed with for the sake of story was the fight between the militia and the Republican Society in the house of James Wilson. This fight actually occurred months after I have it happening. But I used it in my plot to emphasize how the American militia hated Arnold, for they already did so months before this fight took place.

One question I have never been able to resolve is why the Shippens, being Quakers in good standing, did not speak in the traditional Quaker manner, using "thee" and "thou."

No research has explained this. But these terms are not evident in reading the Shippens' personal correspondence. Edward Shippen of Lancaster—Peggy's grandfather—to his sons: "This may inform you that before I came to live here William Allen Esq. made me a present of a small tract of Land in Bucks County."

If they had spoken in the traditional Quaker manner, the passage would begin, "This will inform thee . . ."

Other family correspondence also shows no use of the "thee" and "thou" spoken by Quakers. So I went with the regular mode of speech for the Shippens.

The business of the Arnolds once they embarked upon their course of treason—interviewing people to act as a messenger between them and Andre—is all true. They needed, Flexner tells us, a collaborator, a go-between, who would move messages without involving them. They finally decided to use crockery dealer Joseph Stansbury, a thirty-three-year-old social climber who was loyal to England. Flexner writes: "A servant in Arnold's livery ordered [Stansbury] to wait on the general."

I made that servant Becca.

The date was May 1779. Stansbury later wrote of the experience: "General Arnold sent for me, and after some general conversation, opened his political sentiments respecting the war between Great Britain and America, declaring his abhorrence of a separation of the latter from the former as a measure that would be ruinous to both. General Arnold then communicated to me, under a solemn obligation of secrecy, his intention of offering his services to the commander in chief of the British forces in any way that would most effectually restore the former government and destroy the then usurped authority of Congress, either by immediately joining the British army or cooperating on some concerted plan with Sir Henry Clinton."

Arnold and Peggy had discussed George Monk. Research tells us he signed some letters "Monk," then later gave it up. I applied the name to the note Becca brings to Stansbury.

By now the reader can see how I interweave fiction with history. The rest—how Becca was caught listening at the door and given parole papers and returned home—is obviously of my own making, since Becca herself is someone I made up.

What happened to Arnold and Peggy Shippen in later years? I feel the obligation to tell my readers that, too, since the book does not take the story that far.

· · · · ·

After the treason of her husband was brought to light, General Washington interviewed Peggy Shippen Arnold at West Point and gave her a choice. She could join her husband in British-held New York or rejoin her family in Philadelphia. She chose Philadelphia.

But when she returned home there was much gossip concerning her and her husband. Within two months the authorities forced her to leave, so in November of 1780 she went to live with Arnold in a fine house next door to British headquarters in New York City.

Sir Henry Clinton made Arnold a colonel of a regiment, the highest rank ever given to an American in the British army. But Arnold was not popular in the British army. He was, after all, still a "colonial." His unit was the American Legion Refugees. But he had trouble filling the ranks. And Clinton allowed him to take the field against the Americans only twice: once in Richmond, Virginia, and another time in his native Connecticut.

He and Peggy had a second son before they sailed to London in December of 1781.

For a while it seemed as if Peggy's dreams had come true. Clinton gave her and her husband proper letters of introduction to everyone of importance in England, especially at the Court at St. James Palace. They met the king and the Prince of Wales. The king said that Peggy was "the most beautiful woman he had ever seen."

But foremost British statesmen did not like Arnold. He was, after all, a traitor to his country. He was given no military post. In 1784 he applied for a position in the East India Company and was refused because he had been a traitor.

The Arnolds lived in rented houses in the section of London where other American Loyalists who had fled the United States lived. Peggy and Arnold had another boy in 1783 and a girl in 1784. Both children died in infancy. In 1785 they had another daughter, Sophia, and afterward two more sons, George, born in 1787, and William, born in 1798.

Arnold had money in those early London years, likely from his reward for treason. How much did he get for going over to the British? Flexner, in the October 1967 issue of *American Heritage*, writes, "One [historian] put it as high as '$120,000 in modern purchasing power; another as low as $55,000.' "

But the rewards were more than money. His sons from his first marriage were given commisions in the British army for life. Then King George III gave Arnold a yearly pension of 500 pounds and all Peggy's children, born and as yet unborn, were given a yearly pension of 80 pounds each.

Still Arnold was not happy. As he'd done with the American Congress, he submitted a bill for expenses over and above what he'd been given, to the Comissioners on Loyalist Claims. One claim was for the loss of Mount Pleasant, which his father-in-law had already purchased for his daughter. Another was for losses he figured he incurred for refusing the command of the American Army in

South Carolina. Major General Nathanael Greene got the command, he explained, and for such services was given $20,000 pounds sterling by the Carolinas and Virginia. The truth was that Washington never offered Arnold this command. Eventually, perhaps realizing these claims were not honest, Arnold withdrew them.

In 1785 Arnold purchased a brig and left for Canada, to start business as a merchant. In St. Johns, Canada, he purchased property and started a merchandising enterprise. There is some belief that he also fathered an illegitimate child in that year. A son, John Sage, is mentioned in his will. He returned to England in 1787, left his sons with a private family, and brought Peggy and their daughter to Canada.

Back in St. Johns, he purchased a commodious house and moved his sister Hannah and his sons from his first marriage in. Peggy paid a visit to her family in Philadelphia with her daughter in 1789. She found her parents happy. Her father was again working as a judge. (He would someday become chief justice of Pennsylvania.) Her brother, Edward, and all her sisters were married, and there were many nieces and nephews.

But people snubbed her when she went out. They came in bunches to gather before the Shippen house to catch a glimpse of the traitor's wife. While she was visiting her family, Arnold's warehouse in

St. Johns was mysteriously burned. Arnold was also hated in Canada. In spring of 1791 a mob attacked his home and burned him in effigy, yelling, "Traitor!"

A few weeks later the Arnolds sailed back to England.

In 1794 Benedict Arnold went back to privateering. England and France were at war. He was captured by the French, was scheduled to hang, but escaped.

For two years he served under Sir Charles Grey in the West Indies. But his funds were dwindling and his life was taking a bad turn.

His son Benedict, from his first marriage, died from a wound received while fighting in the West Indies. Daughter Sophia had a paralytic stroke, and his son Edward was also killed fighting with the British.

Arnold returned to England in ill health. Doctors diagnosed dropsy and gout. Benedict Arnold died on June 14, 1801.

They say he called for his old American uniform on his deathbed. But this is legend and not substantiated.

Peggy lived for three more years. She paid off every one of Arnold's debts, put the younger children through good schools, and helped Arnold's remaining son from his first marriage to get started in life.

She counted the children as her blessings. They all grew to honorable adulthood, lived decent and successful lives. None were tainted by their father's act of treason. Perhaps because Peggy worked so hard to shield them from it.

Peggy contracted cancer and suffered very much in the last year of her life. On July 15, 1804, she wrote her last letter to her father. "I am constantly under the effects of opium to relieve a pain that would otherwise be intolerable."

She was forty-four when she died in 1804. The previous summer, she had written to her stepson: "To you I have rendered an essential service; I have rescued your father's memory from disrespect, by paying all his just debts; and his children will now never have the mortification of being reproached with his speculations having injured anybody beyond his own family. . . . I have not even a teaspoon, a towel, or a bottle of wine that I have not paid for."

When Peggy was young, money had been her god. In her later years, the paying of debts gave her a real and personal triumph over all her troubles.

18th Century Vocabulary

CHEMISE—a one-piece loose garment worn by women. The top half has a ruffled neck and three-quarter sleeves and is worn as a blouse, sometimes under a short gown, and the bottom half is worn under a skirt or petticoat.

CONTINENTAL SOLDIER—a soldier of the "regular army," also known as the "Continental Line"

COPPERAS—a green vitriol used as a dye

DROPSY—abnormal accumulation of fluid in the cellular tissue or in the body cavity

FEU DE JOIE—a practice the Americans used of lining up the soldiers, one firing his musket after the other, all down the line. Known as the "firing of joy," it was used to celebrate victory or a joyous occasion.

FOWLING PIECE—a primitive musket used by farmers for shooting fowl

HESSIAN—German soldiers hired by King George III to fight for him

JÄGER—a Hessian rifleman. They wore green uniforms.

LIGHT HORSE—a cavalry unit

LIGHT HORSE HARRY LEE—the nickname given to Harry Lee of the famous Lee family of Virginia. Harry Lee's Light Horse or cavalry unit was the Virginia First Troop. He paid out of his own pocket for the horses and for his men's equipment. Light Horse Harry was the father of General Robert E. Lee, the famous Civil War general.

LOYALIST—the word the Americans gave to those loyal to King George III

MADDER—a red vegetable dye

MANTUA-MAKER—a dressmaker

MILITIAMAN—a citizen soldier who trained on designated weekends to form the defense for their own colony. Much like today's National Guard.

NECESSARY—a privy or outhouse

PAROLE—a prisoner "put on parole" is under his word of honor not to escape

PATROONS—the word applied to those with shady business dealings in Revolutionary War America

PETTICOAT—a skirt

POLTROON—a coward or weakling

POLONAISE—a woman's loose dress

SILLIBUB—a sweet, frothy milk drink, also spelled "syllabub"

SPIRITS—alcoholic beverages

TORY—the word the British applied to those loyal to King George III

TREAT—the word eighteenth-century Americans used to denote negotiations. "Clinton will not allow the Loyalists to treat with Washington."

Bibliography

Armes, Ethel. *Nancy Shippen: Her Journal Book.* New York and London: Benjamin Blom, 1968.

Bakeless, Katherine and John. *Spies of the Revolution.* New York: Scholastic Book Services, 1962.

Bishop, Morris. "You Are Invited to a *Meschianza.*" *American Heritage.* Volume XXV, No. 5 (August 1974).

Flexner, James Thomas. "Benedict Arnold: How the Traitor Was Unmasked." *American Heritage.* Volume XVIII, No. 6 (October 1967).

Flexner, James Thomas. *The Traitor and the Spy: Benedict Arnold and John Andre.* New York: Harcourt Brace and Company, 1953.

Jackson, John W. *With the British Army in Philadelphia.* San Rafael, CA: Presidio Press, 1979.

Kantor, Mackinlay. *Valley Forge*. New York: Ballantine Books, 1975.

Klein, Shirley Randolph. *Portrait of an Early American Family: The Shippens of Pennsylvania Across Five Generations*. Philadelphia: University of Pennsylvania Press, 1975.

National Society Daughters of the American Revolution. *The Great Women of the American Revolution*. Washington, D.C.: The Society, 1976.

Trussell, John B. B., Jr. *Birthplace of an Army: A Study of the Valley Forge Encampment*. Harrisburg: Pennsylvania Historical and Museum Commission, 1979.

Walker, Lewis Burd. "Life of Margaret Shippen: Wife of Benedict Arnold." Philadelphia: *The Pennsylvania Magazine of History and Biography*, 1900.

Weigley, Russell F. *Philadelphia: A Three-Hundred Year History*. New York: W. W. Norton & Co., 1982.

Wheeler, Richard. *Voices of 1776: The Story of the American Revolution in the Words of Those Who Were There*. New York: Penguin Books, 1991.

About the Author

Ann Rinaldi is an award-winning author best known for bringing history vividly to life. Among her books for Harcourt are *A Break with Charity: A Story about the Salem Witch Trials,* an ALA Best Book for Young Adults and a New York Public Library Book for the Teen Age, and *The Fifth of March: A Story of the Boston Massacre,* also a New York Public Library Book for the Teen Age.

A self-made writer, Ms. Rinaldi never attended college but learned her craft through reading and writing. As a columnist for twenty-one years at *The Trentonian* in New Jersey, she learned the art of finding a good story, capturing it in words, and meeting a deadline.

Ms. Rinaldi attributes her interest in history to her son, who enlisted her to take part in historical reenactments up and down the East Coast, where she cooked the food, made the clothing, and learned about the dances, songs, and lifestyles that prevailed in eighteenth-century America.

Ann Rinaldi has two grown children and lives with her husband in central New Jersey.

1. Mama's first commandment is "Nothing we learn is lost to us." What does this mean? In what ways does it gain meaning for Becca during her time with Peggy?

2. What do you think Andre means when he tells Mrs. Shippen, "All rules are made to be broken"? Do you agree?

3. Becca had thought that if you had money you could buy yourself out of bad situations—yet Andre isn't able to buy himself out of trouble in the end. What does Becca learn from Andre's situation? How does her knowledge of Henry Job's role in the war add to this lesson?

4. Becca and Mama keep secrets from each other. Why? Do you think it is wise for a mother and daughter to do?

5. Becca realizes that sometimes "what we become when we find our missing pieces is not always nice." What does she mean by this? Do you have missing pieces? Do you think anyone can ever be "finished"?

Have you read these Great Episodes paperbacks?

SHERRY GARLAND
Indio

KRISTIANA GREGORY
Earthquake at Dawn
Jenny of the Tetons
The Legend of Jimmy Spoon

LEN HILTS
Quanah Parker: Warrior for Freedom,
Ambassador for Peace

DOROTHEA JENSEN
The Riddle of Penncroft Farm

JACKIE FRENCH KOLLER
The Primrose Way

CAROLYN MEYER
Where the Broken Heart Still Beats: The Story of
Cynthia Ann Parker

SEYMOUR REIT
Behind Rebel Lines: The Incredible Story of
Emma Edmonds, Civil War Spy
Guns for General Washington: A Story of
the American Revolution

ANN RINALDI

An Acquaintance with Darkness

*A Break with Charity: A Story about
the Salem Witch Trials*

*Cast Two Shadows: The American Revolution
in the South*

*The Coffin Quilt: The Feud between
the Hatfields and the McCoys*

The Fifth of March: A Story of the Boston Massacre

*Hang a Thousand Trees with Ribbons:
The Story of Phillis Wheatley*

A Ride into Morning: The Story of Tempe Wick

The Secret of Sarah Revere

The Staircase

ROLAND SMITH

*The Captain's Dog: My Journey with
the Lewis and Clark Tribe*

THEODORE TAYLOR

Air Raid—Pearl Harbor!: The Story of December 7, 1941